Mary E. Braddon

The Captain of the Vulture

Mary E. Braddon

The Captain of the Vulture

ISBN/EAN: 9783337080525

Printed in Europe, USA, Canada, Australia, Japan

Cover: Foto ©Andreas Hilbeck / pixelio.de

More available books at **www.hansebooks.com**

THE

CAPTAIN OF THE VULTURE

𝔄 𝔑𝔬𝔟𝔢𝔩

BY THE AUTHOR OF

"LADY AUDLEY'S SECRET," "AURORA FLOYD"

ETC. ETC. ETC.

𝔖𝔱𝔢𝔯𝔢𝔬𝔱𝔶𝔭𝔢𝔡 𝔈𝔡𝔦𝔱𝔦𝔬𝔫

LONDON

JOHN AND ROBERT MAXWELL

MILTON HOUSE, SHOE LANE, FLEET STREET

AND

35 ST. BRIDE STREET, E.C.

CONTENTS.

Contents.

CAPTAIN OF THE VULTURE.

CHAPTER I.

THE WAY TO MARLEY WATER.

" No one by the Highflier to-night ? " asked the blacksmith of Compton-on-the-Moor of the weak-eyed landlord of the Black Bear, first and greatest hostelry in
that parish.

" No one but Captain Duke."

" What ? the Captain has been up in London, then,
maybe ? "

" He has been there three weeks and over," replied
the landlord, who seemed rather of a desponding nature,
and not conversationally inclined.

" Ah ! um ! " said the blacksmith ; " three weeks and
more up in London ; three weeks and more away from
that pretty-spoken lady of his ; three weeks gambling,
and roystering, and fighting, and beating of the watch,
and dancing at that fine roundabout place at Chelsea,
and suppers in Covent Garden ; three weeks spending
of the king's money ; three weeks——"

"Going to the devil; three weeks going to the devil!" said a voice behind him; "why not say it in plain English, John Homerton, while you're about it?"

"Bless us and save us, if it isn't Mr. Darrell Markham!"

"Himself, and nobody else," said the speaker, a tall man in a riding-dress and high boots, wearing a three-cornered hat, drawn very much over his eyes; "but keep it dark, Homerton; nobody in Compton knows I'm here; it's only a business visit and a flying visit. I'm off in a couple of hours. What was that you were saying about Captain George Duke, of His Majesty's ship the Vulture?"

"Why, I was saying, Master Darrell, that if I had such a pretty wife as Mistress Duke, and could only be with her two months out of the twelve, I wouldn't spend half of those two months roystering and gallivanting up in London. I think your cousin might have made a better match of it, Master Darrell Markham, with her pretty face."

"I think she might, John Homerton," said the young man, sadly; "I think she might."

The three men had been standing at the door of the inn during this little dialogue. The blacksmith had the bridle of his sturdy little white pony—five-and-twenty years of age, if a day—in his hand, ready to mount him and ride home to his forge at the furthest end of the straggling country town; but he had been unable to resist the fascination of the weak-eyed landlord's conversational powers. Darrell Markham turned away from the two, and walked out into the dusty high road. He stood for some moments looking thoughtfully along a narrow winding track that crossed the bare black moorland, stretching away for miles before him. The Black Bear stood at the entrance to the town, and on the very edge of the bleak open country.

"We shall have a dark night," said Markham, "and I shan't have a very pleasant ride to Marley Water."

"You'll never go to-night, sir?" said the landlord.

"I tell you I must go to-night, Samuel Pecker. Foul or fair weather, I must sleep at Marley Water this night."

"You always was such a daring one, Mr. Darrell," said the blacksmith admiringly.

"It doesn't need so very much courage for a lonely ride over Compton Moor as all that comes to, John Homerton. I've a pair of pistols that never missed fire yet; my horse is sound, wind and limb; I've a full purse, and I know how to take care of it; I've met a highwayman before to-night, and I've been a match for one before to-night; and what's more to the purpose than all, honest John, I *must* do it."

"Must be at Marley Water to-night, Mr. Markham?"

"I must sleep at the Golden Lion, in the village of Marley Water, this night, Mr. Pecker," replied the young man.

"Landlord, show me the road from here to Marley Water," said a stranger.

The three men looked up: a man on horseback, who had drawn his rein before the door, was looking down at the little group with a sharp scrutinizing gaze. He had ridden up to the inn so softly that they had never heard the sound of his horse's hoofs. How long the horse might have been standing there, or when the horseman had stopped, or where he had come from, not one of the three could guess; but there he was, with the fading light of the autumn evening full upon his face, the last yellow brightness of the low sun glimmering amidst his auburn air.

This face, lit up by the setting sun, was a very handsome one. Regular features, massively cut; a ruddy colour in the cheeks, something bronzed by a foreign sun; brown eyes, with dark clearly defined eyebrows, and waving auburn hair, which the October breeze lifted from the low broad forehead. The horseman was of the average height, stalwart, well proportioned; a model, in short, of manly English beauty. The horse was like its master, broad chested and strong limbed.

"I want to know the nearest road to Marley Water," he said for the second time; for there had been something so sudden in the manner of his appearance that none of the three men had answered his inquiry.

The landlord, Mr. Samuel Pecker, was the first to recover his surprise.

"Yon winding road across the moor will take you straight as an arrow, Captain," he answered civilly, but paradoxically.

The horseman nodded. "Thank you, and good night," he said, and cantered away along the moorland bridle-path, for the road was little better.

"Captain! who is he then?" asked Darrell Markham, as soon as the stranger was gone.

"Your cousin's husband, sir; Captain George Duke."

"Is that George Duke? Why he spoke like a stranger."

"That's his way, sir," said the landlord; "that's the worst of the Captain; hail fellow well met, and what would you like to drink? one day, and keep your distance another. There's no knowing where to have him; but, after all, he's a jolly chap, the Captain, though I can't think what *he* wants at Marley Water to-night, when he hasn't been back from London two hours."

"He's a very handsome chap," said Darrell Markham; "I don't so much wonder that Millicent Markham fell in love with him."

"There's some as says Miss Millicent had fell in love with some one else before ever she saw him," said the landlord insinuatingly.

"They should find something better to do than to talk of a young lady's love-affairs, then," answered Markham gravely. "I tell you what, Samuel Pecker, if I don't set out at once I shan't find Marley Water to-night; it will be as dark as pitch in another hour. Tell them to bring out Balmerino."

"Must you go to-night, Mr. Markham?"

"I tell you I must, Samuel. Come, tell the ostler to bring the horse round. I shall be halfway there before 'tis dark, if I start at once."

"Good night, then, sir," said the blacksmith; "I only wish you was going to stop in Compton. The place is dull enough now, with the old squire dead, and the Hall shut up, and the young squire ruining himself in London, as folks say, and you away. Compton isn't what it was when you was a boy, Mr. Darrell, and the squire, your uncle, used to keep Christmas up at the Hall: those were times—and now——"

"Egad, we must all get old, John Homerton," said Darrell with a sigh.

"But it's hard to sigh, or to talk of growing old either, sir," said the blacksmith, "at eight-and-twenty

years of age.   Good night, Master Darrell, **and—asking**
pardon for the liberty—God bless you!"

Darrell Markham held out his hand in response to
this fervent benediction.   The good man grasped it
with a muscular heartiness, murmured another blessing,
and then mounted the elderly white pony, and jogged
off towards the twinkling lights of the narrow high
street.

Just as the blacksmith rode away, a female voice in
the interior of the inn was heard crying, " Where is he?
where is that foolish boy of mine, I say?   He's not
a-going away to-night; he's not a-going to have his
throat cut or his brains blowed out on the king's highway;" and with these words a ponderous female, of
some fifty summers, emerged from the inn door, and
flung two very red fat arms, ornamented with black
mittens, round Darrell Markham's neck.   " You're not
a-going to-night, Master Darrell?   O, I heard Pecker
asking of you to stay; but in *his* nimiuy-piminy namby-
pamby way, asking isn't asking, somehow," cried ponderous Mrs. Pecker, contemptuously.   "O, I've no
patience with him; as if you was a-going to stay for
dying ducks!"

This rather obscure observation was pointed derisively
at Mr. Samuel Pecker, whose despondent manner drew
upon him the contempt of his magnificent and energetic
better half.

As to the landlord of the Black Bear, it must be here
set down that there was no such thing.   Waiters there
were, chambermaids there were, ostlers there were, but
landlord there was not.   That individual was so entirely
absorbed in the splendour of his large and dominant
spouse that he had much better not have been at all;

for what there was of him was always in the way. If
he gave an order, it was, of course, an insane and utterly
impracticable order; and if by any evil chance some
domestic, unused, perhaps, to the customs of the establishment, attempted to execute that order, why there
was the whole internal machinery of the Black Bear
thrown into confusion for an entire day. If he received
a traveller, he generally gave that traveller such a dismal impression of life in general, and Compton-on-the-
Moor in particular, that nine times out of ten the dispi-
rited wanderer would depart as soon as his horse had
had a mouthful of hay, and a drink of water out of the
great trough under the oak tree before the door. There
never were so many highwaymen on any road as on
the roads he spoke of; there never were going to
be such storms as when he discoursed of the weather;
there never were such calamities coming down upon
poor old England as when he talked politics; or such
bad harvests about to paralyse the country as when he
held forth on agriculture.

Some people said he was gloomy by nature, and that
(like that well-beloved king across the Channel, who
used to tell Madame de Pompadour to stop in the
middle of a funny story) it was pain to him to smile.
Others, on the contrary, affirmed that he had been a
much livelier man before his marriage, and that the
weight of his happiness was too much for him—that
he was sinking under the bliss of being allied to so
magnificent a creature as Mrs. Samuel Pecker, and that
his unlooked-for good fortune in the matrimonial line
had undermined his health and spirits. Be this as it
might, there he was, mildly despondent, and utterly
powerless to combat with the contumely daily heaped

upon his head by his lovely but gigantic partner, Sarah
Pecker.

The stranger, on first becoming a witness of the
domestic felicity within the Black Bear, was apt to
imagine that Mr. Samuel Pecker was in a manner an
intruder there; landlord on sufferance, and nominal
proprietor; or, as one might say, host-consort, only
reigning by right of the actual sovereign, his wife.
But it was no such thing; the august line of Pecker
time out of mind had been regnant at the Black Bear.
The late Samuel Pecker, father of Samuel husband
of Sarah, had been a burly stalwart fellow, six feet
high if an inch, and as unlike his mild and feeble son
as it is possible for one Englishman to be unlike
another Englishman. From this father Samuel had
inherited all those premises, dwelling-house, out-buildings, gardens, farmyard, stables, cowhouses, and pigsties, known as the Black Bear. But Samuel had not
long enjoyed his dominions. Six months after ascending the throne, or rather installing himself in the great
oaken arm-chair in the bar-parlour of the Black Bear,
he had taken to wife Sarah, housekeeper to Squire
Ringwood Markham, of the Hall, and widow of Thomas
Masterson, mariner.

Thus it is that Sarah Pecker's two fat mottled arms
are at this present moment clasped round Darrel Markham's neck. She had known Darrell from his childhood, and had worshipped him after the manner of
honest impulsive womankind, when they set up an
idol of the masculine gender. No mother ever loved
her first-born better than Sarah Pecker loved the bright-
haired boy who seemed a boy still to her at eight-and-
twenty years of age. She believed in him as the supreme

type of all that is noble in manhood, and was firmly convinced that not amongst all the beaux who frequent Ranelagh and the coffee-houses, not in either of the King's services, not in Leicester-fields or Kensington; not at the Cocoa Tree, White's, nor Bellamy's; in the Mall or in Change Alley; at Bath or at Tunbridge Wells; not, in short, 'in any quarter of civilized and fashionable England was there to be met with so handsome, so distinguished, so clever, so elegant, so brave generous fascinating noble and honest a scapegrace as Darrell Markham, gentleman at large, and, what is worse, in difficulties.

"You won't go to-night, Master Darrell," she said. "You won't let it be said that you went away from the Black Bear to be murdered on Compton Moor. Jenny's basting a capon for your supper at this very minute, and you shall have a bottle of your poor uncle's own Burgundy, that Pecker bought at the Hall sale."

"It's no use, Mrs. Pecker; I tell you I mustn't stay. I know how well Jenny can roast a capon, and I know how comfortable you can make your guests, and there's nothing I should like better than to stop, but I mustn't. I want to catch the coach that leaves Marley Water at five o'clock to-morrow morning for York. I had no right to come to Compton at all; but I couldn't resist riding across to shake hands with you, Mrs. Sarah, for the sake of the old times that are dead and gone, and to ask the news of Nat Halloway the miller, and Lucas Jordan the doctor, and Selgood the lawyer, and a few more of my old companions, and——and——"

"And of Miss Millicent? Eh, Master Darrell? For all London's such a wide city, and there's so many oi these fine painted madams flaunting along the Mall, full sail, in their pannier-hoops and French furbelows and rainbow-coloured hoods, you haven't quite forgotten Miss Millicent, eh, Darrell Markham?"

She had nursed him on her ample knees when he was but a tiny swaddled baby, and she sometimes called him Darrell Markham *tout court*.

"There was something wrong in that, Master Darrell," she said reproachfully. "There was a gay wedding a year ago at Compton church, and very grand and very handsome everything was; and sure the bride looked very lovely; but one thing was wrong, and that was the bridegroom."

"If you don't want me to be benighted, or to have these very indifferent brains of mine blown out by some valiant knight of the road upon Compton Moor, you'd better let me be off, Mistress Pecker. Mistress Pecker! O, the good old days, the dear old days! when I used to call you Mistress Sally Masterson, in the housekeeper's room at the Hall." He turned away from her with a sigh, and began to whistle a plaintive old English ditty, as he stood looking out over the wide expanse of gloomy moorland.

The ostler brought the horse round to the inn door— a stout brown hack, sixteen hands high, muscular and spirited-looking, with only one speck of white about him, a long slender streak down the side of his head.

The young man put his arm caressingly round the horse's neck, and drawing his head down, looked at him as he would have looked at a friend, of whose love and truth in a false and cruel world he at least was certain.

"Brave Balmerino, good Balmerino," he said,

"you've to carry me four-and-twenty miles across a rough country to-night. You've to carry me on an errand, the end of which perhaps will be a bad one; you've to carry me away from a great many bitter memories and a great many cruel thoughts; but you'll do it, Balmerino, you'll do it, won't you, old boy?"

The horse nestled his head against the young man's shoulder, and snuffed at his coat-sleeve.

"Brave boy; that means yes," said Markham, as he sprang into the saddle. "Good night, old friends; good-bye, old home! as Mr. Garrick says in Shakespeare's play, 'Richard's himself again!' Good-bye."

He waved his hand and rode slowly off towards the moorland bridle-path, but before he had crossed the wide high road, the usually phlegmatic Samuel Pecker intercepted him, by suddenly rising up, pale of countenance and dismal of mien, under his horse's head.

"Mr. Darrell Markham," said the moody innkeeper very slowly, "don't you go to Marley Water this night! Don't go! Don't ask me why, sir, and don't, sir, ask me wherefore; for I don't know wherefore, and I can't tell why; but don't go! I've got one of those what-you-may-call'ems—I mean one of those feelings that says, as plain as words can speak, 'Don't do it!'"

"What, a presentiment, eh, Pecker?"

"That's the dictionary-word for it, I believe, sir. Don't go!"

"Samuel Pecker, I must," answered Darrell. "If I go to my death through going to Marley Water, so be it; I go!" He shook the bridle on the horse's neck, and the animal sped off at such a rate that by the time Mr. Samuel Pecker had recovered himself suffi-

ciently to look up, all he could see of Darrell Markham
was a cloud of white dust hurrying over the darkening
moorland before the autumn wind.

Mrs. Pecker stood under the wide thatched porch of
the Black Bear watching the receding horseman

"Poor Master Darrell!" she exclaimed with a sigh
and an ominous shake of the head; "brave generous
noble Master Darrell! I only wish, for pretty Miss
Millicent's sake, that Captain George Duke was a little
like him."

"But suppose Captain George Duke wishes nothing
of the kind? how then, Mistress Pecker?"

The person who thus answered Mrs. Pecker's soli-
loquy was a man of average height, dressed in a naval
coat and three-cornered hat, who had come up to the
inn doorway as quietly as the horseman had done half
an hour before.

For once in the course of the landlady's existence
the gigantic bosom of the unflinching Sarah Pecker
quailed before one of the sterner sex. She almost
stammered, that great woman, as she said, "I beg
your pardon, Captain Duke, I was only a-thinking!"

"You were only a-thinking aloud, Mistress Pecker.
So you'd like to see George Duke, of His Majesty's ship
the Vulture, a good-for-nothing idling reckless ne'er-
do-weel like Darrell Markham, would you?"

"I tell you what it is, Captain; you're Miss Millicent's husband, and if—if you was a puppy dog, and
she was fond of you, there isn't a word I could bring
myself to say against you, for the sake of that sweet
young lady. But don't you speak one bad word of
Master Darrell Markham, for that's one of the things
that Sarah Pecker will never put up with while she's

got a tongue in her head and sharp nails of her own at her fingers' ends."

The Captain burst into a long ringing laugh—a laugh that had a silver music peculiar to itself. There were people in the town of Compton-on-the-Moor, in the seaport of Marley Water, and on board His Majesty's frigate the Vulture, who said that there were times when the Captain's laughter had a cruel sound in its music, and was by no means good to hear. But what man in authority ever escaped the poisonous breath of slander; and why should Captain Duke be more exempt than his fellows?

"I forgive you, Mrs. Pecker," he said, "I forgive you. I can afford to hear people speak well of Darrell Markham. Poor devil, I pity him!" With which friendly remark the Captain of the Vulture turned his back upon the portly Sarah, and strolled towards the open door of the inn, through which the rosy glow of fire-light shone out upon the autumn dusk.

On the doorstep of the Black Bear George Duke encountered Mr. Samuel Pecker, who had, after his solemn adjuration to Darrell Markham, re-entered the hostelry by a side door that led through the stabl yard.

If Captain George Duke, of His Majesty's navy, had borne the most terrible shape that ever was assumed by fiend or goblin, his appearance on the step of the inn-door could scarcely have been more appalling to the mild Samuel Pecker. Poor Samuel's face whitened and his knees bent under him as he started back, and stared at the naval officer with his weak blue eyes opened to their very widest extent.

"Then you didn't go, Captain?"

" Then I didn't go?   Didn't go where? "

" You didn't go to Marley Water."

"Go to Marley Water!   No!   Who said I was going there? "

The small remnant of manly courage left in Mr. Samuel Pecker after his surprise was quite knocked out of him by the energetic tone of the Captain, and he murmured mildly,—

" Who said so?   O, no one particular; only—only yourself! "

The Captain laughed his own ringing laugh once more.

" *I* said so?   *I* said so, Samuel?   When? "

"Half an hour ago.   When you asked me the way there."

" When I asked you the way to Marley Water! Why I know the road as well as I know my own quarter-deck."

" That's what struck me at the time, Captain, when you stopped your horse at this door and asked me the way.   I must say I thought it was odd."

" I stopped my horse!   When? "

"Half an hour ago."

"Samuel Pecker, I haven't been across a horse to-day.   I'm not over attached to the brutes at the best of times, but to-night I'm tired out with my journey from London, and I've just come straight from my wife's tea-table, where I've been drinking a dish of sloppy bohea and going to sleep over woman's talk."

" And yet Parson Bendham says there's no such things as ghosts! "

" Samuel Pecker, you're drunk."

"I haven't tasted a mug of beer this day, Captain. Ask Sarah."

"That he hasn't, Captain," responded Samuel's spouse to this appeal. "I keep my eye upon him too sharp for that."

"Then what's the fool woolgathering about, Mistress Sally?" asked the Captain, rather angrily.

"Lord have mercy upon us! I don't know," replied Mrs. Pecker, scornfully; "he's as full of fancies as the oldest woman in all Cumberland; he's always a-seein' of ghosts and hobgoblins and windin' sheets, and all sorts of dismals," added the landlady contemptuously, "and unsettlin' his mind for business and bookkeepin'. I haven't common patience with him, that I han't. He can't pass through the churchyard after dark but honest folks that have had Christian burial must needs come out of their graves to look at him, according to his account—as if any decent corpse would leave a comfortable grave for such as *him.*"

Mrs. Pecker was very fond of informing people of this fact of her small stock of common patience in the matter of Samuel her husband; and as all her actions went to confirm her words, she was pretty generally believed.

" O, never mind, Sarah; never mind, Captain Duke; it's no consequence, and it's no business of mine," said the landlord, with abject meekness; "there was three of us as see him, that's all!"

"Three of you as see whom?" asked the Captain.

" As see him——as see——" the landlord gave a peculiarly dry gulp just here, as if the ghost of something had been choking him, and he were trying to exorcise it by swallowing hard—"there was three of us as see—*it!*"

"It?   What?"

"The man who stopped on horseback at this door half an hour ago, and asked me the way to Marley Water."

"Humph! And what was this man like?" asked the Captain.

"As like you as your own reflection in a looking-glass," answered the landlord. "It's no use looking contemptuously at me, Sarah," he added, in reply to a scornful smile and a disdainful gesture from his better half; "the face that's looking at me now is the face that looked at me half an hour ago. I might have guessed there was something strange in him though from his coming up so quietly," murmured Samuel thoughtfully. "Flesh and blood doesn't creep up to a man unawares like that!"

Captain Duke looked very hard into the face of the speaker; looked thoughtfully, gravely, earnestly at him, with bright searching brown eyes; and then again burst out laughing louder than before. So much was he amused by the landlord's astonished and awe-stricken face, that he laughed all the way across the low old hall—laughed as he opened the door of the oak-panelled parlour in which the genteeler visitors at the Bear were accustomed to sit—laughed as he threw himself back into the great polished oaken chair by the fire, and stretched his legs out upon the stone hearth till the heels of his boots rested against the iron dogs—laughed as he called Samuel Pecker, and could hardly order his favourite beverage, rum punch, for laughing.

The room was empty, and it was to be observed that

when the door closed upon the landlord, Captain Duke, though he still laughed, something contracted the muscles of his face, while the pleasant light died slowly out of his handsome brown eyes, and gave place to a settled gloom.

When the punch was brought him, he drank three glasses one after another. But neither the great wood fire blazing on the wide hearth nor the steaming liquid seemed to warm him, for he shivered as he drank.

He shivered as he drank, and presently he drew his chair still closer to the fire, planted his feet upon the two iron dogs, and sat looking darkly into the red spitting hissing blaze.

"My incubus, my shadow, my curse!" he said. Only six words, but they expressed the hatred of a lifetime.

By-and-by a thought seemed suddenly to strike him ; he sprang to his feet so rapidly that he overset the heavy high-backed oaken chair, and strode out of the room.

On the other side of the hall was situated the common parlour of the inn ; the room in which the trades-men of the town met every evening, the oak room, being sacred to a superior class of travellers, and to such men as the doctor, the lawyer, and Captain Duke. The common parlour was full this evening, and a loud noise of talking and laughter proceeded from the open door.

To this door the Captain went, and removing his hat from his clustering auburn curls, which were tied behind with a ribbon, he bowed to the merry little assembly.

They were on their feet in a moment. Captain George Duke, of his Majesty's ship the Vulture, was a great man at Compton-on-the-Moor. His marriage with the only child of the late squire had identified him with the place, to which he was otherwise a stranger.

"I am sorry to disturb you, gentlemen," he said graciously; "is Pecker here?"

Pecker was there, but so entirely crestfallen and subdued that, on hearing himself asked for, he emerged from his ponderous chair at the head of the table like some melancholy male Aphrodité rising from the sea, and uttered not a word.

"Pecker, I want to know the exact time," said the Captain. "My watch has gone down, and Mistress Duke has been so much occupied with reading Mr. Richardson's romances and nursing her lapdog, that all the clocks at the cottage are out of order. What is the hour by your infallible oaken clock on the stairs, Samuel?"

The landlord rubbed his two little podgy hands through his limp sandy hair, by which process he seemed to communicate a faint stir to his intellectual faculties, and then retired silently to execute the Captain's order. A dozen stout silver turnip-shaped chronometers and great leather-encased Tompion watches were out in a moment.

"Half-past seven by me;" "A quarter to eight;' "Twenty minutes, Captain!" George Duke might have had the choice of half-a-dozen different times had he liked, but he only said quietly,—

"Thank you, gentlemen, very much; but I'll regulate my watch by Pecker's old clock, for I think it keeps truer time than the church, the market, or the gaol."

"The gaol's pretty true to time at eight o'clock on a Monday morning sometimes, though, Captain, isn't it?" said a little shoemaker, who considered himself the wit of the village.

"Not half true enough, sometimes, Mr. Tomkins," answered the Captain, winding up his watch, with a grave smile playing round his well-shaped mouth. "If everybody was hung that deserves to be hung, Mr. Tomkins, there'd be more room in the world for the honest people. Well, Samuel, what's the exact time?"

"Ten minutes to eight, Captain Duke, and such a night! I stopped to look out of the staircase window just now, and the sky's as black as ink, and seems so near the earth that one might fancy it would fall down upon our heads and crush us, if it wasn't for the wind a-stopping of it."

"Ten minutes to eight; that's all right," said the Captain, putting his watch into his pocket. He turned to leave the room, but stopped at the door and said, 'Oh, by the bye, worthy Samuel, at what time did you see my ghost?" He laughed as he asked the question, and looked round at the company with a smile and a malicious wink in the direction of the subdued landlord.

"Compton church clock was striking seven as the man on horseback rode away across the moor, Captain. But don't ask me anything; don't, please, talk to me," he said forlornly; "it's no consequence, it's not any business of mine, it doesn't matter to anybody, but——" he paused and repeated the swallowing process,—"*I saw it!*"

The customers at the Black Bear were not generally apt to pay very serious attention to any remark emanating from the worthy landlord, but these last three words did seem to impress them, and they stared with scared faces from Samuel Pecker to the Captain, and from the Captain back to Samuel Pecker.

"Our jolly landlord has been a little too free with his own old ale, gentlemen, and he must needs take it into his wise head that he has seen my ghost, for no better reason than because some traveller a little like me stopped at his door to ask the way to Marley Water. I hope good ale and good company will set him right again," said George Duke. "Good night, gentlemen all."

He left the room and returned to the oak parlour, where he flung himself once more into his old moody attitude over the blazing logs, and sat staring gloomily into the red chasms in the burning wood—craggy cliffs and deep abysses, down which ever and anon some dying ember fell like a suicide plunging from the summit of a cliff into the fathomless gulf below.

The great brown eyes of the Captain looked straight and steadily into the changing pictures to be seen in the fire. He was so entirely different a creature from that man whose gay voice and light laugh had just resounded in the common parlour of the inn, that it would have been difficult for any one having seen him in one phase to recognize him in the other.

He was not long alone, for presently Nathaniel Halloway the miller dropped in, and joined the Captain over his punch ; and by-and-by attorney Selgood and Mr. Jordan the surgeon—Dr. Jordan *par excellence* throughout Compton—came in arm-in-arm. The four men were very friendly, and they sat drinking, smoking, and talking politics till midnight, when Captain George Duke started from his seat and was for breaking up the party.

" Twelve o'clock from the tower of Compton church," he said, as he rose from the table. " Gentlemen, I've a pretty young wife waiting for me at home, and I've half a mile to walk before I get home ; so I shall leave you to finish your punch and your conversation without me."

Nathaniel Halloway sprang to his feet. " Captain Duke, you're not going to leave us in this shabby fashion. You're not on your own quarter-deck, remember ; and you're not going to have it all your own way. As for the pretty little admiral in petticoats at home, you can soon make your peace with her. Stop and finish the punch, man ! " and the worthy miller, on whom the evening's potations had produced some little effect, caught hold of the Captain's gold-laced cuff in a hearty boisterous fashion, and tried to prevent his leaving the room.

George Duke shook him lightly off, and opening the door that led into the hall, went out, followed by the miller and his boon companions, Dr. Jordan and lawyer Selgood.

The house, which had been so quiet five minutes before, was now all bustle and confusion. First and foremost there was worthy Mistress Sarah Pecker alternately bewailing, lamenting, and scolding at the very extremest altitude of her voice. Then there was Samuel her husband, pale, aghast, and useless, getting feebly into everybody's way, and rapidly sinking beneath the combined effects of mental imbecility and universal contumely. Then there were the ostler and two rosy-faced but frightened-looking chambermaids clinging to each other and to the cook-maid and the waiter; and in the centre of the hall the one cause of all this alarm and emotion lay stretched in the arms of two men, a letter-carrier and a farm labourer. Yes—with Mrs. Sarah Pecker kneeling by his side, adjuring him to speak, to move, to open his heavy eyelids—silent, motionless, and unconscious, lay that Darrell Markham who five hours before had started in full health and strength for the little seaport of Marley Water.

"We kicked over him in the path," said one of the men; "me and Jim Bowlder here, of Squire Morris's at the Grange. We was coming home from Marley market, and we come slap upon him in the dark, so dark that we couldn't see whether he was a man or a dead sheep; but we got him up in our arms and felt that he was stiff with cold and damp—he might be murdered or he might be frozen; there was some wet about his chest and his left arm, and I knew by the feel of it, thick and slimy, that it was blood; and me and Jim Bowlder we raised him between us, heels and head, and carried him straight here."

"Who is it, what is it?" asked Captain Duke, advancing into the very heart of the little crowd.

"Your wife's nearest kinsman and dearest friend, Captain, Miss Millicent's first cousin, Darrell Markham! Murdered! murdered on the moorland road between this and Marley Water."

"Not above a mile from here, missus," interposed the labourer who had picked up the wounded man.

"Darrell Markham! my wife's cousin, Darrell Markham! What did he come here for? What was he doing in Compton?" asked the Captain suspiciously. The dark brown eyes looked straight down at the still face lying on the letter-carrier's shoulder, and dripping wet with the vinegar and water with which Mistress Pecker was bathing the sufferer's forehead.

"What did he come here for! He came here to be murdered! He came here to have his precious life taken from him upon Compton Moor, poor dear lamb, poor dear lamb!" sobbed Mrs. Pecker.

During all this confusion, Lucas Jordan the surgeon slipped quietly behind the little crowd, and taking Darrell Markham's arm in his hand, deliberately slashed open his coat-sleeve from the cuff to the shoulder with the scissors hanging at Mrs. Pecker's waist.

"A basin, Molly, and a silk handkerchief for a bandage," he said quietly. Half-a-dozen silk handkerchiefs were produced from as many pockets and pressed upon the surgeon, while the terrified chambermaid brought him a basin in her shaking hands and held it under Darrell's arm.

"Steadily, my girl," said the doctor, as he drew out a lancet and inserted it in the cold and rigid arm, after having secured his bandage. The blood trickled slowly and fitfully from the vein.

"Is he dead, is he dead, Mr. Jordan?" cried Sarah Pecker.

"No more than I am, ma'am—no more than I am, Mrs. Pecker," answered the surgeon, who had been slashing away with Sarah's big scissors, and making his examination while the bystanders looked on, aghast and admiring. "The gentleman has had the ill luck to get a pistol-bullet through his right arm, shivering the bone above the elbow; but we may be able to make a good job of the arm for all that. He has fainted from the loss of blood and the coldness of the night air. He's

had a baddish fall from his horse, I fancy, and is a good
deal bruised and shaken, and there's a scalp-wound at
the back of his head from the sharp pebbles on the
road; but there's nothing more!"

Nothing more! It seemed so little to these terrified
people, who a minute before had thought Mr. Markham
dead, that Mrs. Pecker, albeit unused to the melting
mood, caught the surgeon's hand between her two fat
palms and covered it with kisses and tears.

"So this is Darrell Markham," said the Captain to
himself thoughtfully; "Darrell the irresistible; Darrell
the handsome; Darrell the brave; Darrell that was
to have married his cousin Millicent, now my wife.
Humph, a fair young man with auburn ringlets and
a straight nose! No fear of his life, you say, doctor?"
he asked aloud.

"None, unless fever should supervene, which Heaven
forbid!"

"But if it should, how then?"

"Every fear. With these excitable temperaments——"

"His temperament is excitable?"

"Extremely excitable! An accident such as this is
very likely to result in fever. Mrs. Pecker, he must be
kept very quiet; he must see no one—that is to say, no
one whose presence can be in the least calculated to
agitate him."

"I'll keep watch at this door myself, doctor; and I
should like to see," said the worthy matron, glaring
vengefully at her small spouse, "I should very much
like to see the person that'll dare to disturb him by so
much as breathing."

The landlord of the Black Bear suspended his respi-
ration on the instant, as if he imagined himself called

upon to exist in future without the aid of that natural function.

"We must get our patient upstairs at once, Mrs Pecker," said the doctor "We must get him into your quietest room, and your most comfortable bed, and we must lose no time about it."

At the doctor's direction, the letter-carrier and the farm-labourer resumed their station at the head and feet of Darrell Markham, the ostler assisting them. The three men had just raised him in their arms, when he lifted his left hand to his damp forehead and slowly opened his eyes.

The three men stopped, and Mrs. Pecker screamed aloud, "O, be joyful, he isn't dead! Master Darrell, speak to us, dear, and tell us you're not dead."

The blue eyes looked dimly at the scared faces crowding round.

"He shot me. He robbed me of the letter to the king, and of my purse. He shot me in my arm."

"Who shot you, my darling? Who shot you, Master Darrell, dear?" cried Mrs. Pecker.

The young man looked at her with a vacant stare; evidently half unconscious of where he was, and of the identity of those around him. Presently he withdrew his bloodshot eyes from her face, and his gaze wandered round amongst the other spectators. From the landlord to the chambermaid, from the chambermaid to the letter-carrier, from the letter-carrier to the doctor, from the doctor to Captain George Duke of his majesty's ship the Vulture.

The blue eyes opened to their widest distension with a wild stare.

"*That*, that's the man!"

" What man, Master Darrell ?"

" The man who shot me."

" I thought we should have him delirious," said the doctor, under his breath.

Captain Duke's dark eyebrows fell loweringly over his brown eyes, and a black shade spread itself about his handsome face.

"You're dreaming, darling," said Mrs. Pecker, soothingly. "What man, dear, and where, where is he ? "

Darrell Markham slowly lifted his unwounded arm and pointed with a steady finger full at the dark face o the Captain of the Vulture.

"There!" he said, half raising himself in the arms of the men supporting him, and with the effort he sank back once more unconscious.

"I thought so," muttered Captain Duke.

"So did I, Captain," responded the doctor. "We shall have him in a high fever, and then he may go off like the snuff of a candle."

"And he must be kept quiet?" asked the Captain, as they carried the wounded man up the wide oak staircase.

"He must be kept quiet, Captain, or I'll not answer for his life. I've known him from a boy, and I know any strong excitement will throw him into a brain-fever."

"Poor fellow ! He's a kinsman of mine, by my marriage with his cousin; though I'm afraid there's not much love lost between us on that score. And this is the first time we've met. Strange !"

"There's a good deal in life that is strange, Captain Duke," said the doctor sententiously.

"There is, doctor," answered the sailor. "So Darrell

Markham, travelling from Compton to Marley Water, has been shot by a person or persons unknown. Very strange!"

CHAPTER II.

MILLICENT.

MILLICENT DUKE sat alone in her little parlour on this autumn night, while the north-east wind howled and whistled without her dwelling, and shook every little square of glass in the narrow windows—she sat alone, trying to read Mr. Richardson's last novel—a well-thumbed little volume, embellished with small oval engravings, which had been lent to her by the wife of the curate of Compton-on-the-Moor. But fond as she was of Mr. Richardson's romances, the Captain's wife was unable to concentrate her attention on the little volume; her thoughts wandered away from poor Clarissa and wicked Lovelace; the book dropped out of her hand, and she fell a-musing over the low fire, and listening to the wind disporting itself in the chimney. It is something to be able to look at Mrs. Millicent Duke, as she sits quietly by her lonely hearth, with one white hand supporting her small head, and with her elbow leaning on the stiff horsehair-cushioned arm of the chair in which she is seated.

It is a very fair and girlish face upon which the fitful firelight trembles; now illumining one cheek with a soft red glow, now leaving it in shadow as the flame shoots up in sudden brightness, or dies out of the scattered embers on the hearth. It is a very fair and girlish face, with delicate features and dark blue eyes in the soft depths of which there lurks a shadow—a shadow as of tears long dried, but not forgotten. There are pensive lines too about the mouth, which do not tell of an entirely happy youth. Looking at that pensive mouth, those sad and thoughtful eyes, it is not difficult to divine that Sorrow and Millicent Duke have met each other face to face, and have been companions and bed-fellows before to-night. But in spite of this pensive sadness which overshadows her beauty, or perhaps by very virtue of this sadness, which refines the beauty it overshadows, Millicent Duke is a very pretty girl. It is not easy to think of her as a married woman; there is such an air of extreme youth about her, such a girlish, almost childish timidity in her manner, that, as her husband—not too loving or tender a husband at the best of times—is apt to say, "it is as difficult to deal with Millicent as with a baby, for you never know when she may begin whimpering—like a spoilt child as she is." There are people in Compton-on-the-Moor who remember the time when the spoilt child never whim-pered, and when a gleam of spring sunshine was scarcely a brighter or more welcome thing to fall across a man's pathway than the radiant face of Millicent Markham; but this was in the good days long departed, when her father, the squire, was living, and when the fair young girl had been wont to ride about the country roads on her pretty white pony, accompanied and pro-tected by her first cousin and dearest friend, Darrell Markham.

She is peculiarly sad this bitter autumn night. The shrill wind whistling at the latticed casements makes her shiver to the heart; she draws the skirt of her grey silk petticoat over her shoulders, and drags the heavy chair nearer to the low fire. She has sent her one servant a strapping country wench, to bed long ago, and she cannot get any more fuel to heap upon the wide hearth The wax candles have burnt low down in the quaint old silver candlesticks; ten, eleven, twelve have struck, with long dreary intervals between each time of striking from the tower of Compton church, and still there is no sign of Captain Duke's return.

"He is happier with them than with me," she said mournfully. "Who can wonder? Their talk amuses him and makes him smile; I can only weary him with my wretched pale face." She looked up as she spoke at an oval mirror on the wainscot opposite to her, and saw this sad pale face reflected by the faint light of the low fire and the expiring candles. "And they once called me a pretty girl!" she murmured, with a sigh, as she contemplated the pale reflection; "I had a colour in my cheeks then, and Darrell used to tell me I had stolen the roses from the Dutch garden. I think he would scarcely know me now!"

The long hour after midnight dragged itself out, and as one o'clock struck with a dismal sound that vibrated drearily along the empty street, Millicent heard the sharp stroke of her husband's footstep on the pavement. She sprang from her chair hurriedly, and ran out into the narrow passage; but just as she was about to withdraw the bolts, she paused suddenly, and laid her hand upon her heart. "What is the matter with me to-night—what is the matter, I wonder?" she murmured; "I feel as if some great sorrow were coming, yet what new sorrow can come to me?"

Her husband knocked impatiently at the door with his sword-hilt, as she fumbled nervously with the bolts.

c

"Were you listening at the door, Millicent, that you open it so quickly?" he asked, as he entered.

"I heard your footstep in the street, George, and hurried to let you in. You are very late," she added, as he strode into the parlour, and flung himself into the chair she had been sitting in.

"O, a complaint, of course," he said, with a sneer. "I've a great deal to keep me at home, certainly," he muttered, looking round—"a crying wife and a bad fire, and half-an-inch of guttering candle." He turned his back upon Millicent, and bent over the embers, trying to warm his hands with the red light left in them. His wife seated herself at the slender-legged polished mahogany table, and taking up Mr. Richardson's neglected novel, pretended to read it by the last glimmer of the two candles.

Presently the Captain spoke, without once turning round to look at his companion, without changing his stooping posture over the fire-place, without once addressing her by name—"There's been an accident down there!" he said briefly.

"An accident!" cried Millicent. She dropped her book, and looked up with an expression of vague alarm. "An accident! O, I am sorry; but what accident?"

Though there was an accent of gentle pity in her voice, there was still a slight bewilderment in her manner, as if she were so preoccupied by some sad thoughts of her own as scarcely to be able to under-stand her husband's words.

As he did not answer her first question, she asked again, "What accident, George?"

"A man has been half killed by highwaymen on Compton Moor."

"But not really killed, George—not killed?" she asked anxiously, but still with that half-preoccupied manner, as if, in spite of herself, she could not quite concentrate her mind upon the subject of which her husband was speaking.

"Not killed, no; but all but killed, don't I tell you?" said the Captain. "It's just the toss-up of a guinea whether he lives or dies. And a handsome fair-haired lad enough," he added, half to himself—"a handsome, fair-faced, fair-haired lad enough. Poor devil!"

"I am very sorry," Millicent murmured gently; and as her husband did not stir from his seat by the fire, or address her further, she took up her book once more, and began again poring over the small, old-fashioned type. There was a pause, during which the Captain kicked the last spark out of the expiring embers; and then George Duke turned and looked at his wife as she sat bending over the light. After watching her for a few minutes with an angry expression in his handsome brown eyes, he cried with a scornful laugh,—

"Heaven bless these novel-reading women! The death of a fellow-creature is little enough to them so long as Miss Clarissa is reconciled to her lover, and Mistress Pamela's virtue is rewarded in the sixth volume! Here's a tender compassionate creature for you! She cries over Sir Charles Grandison, and doesn't so much as ask me who it is that is lying between death and life in the blue room down at the Black Bear!"

Mistress Duke looked up at her husband with a deprecating glance, as if she were used to hard words, and used to warding them off by apologetic speeches.

"I beg your pardon, George," she said hesitatingly. "Indeed I am not unfeeling. I am sorry for this poor wounded, half-dying man, whoever he may be. If I could do anything to serve him, or to comfort him, I would do it. I would do it at whatever cost to myself. What more can I say, George?"

"And they talk about a woman's curiosity!" cried the Captain, with a mocking laugh; "even now she doesn't ask me who the wounded man is."

"His name can make little difference in my pity for him, George. Poor creature! I am very sorry for him, whoever he may be. Is he any friend of yours? Is he any one I know, George?"

Her husband paused for a few moments before he answered this question. Millicent had risen from her seat and stood by the table trying to revive the drooping wick of the candle that had survived its fellow. The Captain turned his chair completely round, and watched her pale face as he said, slowly and distinctly,—

"The man is some one you know—and he is no friend of mine."

"Who is he, George?"

"Your first cousin, Darrell Markham!"

She uttered a cry; not a shrill scream, but a faint pitiful cry; and lifted her hands to her head. She remained in this attitude for some minutes, quite still, quite silent, and then sank quietly into her old position by the table. Her husband watched her all the time with a sneering smile and a mischievous glitter in his eyes.

"Darrell, my cousin Darrell dead?"

"Not dead, Mistress Millicent; not quite so bad as that. Your dear fair-haired pretty-face cousin is not dead, my sweet loving wife; he is only—dying."

"Lying in the blue room at the Black Bear;" she

repeated the words he had said a few minutes before, in a distracted manner, very painful to witness.

"Lying in the blue room at the Bear. Yes, the blue room, No. 4, on the long corridor. You know the chamber well enough. Have you not been to the old inn times and often to see your father's old housekeeper, the mariner's widow—at least the innkeeper's wife?"

"Trembling between life and death," repeated Millicent, in the same half-conscious tone, so piteous to hear.

"He **was**! Heaven knows how he may be now. That was half-an-hour ago; the scale may be turned by this time; he may be dead!"

As George Duke said the last word, his wife sprang from her seat, and, without once looking at him, ran hurriedly to the outer door. She had her hand upon the bolts, when she cried out in a tone of anguish, "O, no, no, no!" and dropped down on her knees, with her head leaning against the lock of the door.

The Captain of the Vulture followed her into the passage, and watched her with hard unpitying eyes.

"You were going to run to him!" he said, as **she** fell on her knees by the outer door.

For the first time since Darrell Markham's name had been mentioned, Millicent looked at her husband; not mournfully, not reproachfully, least of all fearfully; bold, bright, and defiant, her blue eyes looked up to his.

"I was."

"Then why not go? You see I am not cruel; I do not stop you. You are free. Go! Go to your

cousin—and—your lover, Mistress Duke.   Shall I open
the door for you ? ”

She lifted herself with an effort upon her feet, still
leaning for support against the street-door.   “ No, ”
she said, “ I will not go to him; I could do him no
good; I might agitate him; I might kill him!”

The Captain bit his under lip, and the triumphant
light faded from his brown eyes.

“ But understand this, George Duke,” said Millicent,
in a tone that was strange to her husband’s ears, “ it
is no fear of you which keeps me here; it is no dread
of your cruel words or more cruel looks that holds me
from going to his side; for if I could save him by my
presence from one throb of pain—if I could give him
by my love and devotion one moment’s peace and
comfort, and the town of Compton were one raging
fire, I would walk through that fire to do it.”

“ That’s a very pretty speech out of a novel,” said
her husband, “ but I never very much believe in these
pretty speeches—perhaps I’ve a good reason of my
own for doubting them.   I suppose, if Darrell Markham asked for you with his dying breath, you’d go to
see him; especially,” he added, with his old sneer,
“ as the town of Compton *isn’t* on fire.”

Millicent sprang towards him, and caught his arm
convulsively between her two slender little hands, so
feeble at any other time, so strong to-night.

“ Did he, did he, did he?” she cried passionately ;
“ did Darrell ask to see me ?   O, George Duke, on
your honour as a gentleman, as a sailor, as a trusted
servant of his gracious majesty, by your hope in
heaven, by your faith in God, did Darrell Markham
ask to see me ? ”

The Captain kept her waiting for his answer while he went back to the parlour and lighted a wax taper at the flickering flame in the high candlestick.

"I shan't say no, and I shan't say yes," he said; "I'm not going to be go-between for you and him. Good-night," he added, walking past his wife as she stood in the little passage, and going slowly up the stairs; if you've a mind to sit up all night, do so, by all means, Mistress Duke. It's on the stroke of two, and I'm tired. Good-night!"

He went upstairs, and entered a little sleeping-room over the parlour in which they had been seated. It was simply but handsomely furnished, and the most exquisite neatness prevailed in all its arrangements. A tiny fire burned on the hearth, but though the Captain shivered, it was to the window he directed his steps. He opened it very softly, and leaned out, as the clocks struck two. "I thought so," he said, as he heard the faint rattle of bolts and the creaking of a door. "By the heaven above me, I knew she would go to him!"

The faint sound of a light and rapid footstep broke the silence of the quiet street. "And the least agitation might be fatal!" said the Captain of the Vulture, as he softly closed the casement window.

Darrell Markham lay in a death-like stupor in the blue chamber at the Black Bear. Mr. Jordan, the doctor, had declared that his shattered arm, if it ever was set at all, could not be set for some days to come; and the Compton surgeon had thoughts of sending for a distinguished bone-setter in the town of Marley Water, celebrated for twisting distorted limbs into their places, by means of a hideous paraphernalia of racks and pulleys. In the meantime, Mrs. Sarah Pecker had received directions to bathe the swollen limb constantly with a cooling lotion. But on no account, should the young man again return to consciousness, was the worthy landlady of the Black Bear to disturb him with either lamentations or inquiries. Neither was she, at hazard of his life, to admit any one into the room but the doctor himself.

Mrs. Pecker devoted herself to her duties as nurse to the wounded man with a good will, merely remarking that she should very much like to see the individual, male or female, as would come a-nigh him, to worrit or to vex him; "for if it was the parson of the parish," she said, with determination, "he musn't set much account on his eyesight if he tries to circumvent Sarah Pecker."

"No one must come a-nigh him, once for all, and once and for ever," added Mrs. Pecker sharply, as she faced about on the great staircase, and confronted a little crowd of pale faces; for all the household had thronged round her when she emerged from the sick room, in their eagerness to get tidings of Darrell Markham; "and I won't have *you*," she continued, with especial acerbity, to her lord and master, the worthy Samuel, "I won't have *you* a-comin' and a worritin' with your 'Ain't he better, Sarah?' and Don't you think he'll get over it, Sarah?' and such-ike! When a poor dear young gentleman's arm is shivered to a jelly," she said, addressing herself generally, "and when a poor dear young gentleman has been a-lying left for dead on a lonely moor, for ever so many cruel hours on a cold October night, he don't get over

it in twenty minutes, no, nor yet in half an hour either.
So what you've all got to do is just to go back to the
kitchen, and sit there quiet till one or other of you is
wanted; for whatever Master Darrell wants shall be
got. Yes, if he wanted the king's golden crown and
sceptre, one of you should walk to London and fetch
'em!" Having thus declared her supreme pleasure,
Mrs. Pecker reascended the stairs, and re-entered the
sick room; while the doctor, who had declared his
intention of staying all night at the inn, lay down to
take a brief slumber in a neighbouring apartment.

" If a person could be in two places at once, any way
convenient," muttered the landlord, as he withdrew
into the offices of the inn, " why I could account for it
most easy; but seein' they can't, or seein' as how the
parson says they can't, it's too much for me," upon
which Mr. Samuel Pecker seated himself on a great
settle before the kitchen fire, and began to scratch his
head feebly.

" I think as Mr. Markham's had himself shot in the
arm, and she ain't over likely to be a-comin' downstairs,
I might ventur on a mug of the eightpenny," the landlord by-and-by remarked thoughtfully.

It was half-past two by the eight-day clock on the
stairs, and the landlord was going to fetch himself this
very mug of beer, when he was arrested in the hall by
a feeble knocking at the stout oaken door, which had
been closed and barred for the night.

The candle nearly dropped from the hand of the
nervous landlord. "Ghosts, I daresay," he muttered;
" Compton's full of 'em. I used to think the spirits
was confined to the churchyard, and that was bad
enough, but now they've taken to riding straight up to

a man's own door and asking him questions. I wonder what's to become of us. I only wish they'd take to haunting Sarah. Her nerves would be equal to 'em. I don't think if they faced her once when her temper was up, as they'd care to face her again."

The knocking was repeated while the landlord stood meditating thus; this time a little louder.

"They knocks hard for spirits," said Samuel, "and they're pretty persevering." The knocking was still continued—still growing louder. "O, then, I suppose I must," murmured Mr. Pecker, with a groan; but when I undoes the bolts, what's the good? Of course there's no one there; and if them as is there wanted to come in, there's no thickness of oak panel would keep 'em out."

There was some one there, however; for when Mr. Pecker had undone the bolts very slowly and very cautiously, and with a great many half-suppressed but captious groans, a woman slid in at the narrow opening of the door, and before Mr. Pecker had recovered his surprise, crossed the hall and made direct for the staircase, at the top of which was the chamber wherein Darrell Markham lay.

Terror of the vengeance of the ponderous Sarah seized upon the soul of the landlord, and with an unwonted activity he ran forward, and intercepted the woman at the bottom of the stairs.

"You musn't, ma'am," he said, "you musn't; excuse me, ma'am, but it's as much as my life, or even the parson—yes, ma'am, Sarah!" thus vaguely the terrified Samuel.

The woman threw back the large grey hood which had muffled her face.

"Don't you know me, Mr. Pecker?" she asked. "'Tis I, Millicent, Millicent—Duke."

"You, Miss Millicent! You, Mrs. Duke! O miss, O ma'am, your poor dear cousin!"

"Mr. Pecker, for the love of mercy, don't keep me from him. Stand out of the way, stand out of the way," she said passionately; "he may die while you're talking to me here.",

"But, ma'am, you musn't go to him; the doctor, ma'am, and Sarah, Miss Millicent. Sarah, she was quite awful about it, ma'am!"

"Stand aside," cried Mrs. Duke; "I tell you a raging fire shouldn't stop me. Stand aside!"

"No, ma'am—but Sarah!"

Millicent Duke stretched out two slender white hands, and pushed the landlord from her way with a strength that sent him sliding round the polished oak banister of the lowest stair. She flew up the flight of steps, which brought her to the door of the blue room, and on the threshold found herself face to face with Mrs. Sarah Pecker.

The girl fell on her knees, with her hair falling loose about her shoulders, and her long grey cloak trailing round her on the polished oaken floor.

"Sarah, Sarah, darling—Sarah, dear, let me see him."

"Not you, not you, nor any one," said the landlady sternly—"you the last of all persons, Mrs. George Duke."

The name struck her like a blow, and she shivered under the cruelty of the thrust.

"Let me see him!—let me see him!" she said; "his father's brother's only child—his first cousin—his

playfellow—his friend—his dear and loving friend—
his——"

"His wife that was to have been, Mrs. Duke," interrupted the landlady.

"His wife that was to have been; and never, never
should have been another's. His loving, true, and
happy wife that would have been. Let me see him!"
cried Millicent piteously, holding up her clasped hands
to Mrs. Pecker.

"The doctor's in there; do you want him to hear
you, Mrs. Duke?"

"If all the world heard me, I wouldn't stop from
asking you: Sarah, let me see my cousin, Darrell
Markham!"

The landlady—holding a candle in her hand, and
looking down at the piteous face and the tearful eyes
that were almost blinded by the loose pale golden hair
—softened a little as she said,—

"Miss Millicent, the doctor has forbidden a mortal
creature to come a-nigh him—the doctor has forbidden
a mortal soul to say one word to him that could disturb
or agitate him—and do you think the sight of your face
wouldn't agitate him?"

"But he asked to see me, Sarah; he spoke of me!"

"When, Miss Millicent?"

Softening towards this pitiful pale face looking up
into hers, the landlady no longer called her dead master's daughter by the new, hard, cruel name of Mrs.
Duke. "When, Miss Millicent?"

"To-night—to-night, Sarah."

"Master Darrell asked to see you! Who told you
that?"

"Captain Duke."

"Master Darrell hasn't said better than a dozen words this night, Miss Millicent; and those words were mad words, and never once spoke your name."

"But my husband said——"

"The Captain sent you here, then?"

"No, no; he didn't send me here. He told me—at least, he gave me to understand—that Darrell had spoken of me—had asked to see me."

"Your husband's a strange gentleman, Miss Millicent."

"Let me see him, Sarah, only let me see him. I won't speak one word, or breathe one sigh; only let me see him."

Mrs. Pecker withdrew for a few moments into the blue room, and whispered something to the doctor. Millicent Duke, still on her knees on the threshold of the half-opened door, strained her eyes as if she would have pierced through the thick oak that separated her from her prostrate kinsman.

The landlady returned to the door, accompanied by the doctor, who went downstairs to fetch some potion he had ordered for his patient.

"If you want to look at a corpse, Miss Millicent, you may come in and look at him, for he lies as still as one," said Mrs. Pecker.

She took the kneeling girl in her stout arms, and half lifted her into the room, where, opposite a blazing fire, Darrell Markham lay unconscious on a great draperied four-post bed. His head was thrown back upon the pillow, the fair hair dabbled with a lotion with which Mrs. Pecker had been bathing the scalp-wound spoken of by the doctor. Millicent tottered to the bedside, and seating herself in an arm-chair which had been occupied by Sarah Pecker, took Darrel Markham's hand in hers, and pressed it to her tremulous lips. It seemed as if there was something magical in this gentle pressure, for the young man's eyes opened for the first time since the scene in the hall, and he looked at his cousin.

"Millicent," he said, without any sign of surprise "dear Millicent, it is so good of you to watch me."

She had nursed him three years before through a dangerous illness, and it was scarcely strange if in his delirium he confused the present with the past, fancying that he was in his old room at Compton Hall, and that his cousin had been watching by his bedside.

"Call my uncle," he said, "call the squire; I want to see him!" and then after a pause he muttered, looking about him, "surely this is not the old room—surely some one has altered the room."

"Master Darrell, dear," cried the landlady, "don't you know where you are? With friends, Master Darrell, true and faithful friends. Don't you know, dear?"

"Yes, yes," he said, "I know, I know. I've been lying out in the cold, and my arm is hurt. I remember, Sally, I remember; but my head feels strange, and I can scarce tell where I am."

"See here, Master Darrell, here's Mistress Duke has come all the way from the other end of Compton on this bitter black night on purpose to see you."

The good woman said this to comfort the patient, but the utterance of that one name, Duke, recalled his cousin's marriage, and the young man exclaimed bitterly,—

"Mistress Duke! yes, I remember ' and then, turning his weary head upon the pillow, he cried with a sudden energy, "Millicent Duke, Millicent Duke, why do you come here to torture me with the sight of you?"

At this moment there arose the sound of some altercation in the hall below, and then the noise of two voices in dispute, and hurried footsteps upon the staircase. Mrs. Pecker ran to the door, but before she could reach it, it was burst violently open, and the Captain of the Vulture strode into the room. He was closely followed by the doctor, who walked straight to the bedside, exclaiming with suppressed passion, "I protest against this, Captain Duke; and if any ill consequences come of it, I hold you answerable for the mischief."

The Captain took no notice of this speech, but, turning to his wife, said savagely, "Will it please you to go home with me, Mistress Millicent? It is near upon four o'clock, and a sick gentleman's room is scarce a fit place for a lady at such a time."

Darrell Markham lifted himself up in bed, and cried with an hysterical laugh, "I tell you that's the man, Millicent; Sarah, look at him. That is the man who stopped me upon Compton Moor—the man who shot me in the arm, and rifled me of my purse."

"Darrell! Darrell!" cried Millicent; "you do not know what you are saying. That man is my husband."

"Your husband! A highwayman!—a——"

Whatever word was on Mr. Markham's lips remained unspoken, for he fell back insensible upon the pillow."

"Captain George Duke," said the surgeon, laying his hand upon his patient's wrist, "if this man dies, you have committed a murder!"

CHAPTER III.

LOOKING BACK.

JOHN HOMERTON, the blacksmith, only spoke advisedly when he said that the young squire, Ringwood Markham, was ruining himself up in London. The simple inhabitants of villages are apt to exaggerate the dangers and the vices of that unknown metropolis of which they hear such strange stories ; but in this case honest Master Homerton did not exaggerate, for the young squire was hurrying at a good rattling pace along that smooth and easy highway known as the road to ruin.

Ringwood Markham was three years older than his sister Millicent, and six years younger than his cousin Darrell ; for old Squire Markham had married late in life, and had, shortly after his marriage, adopted little Darrell, the only child of a younger brother, who had died early, leaving a small fortune to his orphan boy.

Ringwood Markham in person closely resembled his sister. He had the same pale golden hair, the deep limpid blue eyes, the small features, and delicate pink-and-white complexion. But that style of beauty which was charming in a girl of nineteen was far too effeminate to be pleasing in a man of two-and-twenty, and the old squire had been sorely vexed to see his beloved son grow up into nothing better than a pretty boy—a fair-faced dollish young coxcomb, the admiration of simpering school-girls and middle-aged women, and the type of the Strephons and Damons who at that time overran our English poetry. .

Ringwood had always been his father's favourite, to **the** exclusion even of pretty, lovable, and loving Millicent; and as Darrell grew to manhood, it vexed the old squire to see the elder cousin high-spirited and stalwart, broad-chested and athletic, accomplished in all manly exercises, a good shot, an expert swordsman, a bold horseman, and reckless, daredevil, generous, thought-less, open-hearted lad; while Ringwood only thought of his pretty face and his embroidered waistcoat, and loved the glittering steel ornaments of his sword-hilt far better than the blade of the weapon.

It was hard for the squire to have to confess the humiliating truth, even to himself; but it was not the less a fact that Ringwood Markham was a milksop.

The old man concealed his mortification in the most secret recesses of his heart, and, with a spirit of injustice which is one of the weaknesses of passionate love, hated Darrell for being so superior to his son.

This was how the pale face of sorrow first peeped in upon the little family group at Compton Hall.

Darrell and Millicent had loved each other from that early childish but unforgotten day on which the orphan boy peeped into his baby cousin's cradle, and gazed with admiring wonder at her pretty face and tiny rosy hands, so ready to twine themselves with a warm caressing touch around the boy's coarser fingers.

I am not perhaps justified in saying that love on her side began so soon as this, but I know that it did on his; and I know too that the first syllables cousin Milly ever lisped were those two simple sounds that shaped the name of Darrell.

They loved each other from such an early age, and they loved each other so honestly and truly, that perhaps they were never, in the legitimate sense of the word, lovers,

They had no pretty coquettish jealousies; no charming quarrels and more charming reconciliations; no
stolen meetings by moonlit nights; no interposition of
bribed waiting-maids charged with dainty perfumed
notes. No; they loved each other honestly and openly,
with a calm unchanging affection which had so little
need of words, that few lookers-on would perhaps have
suspected the depth and strength of so tranquil a
passion.

If the squire saw this growing attachment between
the young people, he neither favoured nor discouraged
it. He had never cared very much for Millicent. She
and her brother were the children of a woman whom he
had married for the sake of a handsome fortune, and
who died unnoticed and unregretted—some people said,
of a broken heart—before Millicent was a twelvemonth
old.

So things went on pretty smoothly. Millicent and
Darrell rode together through the shady green lanes,
and over the stunted grass and heather on Compton
Moor, while the squire read his Postboys and Gazeteers
and smoked his pipe in the oak-panelled parlour or
the Dutch garden, and while Ringwood idled about
the village or lounged at the bar of the Black Bear:
and life seemed altogether very easy and pleasant
at Compton Hall, until a catastrophe occurred which
changed the whole current of events.

Darrell and Ringwood Markham had a desperate
quarrel; a quarrel in which blows were struck and hard
words spoken upon both sides, and which abruptly ended
Darrell's residence at Compton Hall.

It has been said that Ringwood Markham was a coxcomb and an idler. There were not wanting those in

Compton who called him something worse than either
of these. There were some who called him a heartless
coward and a liar, but who never so spoke of him in
the presence of his stalwart cousin Darrell.

The day came when Darrell himself called the
uirc's idolized son by these cruel names. He had
iscovered a flirtation between Ringwood and a girl of
seventeen, the daughter of a small farmer; a flirtation
which, but for this timely discovery, might have ended
in shame and despair. Scarlet with passion, the young
man had taken his foppish cousin by the collar of his
velvet coat and dragged him safe into the presence of
the father of the girl, saying, with an oath, such as was
unhappily only too common a hundred years ago,—

"You'd better keep an eye on this young man,
Farmer Morrison, if you want to save your daughter
from a scoundrel."

Ringwood turned very white—he was one of those
who grow pale and not red with passion—and springing
at his cousin like a cat, caught at his throat as if he
would have strangled him; but one swinging blow from
Darrell's fist laid the young man on Farmer Morrison's
sanded floor, with a general illumination glittering
before his dazzled eyes.

Darrell strode back to the Hall, where he packed
some clothes in his saddle-bags, and wrote two letters,
one to his uncle, telling him, abruptly enough, that he
had knocked Ringwood down, because he had found
him acting like a rascal, and that he felt, as there was
now bad blood between them, they had better part.
His second letter was addressed to Millicent, and was
almost as brief as the first. He simply told her of the
quarrel, adding that he was going to London to seek

his fortune, and that he should return to claim her as his wife.

He left the letters on the high chimney-piece in his bedroom, and went down to the stables, where he found his own nag Balmerino, fastened his few possessions to the saddle, mounted the horse in the yard, and rode slowly away from the house in which his boyhood and youth had been spent.

He went away very sad at heart, but possessed and sustained by that hopeful spirit common to generous youth. It seemed such an easy thing to make a fortune to carry back to his cousin Millicent. That great oyster, the world, was waiting to be opened by the bold thrust of an adventurous sword, and who could doubt what rare and priceless pearls were lurking within the shell, ready to fall into the open hands of the valiant adventurer?

Ringwood Markham went home late at night with a pale face and a blood-stained handkerchief bound about his forehead.

He found his father sitting over a spark of fire in the oak parlour on one side of the hall. The door of this parlour was ajar, and as the young man tried to creep past on his way upstairs, the squire called to him sharply, "Ringwood, come here!"

He went sulkily into the room, hanging his dilapidated head, and looking at the floor; altogether an abject creature to behold.

"What's the matter with your head, Ringwood?" asked the squire.

"The pony shied at some sheep on the moor, and threw me against a stone," muttered the young man.

"You're telling a lie, Ringwood Markham!" cried

his father fiercely. "I've a letter from your cousin
Darrell in my pocket. Bah, man! you're the first of
the Markhams who ever took a blow without paying it
back with interest. You've your mother's milk-and-
water disposition, as well as your mother's pink-and-
white face."

"You needn't talk about her," said Ringwood; "you
didn't treat her too well, if folks that I know speak
the truth."

"Ringwood Markham, don't provoke me. It's hard
enough for a Markham of Compton to have a son that
can't take his own part. Go to bed."

The young man left the room with the same slouch-
ing step with which he had entered it. He stole
cautiously upstairs, for he thought his cousin Darrell
was still in the house, and he had no wish to arouse
that gentleman.

So Millicent was left alone at Compton Hall; utterly
alone, for she had now no one to love her.

Perhaps modern physiologists would have discovered
in the nature of Millicent Markham much to wonder at
and to explain. It was a delicate and fragile piece of
mechanism—very exquisite if you could only keep it in
order, but terribly liable to be injured or destroyed.
The squire's daughter was not a clever girl; her intellectual amusements were of the simplest order. An
old romance would make her happy for days, and she
would cry over the mildest verses ever written by
starveling poets in garrets east of Temple Bar. With
her the heart took the place of the mind. Appeal to her
affection, and you might make her what you pleased.
If Darrell had asked her to learn Greek for his
sake, she would have toiled valiantly through dreary

obscurities of grammar, she would have dug patiently at the dryest roots, and would have seated herself meekly by his side to construe the hardest page in Homer. Love her, and her whole nature expanded like some beautiful flower that spreads itself out beneath the morning sun. Withdraw this benign influence, and the same nature contracted into something smaller and meaner than itself—something easily crushed into any shape whatever by a little rough handling.

Darrell, therefore, being gone, and dear old Sally Masterson having left the Hall to become mistress of the Black Bear, poor Millicent was abandoend to the tender mercies of her father and brother, neither of whom cared much more for her than they did for the meek white and liver-coloured spaniel that followed her about the house. So the delicate piece of mechanism got out of order, and Millicent's days were devoted to novel reading and to poring over an embroidered waistcoat-piece that was destined for Darrell, and the colours of which were dull and faded from the tears that had dropped upon the stitches as the patient worker bent over her labour of love, and thought of the absent lover for whose adornment the garment was intended.

She kept Darrell's letter in her bosom. In all the ways of the world she was as unlearned as on that day when Darrell had peeped in upon her as she lay asleep in her cradle, and she had no more doubt that her cousin would make a fortune and return in a few years to claim her as his wife than she had of her own existence. But in spite of this hope, the days were long and dreary, her father neglectful, her brother supercilious and disagreeable, and her home altogether very miserable.

The bitterest misery was yet to come. It came in the person of a certain Captain George Duke, who dropped into Compton on his way from Marley Water to the metropolis, and who contrived to scrape acquaintance with Squire Markham in the best parlour at the Black Bear. Captain George and Master Ringwood became sworn friends in a day or two, and the hearty sailor promised to stop at Compton again on his return to his ship the Vulture.

The simple villagers readily accepted Captain Duke as that which he had represented himself—an officer of his majesty's navy; but there were people in the seaport of Marley Water who said that the good ship whose name was written down as the Vulture in the Admiralty books was quite a different class of vessel from the trim little craft which lay sometimes in a quiet corner of the obscure harbour of Marley. There were malicious people who whispered such words as 'privateer—pirate—slaver;' but the boldest of the slanderers took good care to whisper these things out of the Captain's hearing, for George Duke's sword was as often out of his scabbard as in it, during his brief visits to the little seaport.

However this might be, handsome, rollicking, lighthearted, free-handed George Duke became a great favourite with Squire Markham and his son Ringwood. His animal spirits enlivened the dreary old mansion, and stirred the stagnation of the quiet village life very pleasantly for the Squire and his son. The sailor's roystering stories of sea-going adventures pleased the two landsmen: and the sailor himself, who was a man of the world, and knew how to flatter a profitable acquaintance, seemed the most agreeable of men, and the heartiest of good fellows.

So Compton Hall rang night after night with the gay peals of his cheery laughter; corks flew, and glasses jingled, as the three men sat up till midnight (a terrible hour at Compton) over their Burgundy and claret. It was in one of these half-drunken bouts that Squire Markham promised the hand of his daughter Millicent to Captain George Duke.

"You're in love with her, George, and you shall have her," the old man said. "I can give her a couple of thousand pounds at my death, and if anything should happen to Ringwood, she'll be sole heiress to the Compton property. You shall have her, my boy. I know there's some sneaking courtship been going on between Milly and a broad-shouldered fair-haired nephew of mine, but that shan't stand in your way, for the lad is no favourite with me; and if I choose to say it, my fine lack-a-daisical miss shall marry you in a week's time."

Captain Duke sprang from his chair, and wringing the Squire's hand in his, cried out with a lover's rapture,—

"She's the prettiest girl in England! and I'd sooner have her for my wife than any duchess at St. James's."

"She's pretty enough, as for that," said Ringwood superciliously, "and she'd be a deal prettier if she was not always whimpering."

Farmer Morrison could have told how Master Ringwood himself had gone whimpering out of the sanded kitchen on the day that Darrell Markham knocked him down. The plain-spoken farmer had felt no little contempt for the heir of Compton Hall, whose **wounded** head he had dressed for charity's sake, before dismissing the young man with an emphatic assurance that if he ever came about those premises again, it would be to get such a thrashing as he would easily be able to remember.

Both the children inherited something of the nervous weakness of that poor delicate and neglected mother who had died seventeen years before in Sally Masterson's arms; but timid and sensitive as Millicent was, I think that the higher nature had been given to her, and that beneath that childish timidity and that nervous excitability which would bring tears into her eyes at the sound of a harsh word, there was a latent and quiet courage that had no existence in Ringwood's selfish and frivolous character.

Having promised to bestow his daughter's hand on his new favourite, the Captain, Squire Markham lost no time in carrying out his intention. He summoned Millicent to the oak parlour early on the morning after the drunken carouse, and acquainted her with the manner in which he had disposed of her destiny.

Harsh words on this occasion, as on every other, did their work with Millicent Markham. She heard her father's determination that she should marry George Duke, at first with a stupid apathetic stare, as if the calamity were too great for her to realize its misery at one grasp; then, as he repeated his command, her clear blue eyes brimmed over with big tears, and she fell on her knees at the Squire's feet.

"You don't mean it, sir?" she said piteously, clasping her poor little feeble hands and lifting them towards her father in passionate supplication. "You know that I love my cousin Darrell; that we have loved each

other dearly and truly ever since we were little children; and that we are to be man and wife when you
are pleased to give your consent. You must have known
it all along, sir, though we had not the courage to
tell you. I will be your obedient child in everything
but this; but I never, never can marry any one but
Darrell!"

What need to tell the old story of a stupid, obstinate,
narrow-minded country squire's fury and tyranny? Did
not poor Sophia Western suffer all these torments,
though in the dear old romance all is so happily settled
in the last chapter? But in this case it was different—
Squire Markham would hear of no delay; and before
Darrell could get the letter which Millicent addressed
to a coffee-house near Covent Garden, and bribed one of
the servants to give to the Compton postmaster—before
the eyes of the bride had recovered from long nights
of weeping—before the village had half discussed the
matter—before Mrs. Sarah Pecker could finish the
petticoat she was quilting very sorrowfully for the
wedding clothes—the bells of Compton church were
ringing a cheery peal in the morning sunshine, and
Millicent Markham and George Duke were standing
side by side at the altar.

When Darrell Markham received the poor little tear-
stained letter, telling him of this ill-omened marriage,
he fell into an outburst of rage; an outburst of blind
fury which swept alike upon the Squire, young Ringwood, Captain George Duke, and even poor unhappy
Millicent herself. It is so difficult for a man to understand the influence brought so bear upon a weak helpless woman by the tyranny of a brutal father. Darrell
cried out passionately that Millicent ought to have been

true to him in spite of the whole world, as he would
have been to her through every trial. He hurried down
to Compton to creep stealthily about the village after
dusk, lest his presence should bring evil upon the
woman he loved, and to discover that he was indeed too
late—that the piteous blotted letter had told him no
more than the cruel truth, and that the Squire had
kept his word.

Made desperate by the shipwreck of his happiness, the young man went back to London with
angry feelings burning in his breast. He rushed for
a brief period into the dissipations of the town, and
tried to drown Millicent's fair face in tavern mea-
sures and long draughts of Burgundy, and to forget
his troubles among the patched and painted beauties
of Spring Gardens.

A marriage contracted under such circumstances
was not likely to be a very happy one. Light-hearted,
rollicking George Duke was by no means a delightful
person by the domestic hearth. The man whose lively
spirits are the delight of his tavern acquaintances is apt
to be rather a dull companion in the family circle. At
home the Captain was moody and ill-tempered, always
ready to grumble at Millicent's pale face and tear-
swollen eyes. For the best part of the year he was away
with his ship, on some of those mysterious voyages
of which the Admiralty knew so little; and in these
long absences, Millicent, if not happy, was at least at
rest. Three months after the wedding the old Squire
was found dead in his arm-chair, a victim to apoplexy
engendered of sedentary habits and high living; and
Ringwood, succeeding to the estate, shut up the Hall,
and rushed away to London, where he was soon lost to

the honest folks of Compton in a whirlpool of vice and dissipation.

This was how matters stood when George and Millicent had been married fifteen months, and Darrell Markham well-nigh lost his life at the hands of a highway robber upon the dreary moorland road to Marley Water.

CHAPTER IV.

CAPTAIN DUKE PROVES AN ALIBI.

DARRELL MARKHAM did not die from the effects of that excitement which the doctor said might be so fatal. The surgeon fought bravely with the fever, and the bone-setter from Marley Water did his work well, though not without agony to the patient; for there were no blessed anæsthetics in those days, whereby a man might be lulled into peaceful repose while the operator's knife hacked his flesh, or the surgeon's relentless hand dragged his unwilling muscles and distorted bones back to their proper places.

Darrell was very slow to recover, so slow that the snow lay white upon the moorland beneath the windows of the Black Bear before the shattered arm was firmly knit together, or the enfeebled frame restored to its native vigour. It was a dreary and a tedious illness. Honest Sarah Pecker was nearly worn out with nursing her sick boy, as she insisted on calling Darrell. The weak-eyed and weak-minded Samuel was made to wear list shoes and to creep like a thief about his roomy hostelry. The evening visitors were sent into a dark tap-room at the back of the house, in order that the sound of their revelry might not disturb the sick man. Gloom and sadness reigned in the Black Bear until that happy day upon which Dr. Jordan pronounced his patient to be out of danger. Sarah Pecker gave away a barrel of the strongest ale upon that joyous afternoon, pouring the generous liquor freely out for every loiterer who stopped at the door to ask after poor Maister Darrell.

Captain George Duke was away on a brief voyage on the Spanish coast when Darrell began to mend; but by the time the young man had completely recovered, the sailor returned to Compton.

The snow was thick in the narrow street when the Captain came back. He came without warning, and walked quietly into the little parlour, where he found Millicent sitting in her old attitude by the fire, reading a novel.

But he was in a better temper than usual on this particular occasion, and looked wonderfully handsome and dashing in his weather-beaten uniform. It was not quite the king's uniform, as some people said; very like it; but yet with slight technical differences that told against the Captain.

George Duke caught Millicent in his arms and gave her a hearty kiss upon each cheek before he had time to notice her faint repellent shudder.

"I've come home to you laden with good things, Mistress Milly," he said, as he seated himself opposite to her, while the stout servant-maid piled fresh logs upon the blazing fire. "A chest of oranges, and a cask of wine from Cadiz—liquid gold, my girl, and almost as precious as the sterling metal; and I've a heap of pretty barbarous trumpery for you to fasten on

your white neck and arms, and hang in your rosy little
ears."

The Captain took an old-fashioned, queerly-shaped
leather case from his pocket, and opened it on the little
table where he spread out a quantity of foreign jewellry
that glittered and twinkled in the firelight. Arabesqued
gold of wonderful workmanship glimmered in that rosy
firelight, and strange outlandish many-coloured gems
sparkled upon the dark oak table and reflected themselves deep down in the polished wood, like stars in a river.

Millicent blushed as she bent over the trinkets, and
stammered out some gentle grateful phrases. She was
blushing to think how little she cared for all these gew-
gaws, and how her soul was set on another treasure
which never could be hers—the forbidden treasure of
Darrell's deep and honest love.

As she was thinking this, the Captain looked up at
her, carelessly as it seemed, but in reality with a very
searching glance in his flashing brown eyes.

"O, by the bye," he said, "how is that pretty fair-
haired cousin of yours ?   Has he recovered from that
affair? or was it his death ?"

There was a malicious sparkle in his eyes, as he
watched his wife shiver at the sound of that cruel word
"death."

"That's another figure in the long score between you
and me, my lady," he thought.

"He is much better.   Indeed, he is nearly well,"
Millicent said quietly.

"Have you seen him ?"

"Never since the night on which you found me at
his bedside."

She looked up at him calmly, almost proudly, as she

spoke. It was a look that seemed to say, " I have a
clear conscience, and, do what you will, you cannot
make me blush or falter."

She had indeed a clear conscience. Many times
Sarah Pecker had come to her, and said, " Your cousin
is very low to-night, Miss Millicent; come and sit
beside him, if it's only for half an hour; to cheer him
up a bit. Poor old Sally will be with you, and where
she is, the hardest can't say there's harm."

But Millicent had always steadily refused, saying,
"It would only make us both unhappy, Sally, dear.
I'd rather not come."

None knew how, sometimes late at night, when the
maid-servant had gone to bed, and the lights in the
upper windows of Compton High Street had been
one by one extinguished, this same inflexible Millicent
would steal out, muffled in a long cloak of shadowy
grey, and creep to the roadway under the Black Bear,
to stand for ten minutes in the snow or rain, watching
the faint light that shone from the window of the room
where Darrell Markham lay.

Once, standing ankle-deep in snow, she saw Sarah
Pecker open the window to look out at the night, and
heard her cousin's voice asking if it were snowing.

She burst into tears at the sound of this feeble voice.
It seemed so long since she had heard it, she half
fancied that she might never hear it again.

One of the Vulture's men brought the case of oranges
and the cask of sherry from Marley to Compton upon
the very night of the Captain's return, and George
Duke drank half a bottle of the liquid gold before he
went to bed. He tried in vain to induce Millicent to
taste the topaz-coloured liquor. She liked Sarah Pecker's

cowslip wine better than the finest sherry ever grown in the Peninsula.

Early the next morning the Compton constable came to the cottage armed with a warrant for the apprehension of Captain George Duke on a charge of assault and robbery on the king's highway. Pale with suppressed fury, the Captain strode into the little parlour where Millicent was seated at breakfast.

"Pray, Mistress Millicent," he said, "who has set on your pretty cousin to try and hang an innocent man, with the intent to make a hempen widow of you, as I suppose? What is the meaning of this?"

"Of what, George?" she asked, bewildered by his manner.

He told her the whole story of the warrant. "Of course," he said, "you remember this Master Darrell's crying out that it was I who shot him?"

"I do, George; I thought then that it was some strange feverish fancy, and I think so now."

"I scarcely expected so much of your courtesy, Mistress Duke," answered her husband. "Luckily for me, I can pretty easily clear myself from this mad-brained charge; but I am not the less grateful to Darrell Markham for his kind intent."

The constable took Captain Duke at once to the magistrate's parlour, where he found Darrell Markham seated, pale from his long illness, and with his arm still in a sling.

"Thank you, Mr. Markham, for this good turn," said the Captain, folding his arms and placing himself against the doorway of the magistrate's room; "we shall find an opportunity of squaring our accounts some of these days, I daresay."

The worthy magistrate was not a little puzzled as to how to deal with the case before him. Little as was known in Compton of Captain George Duke, it seemed incredible that so fine a gentleman and the husband of Squire Markham's daughter could be guilty of highway robbery. But in those days highway robbery was a very common offence, and the public had been astonished by more than one strange discovery. Finer gentlemen than Captain Duke had tried to mend their desperate fortunes on the king's highway.

Darrell stated his charge in the simplest and most straightforward fashion. He had ridden away from the Black Bear to go to Marley Water. Three miles from Compton, a man whom he swore to have been no other than the accused, rode up to him and demanded his purse and watch. He drew his pistol from his belt, but while he was cocking it, the man, Captain Duke, fired, shot him in the arm, dragged him off his horse, and threw him into the mud. He remembered nothing more until he awoke in the hall at the Black Bear, and recognized the accused amongst the bystanders.

The magistrate coughed dubiously.

"Cases of mistaken identity have not been uncommon in the judicial history of this country," he said, sententiously. "Can you swear, Mr. Markham, that the man who attacked you was Captain George Duke?"

"If that man standing against the door is Captain Duke, I can solemnly swear that he is the man who robbed me."

"When you were found by the persons who picked you up, was your horse found also?"

"No, the horse was gone."

ᴇ

"Would you know him again?"

"Know him again? What, honest Balmerino? I should know him amongst a thousand."

"Hum!" said the magistrate, "that is a great point; I consider the horse a great point."

He pondered so long over his very important part of the case, that his clerk had occasion to nudge him respectfully and to whisper something in his ear before he went on again.

"O, ah, yes, to be sure, of course," he muttered helplessly; then clearing his throat, he said in his magisterial voice, "Pray, Captain Duke, what have you to say to this charge?"

"Very little," said the Captain quietly; "but before I speak at all, I should be glad if you would send for Mr. Samuel Pecker, of the Black Bear."

The magistrate whispered to the clerk, and the clerk nodded, on which the magistrate said, "Go, one of you, and fetch the aforesaid Samuel Pecker."

While one of the hangers-on was gone upon this errand, the worthy magistrate nodded over his *Flying Post*, the clerk mended the fire, and Mr. Darrell Markham and the Captain stared fiercely at each other—an ominous red glimmer burning in the sailor's brown eyes.

Mr. Pecker came, with a white face and limp disordered hair, to attend the magisterial summons. He had some vague idea that hanging by the neck till he was dead might be the result of this morning's work; or that, happily escaping that last penalty of the law, he would suffer a hundred moral deaths at the hands of Sarah, his wife. He could not for a moment imagine that he could possibly be wanted in the magistrate's

parlour unless accused of some monstrous though un-
consciously committed crime.

He gave a faint gasp of relief when some one in
the room whispered to him that he was required as a
witness.

"Now, Captain Duke," said the magistrate, "what
have you to say to this?"

"Will you be good enough to ask Mr. Darrell Markham two or three questions?"

The magistrate looked at the clerk, the clerk nodded
to the magistrate, and the magistrate nodded an assent
to Captain Duke's request.

"Will you ask if he knows at what time the assault
was committed?"

Before the magistrate could interpose, Darrell Markham spoke.

"I happen to be able to answer that question with
certainty," he said. "The wind was blowing straight
across the moor, and I distinctly heard Compton church
clock chime the three-quarters after seven as the man
rode up to me."

"As I rode up to you?" asked George Duke.

"As *you* rode up to me," answered Darrell.

"Mr. Samuel Pecker, will you be so good as to
tell the magistrate where I was at a quarter to
eight o'clock upon the night of the 27th of October?"

"You were in the parlour of the Bear, Captain,"
answered Samuel, in short gasps; "and you came in
and asked the time, which I went out to look at our
eight-day on the stairs, and it were ten minutes to
eight exact by father's eight-day, as is never a minute
wrong."

"There were other people in the parlour that night who saw me and who heard me ask the question, were there not, Mr. Pecker?"

"There were a many of 'em," replied Samuel; "which they saw you wind your watch by father's eight-day; for it weren't you, Captain Duke, as robbed Master Darrell, but *I* know who it were."

. There was stupefaction in the court at this extraordinary assertion.

"You know!" cried the magistrate; "then, pray, why have you withheld the knowledge from those entitled to hear it?   This is very bad, Mr. Pecker; very bad indeed!"

The unhappy Samuel felt that he was in for it.

"It were no more Captain Duke than it were me," he gasped; "it were the other."

"The other!   What other?"

"Him as stopped his horse at the door of the Black Bear, and asked the way to Marley Water."

Nothing could remove Samuel Pecker from his position.   Questioned and cross-questioned by the magistrate, the clerk, and Darrell Markham, he steadfastly declared that a man so closely resembling Captain Duke as to deceive both himself and John Homerton the blacksmith had stopped at the Black Bear and asked the way to Marley.

He gasped and stuttered and choked and bewildered himself, but he neither prevaricated nor broke down in his assertions, and he begged that John Homerton might be summoned to confirm his statement.

John Homerton was summoned, and declared that, to the best of his belief, it was Captain Duke who stopped at the Black Bear, while he, Master Darrell

Markham, and the landlord were standing at the door.

But this assertion was shivered in a moment by an *alibi*. A quarter of an hour after the traveller had ridden off towards Marley, Captain Duke walked up to the inn from the direction of the High Street.

Neither the magistrate nor the clerk had anything to say to this. The affair seemed altogether a mystery, for which the legal experience of the Compton worthies could furnish no parallel.

If James Dobbs assaulted Farmer Hobbs, upon some question of wheat or turnips, it was easy to deal with him according to the precedent afforded by the cele-brated case of Jones *v.* Smith; but the affair of to-day stood alone in the judicial records of Compton.

While the magistrate and his factotum consulted together in whispers, without getting any nearer to a decision, George Duke himself came to their rescue.

" I suppose, after the charge having broken down in this manner, I need not stop here any longer, sir ? " he said.

The magistrate caught at this chance of extrica-tion.

" The charge *has* broken down," he replied, with solemn importance, "and as you observe, Captain Duke, and as indeed I was about to observe myself, we need not detain you any longer. You leave this room with as good a character as that with which you entered it," he added, while a slight titter circulated amongst some of the bystanders at this rather ambi-guous compliment. " I am sorry, Mr. Markham, that this affair is so involved in mystery. It is evidently a case of mistaken identity, one of the most difficult class of cases that the law ever has to deal with; but, as I said before, I consider the missing horse a great point —a very strong point."

The Captain and Darrell Markham left the room at the same time.

"I have an account to settle with you, Mr. Markham, tor this morning's work," Captain Duke whispered to his accuser.

"I do not fight with highwaymen," Darrell answered proudly.

"What, you still dare to insinuate——"

"I dare to say that I don't believe in this story of George Duke and his double. I believe that you proved an *alibi* by some juggling with the clock at the Black Bear, and I most firmly believe that you are the man who shot me!"

"You shall pay for this," hissed the Captain through his set teeth; "you shall pay double for every insolent word, Darrell Markham, before you and I have done with each other."

He strode away, after flinging one dark wicked look at his wife's cousin, and returned to the cottage, where Millicent, pale and anxious, was awaiting the result of the morning.

Darrell Markham left Compton by the mail coach that very night; and, poorer by the loss of his horse, his watch, and purse, set forth once more to seek his fortunes in cruel stony-hearted London.

CHAPTER V.

MILLICENT MEETS HER HUSBAND'S SHADOW.

A FORTNIGHT after Darrell's departure the good ship Vulture was nearly ready for another cruise, and Captain Duke rode off to Marley Water to superintend the final preparations.

"I shall sail on the thirtieth, Milly," he said, the day he left Compton; "and as I shan't have time to ride over here and say good-bye to you, I should like you to come to Marley, and see me before I start."

"I will come, if you wish me to come, George," she answered quietly. She was always gentle and obedient, something as a child might have been to a hard taskmaster, but in no way like a wife who loved her husband.

"Very good. There's a branch coach passes through here three times a week from York to Carlisle; it stops at Marley Water. You can come by that, Millicent."

"Yes, George."

The snow never melted upon Compton Moor throughout the dark January days. Millicent felt a strange dull aching pain at her heart as she stood before the door of the Black Bear, waiting for the Carlisle coach, and watching the dreary expanse of glistening white that stretched far away to the chill leaden-hued horizon, darkening already in the early winter afternoon. She had seen it often under the tremulous moonlight when Darrell Markham was lying on his sick bed. Dismal as that sad time had been, she looked back to it with a sigh. He was near her then, she thought, and now he was lost in the wild vortex of terrible London—sucked into that great Maelstrom of which she was so ignorant—far away from her and all thoughts of her—happy, it might be, amongst pleasant friends and companions, beautiful women and light-hearted men—lost to her perhaps for ever.

Mrs. Sarah Pecker cried out indignantly at this wintry journey.

"What does the Captain mean by it," she said, "sending of a poor delicate lamb like you four-and-twenty mile in an old fusty stage-coach upon such a afternoon as this? If he wants you to catch your death, Miss Milly, he's a-going the right way to bring about his wicked wishes."

The great heavy lumbering broad-shouldered coach drove up while Mrs. Pecker was still holding forth upon this subject. One or two of the inside passengers looked out and asked for brandy-and-water while the horses were being changed. Some of the outsides clambered down from the roof of the vehicle, and went into the Black Bear to warm themselves at the blazing fire in the parlour, and drink glasses of raw spirits. One man seated upon the box refused to alight, when asked to do so by another passenger. He sat with his face turned away from the inn, looking straight out upon the snowy moorland, while his fellow-travellers refreshed themselves; and he preserved the same attitude so long as the coach stopped.

Even if this man's face had been turned towards the little group at the door of the Black Bear, they would have had considerable difficulty in distinguishing his features, for he wore his three-cornered hat slouched over his eyes, and the collar of his thick horseman's coat drawn close up to his ears.

"He's a grim customer up yonder," said the man who had spoken to this outside passenger, designating him by a jerk of the head—"a regular grim customer. I wonder what he is, and where he's going to."

Mistress Pecker assisted Millicent into the coach, settled her in a warm corner, and wrapped her camlet cloak about her.

"You'd better have one of Samuel's comforters for your throat, Miss Milly," she said, "and one of his coats to wrap about your feet. It's bitter weather for such a journey."

Millicent declined the coat and the comforter; but she kissed her old nurse as the coachman drew his horses together for the start.

"God bless you, Sally," she said; "I wish the journey was over and done with, and that I was back again with you."

The coach drove off before Mrs. Pecker could reply.

"Poor dear child," said the innkeeper's wife, "to think of her going out alone and friendless on such a day as this. She wishes she was back with us, she says. I sometimes think there's a look in her poor mournful blue eyes, as if she wished she was lying quiet and calm in Compton churchyard."

The high road from Compton to Marley Water wound its way across bleak and sterile moors, passing now and then a long straggling village or a lonely farm-house. The journey was longer by this road than by the moorland bridle-path, and it had been dark some time when the stage-coach drove over the uneven pavement of the High Street of Marley Water.

Millicent found her husband waiting for her at the inn where the coach stopped.

"You're just in time, Milly," he said; "the Vulture sails to-night."

Captain Duke was stopping at a tavern on the quay. He put Millicent's arm in his, and led her through the narrow High Street.

This principal street of Marley Water was lighted here and there by feeble oil-lamps, which shed a wan light upon the figures of the foot-passengers.

Glancing behind her once, bewildered by the strange bustle of the busy little sea-port town, Millicent was surprised to see the outside passenger whom she had observed at Compton following close upon their heels.

Captain Duke felt the little hand tighten upon his arm with a nervous shiver.

"What made you start?" he asked.

"The—the man!"

"What man?"

"A man who travelled outside the coach, and whose face was quite hidden by his hat and cloak. I heard the other passengers talking of the man. He was so rude and silent that people took a dislike to him. He is just behind us."

George Duke looked back, but the outside passenger was no longer to be seen.

"What a silly child you are, Millicent!" he said. "What is there so wonderful in your seeing one of your fellow-passengers in the High Street ten minutes after the coach has stopped?"

"But he seemed to be following us."

"Why, my country wench, people walk close behind one another in busy towns without any such thought as following their neighbours. Millicent, Millicent, when will you learn to be wise?"

The Captain of the Vulture seemed in unusually good spirits upon this bitter January night.

"I shall be far away upon the blue water in twenty-four hours, Milly," he said. "No one but a sailor can tell a sailor's weariness of the land. I heard of your brother Ringwood last night."

"Bad news?" asked Millicent anxiously.

"No good news for you, who will come in for his money if he dies unmarried. He's leading a wild life, and wasting his substance in taverns, and worse places than taverns. Luckily for you, the Compton property is safely secured, so that he can neither sell nor mortgage it."

The little inn at which George Duke was stopping faced the water, and Millicent could see the lights on board the Vulture gleaming far away through the winter night, from the window of the little parlour where supper was laid out ready for the traveller.

"At what o'clock do you sail, George?" she asked.

"A little before midnight. You can go down to the pier with me, and see the last of me, and you can get back to Compton by the return coach to-morrow morning."

"I will do exactly as you please. Will this voyage be a long one, George?"

"Not long. I shall be back in three months at the latest."

Her heart sank at his ready answer. She was always so much happier in her husband's absence than when he honoured her with his company—happy in her trim little cottage, her stout good-tempered servant, the friends who had known her from childhood, her favourite romances, her old companion the faithful brown and white spaniel — happy in all these — happy too in her undisturbed memories of Darrell Markham.

While George and his wife were seated at the little supper-table, one of the servants of the inn came to say that Captain Duke was wanted.

"Who wants me?" he asked impatiently.

"A man wrapped in a horseman's coat, and with his hat over his eyes, Captain."

"Did you tell him that I was busy; that I was just going to sail?"

"I did, Captain; but he says that he must see you. He has travelled above two hundred miles on purpose."

An angry darkness spread itself over the Captain's handsome face.

"Curse all such unseasonable visitors!" he exclaimed savagely. "Let him come up-stairs. Here, Millicent," he added, when the waiter had left the room, "take one of those candles, and go into the opposite chamber, it is my sleeping-room. It will be best for me to see this man alone. Quick, girl, quick."

Captain Duke thrust the candlestick into his wife's hand with an impatient gesture, and almost pushed her out of the room in his flurry and agitation.

She hurried across the landing-place into the opposite chamber, but not before she had recognized in the man ascending the stairs the outside passenger who had followed the Captain and herself in the High Street; not before she had heard her husband say, as he shut the parlour door upon himself and his visitor,—

"You here! By heaven, I guessed as much."

Some logs burned upon the open hearth in the

Captain's bed-chamber, and Millicent seated herself on a low stool before the warm blaze. She sat for upwards of an hour wondering at this stranger's lengthened interview with her husband. Once she went on to the landing to ascertain if the visitor had left. He was still with the Captain. She heard the voices of the two men raised as if in anger, but she could not hear their words.

The clock was striking eleven as the parlour door opened and the stranger descended the stairs. Captain Duke crossed the landing-place and looked into the bedroom where Millicent sat brooding over the fire.

"Come," he said; "I have little better than half an hour to get off; put on your cloak and come with me."

It was a bitter cold night. The moon was nearly at the full, and shone upon the long stone pier and the white quays with a steely light that gave a ghostly brightness to every object upon which it fell. The outlines of the old-fashioned houses along the quay were cut black and sharp against this blue light; every coil of rope and idle anchor, every bag of ballast lying upon the edge of the parapet, every chain and post, and iron ring attached to the solid masonry, was distinctly visible in this winter moonlight. The last brawlers had left the tavern on the quay, the last stragglers had deserted the narrow streets, the last dim lights had been extinguished in the upper windows, and Marley Water, at a little after eleven o'clock, was as tranquil as the quiet churchyard at Compton-on-the-Moor.

Millicent shivered as she walked by her husband's side along the quay. He had not spoken to her since he had bade her accompany him to the pier. Once or

twice she glanced at him furtively. She could see the
sharp lines of his profile clearly defined against the
luminous atmosphere, and she could see by his face that
he had some trouble on his mind. They turned off
the quay on to the pier, which stretched far out into
the water.

"The boat is to wait for me at the other end," said
Captain Duke. "The tide has turned and the wind is
in our favour."

He walked for some time in silence, Millicent watching him timidly all the while ; presently he turned to
her and said, abruptly,—   .

"Mistress George Duke, have you a ring or any such
foolish trinket about you ?"

"A ring, George ?" she said, bewildered by the suddenness of the question.

"A ring, a brooch, a locket, a ribbon, anything
which you could swear to twenty years hence if need
were ?"

She had a locket hanging about her throat which
had been given to her by Darrell on her sixteenth birthday ; a locket containing one soft ring of her cousin's
auburn hair, than which she would have sooner parted
with her life.

"A locket !" she said, hesitating.

"Anything ! Haven't I said before, anything ?"

"I have the little diamond earrings in my ears, George,
the earrings you brought me from Spain."

"Give me one of them, then ; I have a fancy to take
some token of you with me on my voyage. The earring will do."

She took the jewel from her ear and handed it to
him. She was too indifferent to him and to all things

in her weary life even to wonder at his motive in asking
for the trinket.

"This is better than anything," he said, slipping the
jewel into his waistcoat pocket; "the earrings are of
Indian workmanship and of a rare pattern. Remember,
Millicent, the man who comes to you and calls himself
your husband, yet cannot give you this diamond earring,
will not be George Duke."

"What do you mean, George?"

"When I return to Compton, ask me for the fellow
jewel to that in your ear. If I cannot show it to you—"

"What then, George?"

"Drive me from your door as an impostor."

"But I should know you, George; what need should
I have of any token to tell me who you were?"

"You might have need of it. Strange things happen
to men who lead such a life as mine. I might be taken
prisoner abroad, and kept away from you for years. But
whether I come back three months hence, or ten years
hence, ask me for the earring, and if I cannot produce
it, do not believe in me."

"But you may lose it."

"I shall not lose it."

"But I can't understand, George——"

"I don't ask you to understand," replied the Captain impatiently; "I only ask you to remember what I
say, and to obey me."

He relapsed into silence. They walked on towards
the farther end of the long pier, the moon sailing high
in the cloudless sky before them, their shadows stretching out behind them black upon the moonlit stones.

They were half a mile from the quay, and they were
alone upon the pier, with no sound to wake the silence

but the echoes of their own footsteps and the noise of the waves dashing against the stone bulwarks.

The Vulture's boat was waiting at the end of the pier. Captain George Duke took his wife in his arms and pressed his lips to her cold forehead.

"You will have a lonely walk back to the inn, Millicent," he said; "but I have told 'lem to make you comfortable, and to see you safely off by the return coach to-morrow morning. Good-bye, and God bless you. Remember what I have told you to-night."

Something in his manner—a tenderness that was strange to him—touched her gentle heart.

She stopped him as he was about to descend the steps.

"It has been my unhappiness that I have never been a good wife to you, George Duke. I will pray for your safety while you are far away upon the cruel sea."

The Captain pressed her trembling little hand.

"Good-bye, Millicent," he said, "and remember."

Before she could answer him he was gone. She saw the men push the boat off from the steps; she heard the regular strokes of the oars splashing through the water, the little craft skimming lightly over the surface of the waves.

He was gone; she could return to her quiet cottage at Compton, her novel reading, her old friends, her undisturbed recollections of Darrell Markham.

She stood watching the boat till it grew into a black speck upon the moonlit waters; then she slowly turned and walked towards the quay.

A long lonely walk at that dead hour of the night for such a delicately nurtured woman as Millicent

Duke! She was not a courageous woman either; rather over-sensitive and nervous, as the reader knows; fond of reading silly romances such as people wrote a century ago, full of mysteries and horrors, of haunted chambers, secret passages, midnight encounters, and masked assassins.

The clocks of Marley Water began to strike twelve as she approached the centre of the desolate pier. One by one the different iron voices slowly rang out the hour; smaller voices in the distance taking up the sound, until all Marley and all the sea, seemed to Millicent's fancy, tremulous with the sonorous vibration. As the last stroke from the last clock died away and the sleeping town relapsed into silence, she heard the steady tramp of a man's footsteps slowly approaching her.

She must meet him and pass by him in order to reach the quay.

She had a strange vague fear of this encounter. He might be a highwayman; he might attack and attempt to rob her.

The poor girl was prepared to throw her purse and all her little trinkets at his feet—all but Darrell's locket.

Still the footsteps slowly approached. The stranger came nearer and nearer in the ghastly moonlight—nearer, until he came face to face with Millicent Duke, and stood looking at her with the moonlight shining full upon him.

Then she stopped. She meant to have hurried by the man, to have avoided even being seen by him, if possible. But she stood face to face with him, rooted to the ground, a heavy languor paralyzing her limbs.

F

an unearthly chill creeping to the very roots of her hair.

Her hands fell powerless at her sides. She could only stand white and immovable, with dilated eyes staring blankly into the man's face. He wore a blue coat, and a three-cornered hat, thrown jauntily upon his head, so as in nowise to overshadow his face.

She was alone, half a mile from a human habitation or human help—alone at the stroke of midnight with her husband's ghost.

It was no illusion of the brain ; no self-deception born of a fevered imagination. There, line for line, shade for shade, stood a shadow that wore the outward seeming of George Duke.

She reeled away from the phantom figure, tottered feebly forward for a few paces, and then summoning a desperate courage, rushed blindly on towards the quay, her garments fluttering in the sharp winter air. She was breathless and well-nigh exhausted when she reached the inn. A servant had waited up to receive her; the fire burned brightly in the wainscoted little sitting-room ; all within was cheerful and pleasant.

Millicent fell into the girl's arms and sobbed aloud. "Don't leave me," she said ; "don't leave me alone this terrible night. I have often heard that such things were, but never knew before how truly people spoke who told of them. This will be a bad voyage for the ship that sails to-night. I have seen my husband's ghost."

CHAPTER VI.

SALLY PECKER LIFTS THE CURTAIN OF THE PAST.

THE best part of a year had dragged out its slow monotonous course since that moonlit January night on
which Millicent Duke had stood face to face with the
shadow of her husband upon the long stone pier at
Marley Water. The story of Captain George Duke's
ghost was pretty well known in the quiet village of
Compton-on-the-Moor, though Millicent had only told
it under the seal of secrecy to honest Sally Pecker.

The wisest of womankind is not without some touch
of human frailty. Mrs. Sally had tried to keep this
solemn secret, but her very reticence was overstrained.
There was something more suggestive than words in
her pursed-up lips, and the solemn shake of her head,
to say nothing of many a hint and insinuation dropped
in the hearing of her intimates. So in three days all
Compton knew that the hostess at the Black Bear had
something wonderful on her mind which she "could,
an' if she would," reveal to her especial friends and
customers.

Again, though Millicent might be sole proprietress
of that midnight encounter at Marley, had not Samuel
Pecker himself a prior claim upon the Captain's ghost?
Had he not seen and conversed with the apparition?
"I see him as plain, Sarah, as I see the oven and the
spit as I'm sitting before at this present time," Samuel
protested. It was scarcely strange, then, if little by
little, dark hints of the mystery oozed out until the
story became common talk in every village household.

The simple country people were very willing to believe
in Captain Duke's double, and had no idea of attempting to find some commonplace rational explanation of
the apparition which had startled Mr. Pecker and Mrs.
Duke. Everybody agreed in the conviction that the
appearance of the shadow boded evil to the substance;
and when the three months appointed for the voyage of
the Vulture expired, and Captain Duke did not return
to Compton, the honest Cumbrians began to look
solemnly at one another, and to mutter ominously that
they had never looked to see George Duke touch
British ground alive.

But Millicent heard none of these whispers. Shut
up in her cottage, she read her well-thumbed romances,
sitting in the high-backed arm-chair, with the white
and brown spaniel at her feet and Darrell Markham's
locket in her bosom. The stout servant-girl went out
in the evenings now and then, and heard the Compton
gossip; but if ever she thought of repeating it to her
mistress, she felt the words die away upon her lips as
she looked at Millicent's pale face and mournful blue
eyes.

"Madam has trouble enough," she thought, "without hearing their talk." So she held her peace; and
Mrs. Duke waited patiently for her husband's return,
tormented by none of those anxieties which besiege the
heart of a loving wife, and content to wait his coming
patiently to the end of her life if need were.

She waited a long time. Month after month passed
away; the long grass grew deep in the meadows round
Compton, and fell in rich waves of dewy green under
the mower's scythe; the stackers spread their smooth
straw thatch over groops of noble hayricks clustering

about the farm-houses; the corn began to change colour, and undulating seas of wheat and rye faded from green to sickly yellow, which deepened slowly into gold; the ponderous waggons staggered homeward through the perfumed evening air, groaning under their rich burdens of golden grain; the flat stubble-fields were laid bare to the autumn breezes, and the ripening berries grew black in the hedges; the bright foliage in the woods slowly faded out, and the withered leaves fell rustling to the ground; the early frost began to sparkle upon the whitened moors in the chilly sunrise; the pale November fog came stealing over the wide open country, and creeping into Compton High Street in the early twilight; as Time, the inexorable, with every changing sign by which he marks his course upon the face of nature, pursued that one journey which knows no halting-place; and still no tidings of Captain George Duke and the good ship Vulture were heard in Compton. It seemed as if the honest villagers had indeed been strangely near the truth when they said that the Captain would never touch British ground again. In all Compton, Millicent Duke was perhaps the only person who thought differently.

"It is but ten months that he has been away," she said, when Mrs. Sally Pecker hinted to her that the chances seemed to be against the Captain's return, and that it might be only correct where she to think of putting on mourning; "it is not ten months, and George Duke was never an over-anxious husband. If it seemed pleasant or profitable to him to stay away, no thought of me would bring him back any the sooner. If it was three years, Sally, I should think little of it, and expect any day to see him walk into the cottage."

"Him as you saw upon the pier at Marley, perhaps Miss Milly," answered Sally solemnly, "but not Captain Duke! Such things as you and Samuel see last winter aren't shown to folks for nothing; and it seem▲ a'most like doubting Providence to doubt that the Captain's been drowned. I dreamt three times that I see my first husband, Thomas Masterson, lying dead upon a bit of rock in the middle of a stormy sea; and I put on widow's weeds after the third time."

"But you had news of your husband's **death,** Sally, hadn't you?"

"No more news than his staying away seventeen year and more without sending letter or message to tell that he was living in all those years, Miss Milly; and if that ain't news enough to make a woman a widow, I don't know what is!"

Millicent was sitting on a low stool at Mrs. Sally Pecker's feet before a cheerful sea-coal fire in the landlady's own snug little parlour at the Black Bear. It was a comfort for the poor girl to spend these long wintry evenings with honest Sally, listening to the wind roaring in the wide chimneys, counting the drops of rain beating against the window-panes, and talking of the dear old times that were past and gone.

The ordinary customers at the Black Bear were a very steady set of people, who came and went at the same hours, and ordered the same things from year's end to year's end; so when Sally had her dear young mistress to visit her, she left the feeble Samuel to entertain and wait upon his patrons, and, turning her back to business and the bar, took gentle Millicent's pale golden head upon her knee, and smoothed the soft curls with loving hands, and comforted the forlorn heart with

that talk of the days gone by which was so mournfully
sweet to Mistress George Duke.

Long as Sarah Masterson had been housekeeper at
the Hall, Millicent never remembered having heard
any mention whatever of the name of Thomas Masterson, mariner, nor had she ever questioned honest
Sally about that departed individual ; but on this dark
November evening some chance word brought Sarah's
first husband into Mrs. Duke's thoughts, and she felt a
strange curiosity about the dead seaman.

" Was he good to you, Sally?" she asked ; " and did
you love him?"

Sally looked gloomily at the fire for some moments
before she answered this question.

" It's a long while ago, Miss Millicent," she said ,
" and it seems hard, looking back so far, to remember
what was and what wasn't.   I was but a poor stupid
lass when Masterson first came to Compton."   She
paused for a moment, still staring thoughtfully at the
fire, and then said with a suddenness that was almost
spasmodic, " I *did* love him, Miss Milly, and he warn't
good to me."

" Not good to you, Sally?"

" He was bitter bad, and cruel to me," answered
Sally in a suppressed voice, her eyes kindling with
the angry recollection.   " I had a bit of money left
me by poor old grandfather, and it was that the hard-
hearted villain wanted, and not me.   I had a few bits of
silver spoons and a tea-pot as had been grandmother's,
and he cared more for them than for me.   I had my
savings that I'd been keeping ever since I first went
to service, and he wrung every guinea from me, and
every crown-piece, and shilling, and copper, till he left

me without clothes to cover me, and almost without
bread to eat. You see me here, miss, with Samuel,
having of my own way in everything, and managing
of him like; and perhaps it's my recollection of having
been ill-used myself, and the thought of what a man
can be if once he gets the upper hand, that makes
me rather sharp with Pecker. You wouldn't believe I
was the same woman if you'd seen me with Masterson.
I was afraid of him, Miss Millicent—I was afraid of
him!"

The very recollection of her dead husband seemed to
strike terror to the stout heart of the ponderous Sarah.
She cowered down over the fire, clinging to Millicent as
if she would have turned for protection even to that
slender reed, and, glancing across her shoulder, looked
towards the window behind her, as if she expected to
see it shaken by some more terrible touch than that of
the wind and the rain.

"Sally! Sally!" exclaimed Millicent soothingly—for
it was now her turn to be the comforter—"why were
you afraid of him?"

"Because he was——I haven't told you all the truth
about him yet, Miss Millicent, and I've never told it to
mortal ears, and never will except to yours. I've called
him a mariner, miss, for this seventeen years and past.
It's not a hard word, and it means almost anything
in the way of sailoring; but he was one of the most
desperate smugglers as ever robbed his king and
country; and I found it out three months after we
was married."

It was some little time before Millicent uttered a
word in reply to this. She sat with her slender hands
clasped round one of Sarah's plump wrists, with her

large blue eyes fixed upon the red blaze, with the
thoughtfully-earnest gaze peculiar to her. Perhaps she
was thinking how little she knew of the Captain of the
Vulture, or the nature of the service in which that
vessel was engaged.

"My poor, poor Sally! it was very hard for you,"
she said at last. "Compton seems so far away from
the world, and we so ignorant, that it was little wonder
you were deceived. Others have been deceived, Sally,
since then."

Mrs. Sarah Pecker nodded her head. She had heard
the dark reports current among the Compton people
about the good ship Vulture and her Captain. She
only sighed thoughtfully as she murmured,—

"Ah, Miss Milly, if that had been the worst, I might
have borne it uncomplaining, for I was milder-tempered
in those days than I am now. We didn't live at
Compton, but in a little village on the coast, as was
handy for my husband's unlawful trade. We'd lived
together five years, me never daring to complain of
any hardships, nor of the wickedness of cheating the
king as Thomas Masterson cheated him every day of
his life. I seemed not much to care what he did, or
where he went, for I had my comfort and my happiness.
I had my boy, who was born a year after we left
Compton—such a beautiful boy, with great black eyes
and dark curly hair—and I was as happy as the day
was long while all went well with him.

"But the bitterest was to come, Miss Milly; for
when the child came to be four years old, I saw that
the father was teaching him his own bad ways, and
putting his own bad words into the baby's innocent
mouth, and bringing him up in a fair way to be a curse

to himself and them that loved him. I couldn't bear
this; I could have borne to have been trampled on
myself, but I couldn't bear to see my child going to
ruin before his mother's eyes. I told Masterson so one
night. I was violent, perhaps; for I was almost wild
like, and my passion carried me away. I told him that
I meant to take the child away with me out of his reach,
and go into service and work for him, and bring him
up to be an honest man. He laughed, and said I was
welcome to the brat; and I took him at his word,
thinking he didn't care. I went to sleep that night
with the boy in my arms, meaning to set out early the
next morning, and come back to Compton, where I had
friends, and where I fancied I could get a living for
myself and my darling; and I thought we might be
so happy together. O, Miss Millicent, Miss Millicent,
may you never know such a bitter trial as mine! When
I woke from pleasant dreams about that new life which
never was to be, my child was gone. His cruel father
had taken him away, and I never saw either Masterson
or my boy again."

"You waited in the village where **he** left you?"
asked Millicent.

"For a year and over, Miss Milly, hopin' that he'd
come back, bringing the boy with him; but no tidings
ever came of him or of the child. At the end of that
time I left word with the neighbours to say I was gone
back to Compton; and I came straight here. I'd been
housemaid at the Hall when I was a slip of a girl, and
your father took me as his housekeeper, and I lived
happy in the dear old house for many years, and I
loved you and Master Darrell as if you'd been my own
children; but I've never forgotten my boy, Miss Milli-

cent, and it's very seldom that I go to sleep without
seeing his beautiful black eyes shining upon me in my
dreams."

"O Sally, Sally, how bitterly you have suffered, and
what reason you have to hate this man's memory!"

"We've no call to talk harsh of them that's dead
and gone, Miss Milly. Let 'em rest with their sins
upon their own heads, and let us look to happier times.
When Thomas Masterson went away and left me without a sixpence to buy a loaf of bread, I never thought
to be mistress of the Black Bear. Pecker has been a
good friend to me, miss, and a true, and I bless the
providence that sent him courting to the Hall. I fancy
I can see him now, poor creature," said Mrs. Pecker,
meditatively, "sitting of evenings in the housekeeper's
room, never talking much, but always looking melan-
cholic like, and dropping sudden on his knees one
night, saying, 'Sarah, will you have me?'"

Mr. Samuel Pecker here venturing to put his head
into the room, and furthermore presuming to ask some
question connected with the business of the establishment, was answered so sharply by his beloved wife that
he retreated in confusion without obtaining what he
wanted.

For the worthy Sarah, in common with many other
wives, made a point of scrupulously concealing from
her weaker helpmate any tender or grateful feeling that
she might entertain for him; being possessed with an
ever-present fear that if treated with ordinary civility,
he might, to use her own words, try to get the better
of her.

So the dreary winter time set in, and, except for this
honest-hearted Sally Pecker, and the pale curate's busy

little wife, who had much ado to keep seven children fed and clothed upon sixty pounds a year, Millicent Duke was almost friendless. She was so gentle and retiring, of so reserved and diffident a nature, that she had never made many acquaintances. In the happy old time at the Hall, Darrell had been her friend, confidant, and playfellow; and she had neither needed nor wished to have any other. So now she shut herself up in her little cottage, with its quaint old mirrors and spindle-legged tables, and little casement windows looking out upon a patch of old-fashioned garden—she shut herself up in her prim orderly little abode, and the Compton people seldom saw her except at church, or on her way to the Black Bear.

Millicent received no news of Darrell from his own hand; but the young man wrote about once in six weeks to Mrs. Sarah Pecker, who was sorely put to it to scrawl a few lines in reply, telling him how Miss Millicent was but weakly, and how Captain Duke was still away with his ship the Vulture. Through Sally, therefore, Mrs. Duke had tidings of this dear cousin. He had found friends in London, and had been engaged as secretary by a noble Scottish lord, suspected of no very strong attachment to the Hanoverian cause. It was not so long since other noble Scottish lords had paid the terrible price of their loyalty. There were ghastly and hideous warnings for those who went under Temple Bar. So whatever was done for the exiled family was done in secret—for the failures of the past had made the bravest men cautious.

———

CHAPTER VII.

HOW DARRELL MARKHAM FOUND HIS HORSE.

WHILE Millicent sat in the little oaken parlour at the Black Bear, with her head on Sarah Pecker's knee, and her melancholy blue eyes fixed upon the red recesses in the hollow fire, Darrell Markham rode westward through the dim November fog, charged with letters and messages from his patron, Lord C——, to some noble Somersetshire gentlemen, whose country seats lay very near Bristol.

On the first night of his journey, Darrell was to put up at Reading. It was dark when he entered the town, and rode between the two dim rows of flickering oil-lamps straight to the door of the inn to which he had been recommended. The upper windows of the hostelry were brilliantly illuminated, and the traveller could hear the jingling of glasses, and the noise of loud and riotous talk within. Though dark, it was but early, and the lower part of the house was crowded with stalwart farmers, who had ridden over to Reading market, and the townspeople who had congregated about the bar to discuss the day's business.

Darrell flung the reins to the ostler, to whom he gave particular directions about the treatment of his horse.

"I will come round to the stable after I've dined," said Mr. Markham, in conclusion, "and see how the animal looks; for he has a hard day's work before him to-morrow, and he must start in good condition."

The ostler touched his hat, and led the horse away.

The animal was a tall bony grey, not over handsome to look at, but strong enough to make light of the stiffest work.

The landlord ushered Darrell up the broad staircase, and into a long corridor, in which he heard the same loud voices that had attracted his attention outside the inn.

"You have rather a riotous party," he said to the landlord, who was carrying a pair of wax lights, and leading the way for his visitor.

"The gentlemen are merry, sir," answered the man. "They have been a long time over their wine. Sir Lovel Mortimer seems a rare one to keep the bottle moving amongst his friends."

"Sir Lovel Mortimer?"

"Yes, sir. A rich baronet from Devonshire, travelling to London with some of his friends."

"Sir Lovel Mortimer," said Darrell thoughtfully; "I know of no Devonshire man of that name."

"He seems a gentleman used to great luxury;" answered the landlord; "he has kept every servant in the house busy waiting upon him ever since he stopped here to dine."

Darrell felt very little interest in the customs of this Devonshire baronet. He ate a simple dinner, washed down with half a bottle of claret, and then went down stairs to ask the way to the stables. The ostler came to him with a lantern, and after leading him through a back-door and acoss a yard, ushered him into a roomy six-stalled stable. The stalls were all full, and as Darrell's grey horse was at the further extremity of the stable, he had to pick his way through wet straw and clover, past the other animals.

"Them there bay horses belongs to Sir Lovel Mortimer and his friends," said the man; "and very handsome beasts they be. Sir Lovel himself looks a pictur' mounted on this here bay."

He slapped his hand upon the haunch of a horse as he spoke. The animal turned round as he did so, and tossing up his head, looked at the two men.

"A tidy bit of horse-flesh, sir," said the ostler; "a hundred guineas' worth in any market, I should say."

Darrell nodded, and striding up to the animal's head, threw one strong arm round the arched neck, and catching the ears with the other hand, dragged the horse's face to a level with his own.

"I'd have you be careful, sir, how you handle him," cried the ostler, with a tone of considerable alarm; "the beast has a temper of his own; he tried to bite one of our boys not half an hour ago."

"He won't bite me," said Darrell quietly. "Give me the lantern here, will you?"

"You'd better let go of his head, sir; he's a stiffish temper," remonstrated the ostler, drawing back.

"Give me the lantern, man; I know all about his temper."

The ostler obeyed very unwillingly; and handed Darrell the lantern.

"I thought so," said the young man, holding the glimmering light before the horse's face. "And you knew your old master, Balmerino, eh, boy?"

The horse whinnied joyously, and snuffed at Darrell's coat-sleeve.

"The animal seems to know you, sir," exclaimed the ostler.

"We know each other as well as ever brothers did,"

said Darrell, stroking the horse's neck. "I have ridden him for seven years and more, and I only lost him a twelvemonth ago. Do you know anything of this Sir Lovel Mortimer who owns him?"

"Not over much, sir, except that he's a fine high-spoken gentleman. He always uses our house when he's travelling between London and the west."

"And is that often?" asked Darrell.

"Maybe six or eight times in a year," answered the ostler.

"The gentleman is fonder of the road than I am," muttered the young man. "Has he ever ridden this horse before to-day?"

The ostler hesitated and scratched his head thoughtfully.

"I see a many bay horses," he answered, after a pause; "I can't swear to this here animal; he may have been here before, you see, sir; but then lookin' at it the other way, you see, sir, he mayn't."

"Anyhow, you don't remember him?" said Darrell.

"Not to swear to," repeated the man.

"I wouldn't mind giving a hundred pounds for this meeting of to-night, Balmerino, old friend," murmured Darrell, "though it was the last handful of guineas I had in the world!"

He returned to the house, and went straight to the bar, where he called the landlord aside.

"I must speak to one of your guests upstairs, my worthy host," he said. "Sir Lovel Mortimer must answer me two or three questions before I leave this house."

The landlord looked alarmed at the very thought of an intrusion upon his important customer.

"Sir Lovel is not one to see over much company," he said; "but if you're a friend of his——"

"I never heard his name till to-night," answered Darrell; "but when a man rides another man's horse, he ought to be prepared to answer a few questions."

"Sir Lovel Mortimer riding another man's horse?" cried the landlord aghast. "You must be mistaken, sir!"

"I have just left a horse in your stable that I could swear to as my own before any court in England."

"A gentleman has often been mistaken in a horse," muttered the landlord.

"Not after he has ridden him seven years," answered Darrell. "Be so good as to take my name to Sir Lovel, and tell him I should be glad of five minutes' conversation at his convenience."

The landlord obeyed very reluctantly. Sir Lovel was tired with his journey, and would take it ill being disturbed, he muttered; but as Darrell insisted. he went upstairs with the young man's message, and returned presently to say that Sir Lovel would see the gentleman.

Darrell lost no time in following the landlord, who ushered him very ceremoniously into Sir Lovel's apartment. The room occupied by the West-country baronet was a long wainscoted chamber, lighted by wax candles set in sconces between the three windows and the panels in the opposite walls. It was used on grand occasions as a ball-room, and had all the stiff old-fashioned grandeur of a state apartment. The flames from a pile of blazing logs went roaring up the wide chimney, and in an easy-chair before the open hearth lolled an effeminate-looking young man, in a brocade

G

dressing-gown, silk stockings with embroidered clocks, and shoes adorned with red heels and glittering diamond buckles that emitted purple and rainbow sparks in the firelight. He wore a flaxen wig, curled and frizzed to such a degree that it stood away from his face, round which it formed a pale-yellow frame, contrasting strongly with a pair of large restless black eyes and the blue stubble upon his slender chin. He was quite alone, and in spite of the two empty punchbowls and the regiment of bottles upon the table before him, he seemed perfectly sober.

"Sit ye down, Mr. Markham," he said, waving a hand as small as a woman's, and all of a glitter with diamonds and emeralds, " sit ye down ; and hark ye, Mr. William Byers, bring me another bottle of claret, and see that it's a little better than the last. My two worthy friends have staggered off to bed, Mr. Markham, a little the worse for this evening's bout, but you see I've contrived to keep my brains pretty clear of cobwebs, and am your humble servant to command."

Sir Lovel Mortimer was as effeminate in manners as in person. He had a clear treble voice, and spoke in the languid drawling manner peculiar to the maccaronis of Ranelagh and the Ring. He was the sort of fopling one reads about in the *Spectator*, and would have been a spectacle alike miraculous and disgusting to good country-bred Sir Roger de Coverley.

Darrell Markham told the story of his recognition of the horse in a few words.

" And you lost the beast——" drawled Sir Lovel.

" A year ago last month."

"Strange ! " lisped the baronet. "I gave fifty guineas for the animal at a fair at Barnstaple last July."

" Do you remember the person of whom you bought him ? "

" Yes, perfectly. He was an elderly man, with white hair ; he represented himself as a farmer from Dorsetshire."

" Then the trace of the villain who robbed me is lost," said Darrell. " I would have given much had you got the horse straight from the scoundrel who robbed me of my purse and watch, and some documents of value to others besides myself, upon Compton Moor, last October."

Sir Lovel Mortimer's restless black eyes flashed with an eager light as he looked at the speaker. Those ever-restless eyes were strangely at variance with the young baronet's drawling treble voice and languid manner. It was as if the man's effeminate languor were only an assumption, the falsehood of which the eager burning eyes betrayed in spite of himself.

" Will you tell me the story of your encounter with the knight of the road ? " he asked.

Darrell gave a brief description of his meeting with the highwayman, omitting all that bore any relation to either Millicent or Captain George Duke.

" I scarcely expect you to believe all this," said Darrell, in conclusion, " or to acknowledge any claim of mine to the horse ; but if you like to come down to the stable, you will see at least that the faithful creature remembers his old master."

" I have no need to go to the stable for confirmation of your words, Mr. Markham," answered the young baronet ; " I should be the last to doubt the truth of a gentleman's assertion."

The landlord brought the claret and a couple of

clean glasses, while the two men were talking, and Sir Lovel pledged his visitor in a bumper.

The West-country baronet seemed delighted to secure Darrell's society. He talked of the metropolis, boasted of his conquests among the fair sex as freely as if he had been a second Beau Fielding, and, slipping from one object to another, began presently to speak of politics. Darrell, who had listened patiently to his companion's silly prattle, grew grave immediately.

"You seem to take but little interest in either party, Mr. Markham," Sir Lovel said at last, after vainly trying to discover the bent of Darrell's mind.

"Not over much," answered the young man. "I was bred in the country, where all the share we had in public affairs was to set the bells ringing on the king's birthday, and pray for his majesty in church on Sundays and holidays. We got our political opinions as we got the fashion of our waistcoats and wigs, a twelvemonth after they were out of date in London."

Sir Lovel shrugged his shoulders.

"I see you don't care to trust strangers with your real sentiments, Mr. Markham, and I make no doubt you are wise," he said, with perfect good temper. "What say you to our eating a broiled capon together?" he asked presently. "My friends were too far gone to hold out for supper, and I shall be very glad of your company over a bowl of punch."

Darrell begged to be excused. He had to be on the road early the next morning he said, and sadly wanted a good night's rest. But the baronet would take no refusal. He rang the bell, summoned Mr. William Byers, the landlord, who waited in person upon his important guest, and ordered the capon and the punch.

" We can come to a friendly understanding about the horse while we sup, Mr. Markham," said Sir Lovel.

Darrell bowed. The friendly understanding the two men came to was to the effect that Markham should pay the baronet twenty guineas and give him the grey horse in exchange for Balmerino—the grey being worth about twenty pounds, and Sir Lovel being willing to lose ten by his bargain. So Darrell and the baronet parted excellent friends, and early the next morning Balmerino was brought round to the front door of the inn, saddled and bridled for his old master.

The animal was in splendid condition, and Darrell felt a thrill of pleasure as he sprang into the saddle. It seemed as if the horse recognized the light hand of his familiar rider. The pavement of the Reading street clattered under his hoofs, and in ten minutes the traveller was out upon the Bath road with the town melting into the distance behind him.

Darrell dined at Marlborough, where he gave Balmerino two or three hours' rest. It was dusk when he left the inn door, and a thick white fog shut out the landscape on either side of the high road. This fog had grown dark and dense when Darrell found himself in the loneliest part of the road between Marlborough and Bath. He had a well-filled purse, heavy enough to tempt the marauding hands of highway robbers; but he had a good pair of pistols, and felt safely armed against all attack. But, for the second time in his life, he had reason to repent of his rashness, for in the very loneliest turn of the road he heard the clattering of many hoofs close behind him, and by the time he had his pistols ready he was surrounded by three men, one of whom, coming behind him, threw up his arm as he was about to fire at the first of his assailants, while the third struck the same kind of swinging blow upon his head that had laid him prostrate a year before upon the moorland road between Compton and Marley.

When Darrell Markham recovered his senses he found himself lying on his back in a shallow dry ditch; the fog had cleared away, and the stars shone with a pale and chilly glimmer in the wintry sky. The young man's pockets had been rifled and his pistols taken from him; but tied to the hedge above him stood the grey horse which he had left in the custody of Sir Lovel Mortimer.

Stupefied by the blow that had prostrated him, and with every bone in his body stiff from lying for four or five hours in the cold and damp, Darrell was just able to get into the saddle and ride about a mile and a half to the nearest roadside inn.

The country people who kept this hostelry were almost frightened when they saw the traveller's white face and blood-stained forehead; but any story of outrage upon the high road found ready listeners and hearty sympathy.

The landlord stood open-mouthed as Darrell told of his adventure of the night before, and the exchange of the horses.

"Was the West-country baronet a fine ladyfied little chap, with black eyes and small white hands?" he asked eagerly.

"Yes."

The man looked triumphantly round at the bystanders. "I'm blest if I didn't guess as much," he said. "It's Captain Fanny."

"Captain Fanny?"

"Yes; one of the most daring villains in all the West of England, and one that is like an eel for giving folks the slip when they fancy they've caught him. He has been christened Captain Fanny on account of his small hands and feet and his lackadaisical ways."

The ostler came in as the landlord was speaking.

"I don't know whether you knew of this, sir," he said, handing Darrell a slip of paper; "I found it tied to the horse's bridle."

The young man unfolded the paper and read these words :

"With Sir Lovel Mortimer's compliments to Mr. Markham, and in strict accordance with the old adage which teaches us that exchange is no robbery."

CHAPTER VIII.

HOW A STRANGE PEDLAR WORKED A GREAT CHANGE IN THE MIND AND MANNERS OF SALLY PECKER.

DARRELL MARKHAM waited at the roadside inn till the tedious post of those days brought him a packet containing money from his friend and patron, Lord C——. He was vexed and humiliated by his encounter with Captain Fanny. For the second time in his life he had been worsted, and for the second time he found himself baulked of his revenge. The rural constable to whom he told the story of the robbery only shrugged his shoul-

ders, and offered to tell him of a dozen more such adventures which had occurred within the last week or
two; so Darrell had nothing to do but to submit quietly
to the loss of his money and his horse, and ride on to
execute his commissions in Somersetshire—commissions
from which little good ever came, as the reader knows;
for it seemed as if that kingly house on which misfor-
tune had so long set her seal, was never more to be
elevated from the degradation to which it had sunk.

All this time, while Darrell turned his horse's head
from the west and journeyed by easy stages slowly back
to town; while Sally Pecker at the Black Bear, and
everybody in Compton, from the curate, the lawyer,
and the doctor, to the lowliest cottager in the village,
was busy with preparacions for the approaching Christmas, Millicent Duke waited and watched day after day
for the return of her husband. All Compton might
think the Captain dead, but Millicent could not think
so. She seemed possessed by some settled conviction
that all the storms which ever rent the skies or shook
the ocean would never cause the death of George Duke.
She watched for his coming with a sick dread that
every day might bring him. She rose in the morning
with the thought that ere the early winter's night
closed in he would be seated by the hearth. She never
heard a latch lifted without trembling lest his hand
should be upon it, nor listened to a masculine footfall
in the village High Street without dreading lest she
should recognize his familiar step. Her meeting with
George Duke's shadow upon the moonlit pier at Marley
had added a superstitious terror to her old dread and
dislike of her husband. She thought of him now as a
being possessed of unholy privileges. He might be near

her, but unseen and impalpable ; he might be hiding in
the shadowy corners of the dark wainscot, or crouching
in the snow outside the latticed window. He might be
a spy upon her inmost thoughts, and knowing her dis-
trust and aversion, might stay away for long years, only
to torment her the more by returning when she had
forgotten to expect him, and had even learned to be
happy.

You see there is much allowance to be made for her
lonely life, her limited education, and the shade of super-
stition inseparable from a poetic temperament, and a
mind whose sole aliment had been such novels as people
wrote and read a hundred years ago.

She never heard from her brother Ringwood, and the
few reports of him that came to her from other sources
only told of riot and dissipation, of tavern brawls and
midnight squabbles in the streets about Covent Garden.
She knew that he was wasting his substance amongst
bad men, but she never once thought of her own interest
in his fortune, or of the possibility that her brother's
death might make her mistress of the stately old mansion in which she had been born.

Sally Pecker was in the full flood-tide of her Christmas preparations. Fat geese dangled from the hooks in
the larder, with their long necks hanging within a little
distance of the ground ; brave turkeys and big capons
hung cheek by jowl with the weighty sirloin of beef
which was to be the principal feature of the Christmas
dinner. Everywhere, from the larder to the scullery,
from the cellars to the sink, there were the tokens of
plenty and the abundant promise of good cheer. Samuel
was allowed to employ himself in the decoration of the
old hostelry ; he was permitted to get on rickety ladders

and endanger his neck in the process of hanging up
holly and mistletoe; but all the more serious and substantial preparations devolved upon Sarah.   In the
kitchen, as in the pantry, Sally was the presiding deity.
Betty the cookmaid plucked the geese, while her mistress made the Christmas pies and prepared the ingre-
dients for the pudding, which was to be carried into the
oak parlour on the ensuing day, garnished with holly
and all ablaze with burnt brandy.   So important were
these preparations, that as late as nine o'clock on the
night of the twenty-fourth of December, the maid and
her mistress were still hard at work in the great kitchen at the Black Bear.   This kitchen lay at the back
of the house, and was divided from the principal rooms
and the entrance-hall and bar by a long passage, which
kept the clatter of plates and dishes, the smell of cooking, and all the other tokens of preparation, from the
ears and noses of Mrs. Pecker's customers, who knew
nothing of the dinner they had ordered until they saw
it smoking upon the table before them.

   Sally Pecker and her maid were quite alone in the
kitchen, for Samuel was busy with his duties in the
bar, and the two chambermaids were waiting upon the
visitors who had been dropped at the Bear by the Carlisle coach.   The pleasant seasonable frost, in which all
Compton had rejoiced, had broken up with that perti-
nacious spirit of contradiction with which a hard frost
generally does break up just before Christmas, and a
drizzling rain fell silently without the closely barred
window-shutters.

   "I never see such weather," said Mrs. Pecker,
slamming the back door with an air of vexation after
having taken a survey of the night; "nothing but rain,

rain, rain, coming down as straight as one of Samuel's pencil streaks between the figures in a score. Christmas scarcely seems Christmas in such weather as this. We might as well have ducks and green peas and cherry pie to-morrow, for all I can see, for it's so close and muggy that I can scarcely bear to come nigh the fire."

The servants at the Black Bear knew the value of a good place and a peaceful life far too well ever to contradict their mistress, so Betty the cookmaid coincided immediately with Mrs. Pecker, and declared that the weather certainly was uncomfortably warm; very much in the same spirit as that of the Danish courtier who was so eager to agree with Prince Hamlet.

The back door communicating with this kitchen at the Black Bear was the entrance generally used by any of the village tradesmen who brought Mrs. Pecker their goods; as well as by tramps and beggars and such idle ne'er-do-weels, who were apt to hang about the premises with an eye to broken victuals or silver spoons, and who were generally sent off with a sharp answer from Sarah or her handmaidens.

On this Christmas-eve Mrs. Pecker was expecting a parcel of groceries from the nearest market town—a parcel which was to be brought to her by the Compton carrier.

"Purvis is late, Betty," she said, as the clock struck nine, "and I shall want the plums for my next batch of pies. Drat the man! he's gossiping and drinking at every house he calls at, I'll be bound."

Betty murmured something about Christmas, and taking a friendly glass like, for the sake of the season; but Mrs. Pecker cut short her maid's apology for the delinquent carrier, and said sharply,—

"Christmas or no Christmas, folks should attend to the business they live by; and as for friendly glasses out of compliment to the season, it's a rare season that isn't a good season for drink with the men; for every wind that blows is an excuse for a fresh glass with them. I haven't kept the head inn in Compton without finding out what *they* are."

It seemed as if the carrier had been aware of the contumely showered on his guilty head, for at this very moment a sharp rap at the window-shutters arrested Mrs. Pecker in the full torrent of her scorn.

"That's Purvis, I'll lay my life," she exclaimed; "the fool don't know the door from the window, because it's Christmas time, I suppose. Run, Betty, and fetch the parcel. You'll have to feel in my pocket for the six pence that's to pay him, for I can't take my hands out of the flour."

The girl hurried to open the door, and went out into the yard; but she presently returned to say that it was not Purvis, but a pedlar who wanted to show Mrs. Pecker some silks and laces.

"Silks and laces!" cried Sally; "I want no such furbelows. Tell the man to go about his business directly. I won't have any such vagabonds prowling about the premises."

The girl went back to the door and remonstrated with the man, who said very little, and spoke in an indistinct mumbling voice that scarcely reached Mrs. Pecker's ears; but whatever he did say, it was to the effect that he would not leave the place until he had seen the mistress of the Black Bear.

Betty came back to tell Mrs. Pecker this.

"Won't he?" exclaimed the redoubtable Sarah,

raising her voice for the edification of the pedlar; "we'll soon see about that. Tell him that we're not without constables in Compton, and that our magistrates are pretty hard against tramps and vagabonds."

"But you won't be hard upon me, will you, Mrs. Pecker? I don't think you'll find it in your heart to be hard upon me," said the man, putting his head into the kitchen.

He was a stalwart broad-shouldered fellow, with a big hook-nose, twinkling black eyes, and a complexion that had grown almost copper-coloured by exposure to all kinds of weather. He wore a three-cornered hat, which was trimmed with tarnished lace, and perched carelessly on one side of his head. His sleek hair was of a purplish black; and he wore a stiff black beard upon his fat double chin. Gold earrings twinkled in his ears, and something very much like a diamond glittered amongst the dingy lace of his ragged cravat. The bronzed dirty hand with which he held open the box while he addressed Mrs. Pecker was bedizened by rings, which might have been either copper or rich barbaric gold.

"You'll not refuse to look at the silks, Mrs. Sally," he said, in an insinuating tone; "or to give a poor tired wayfarer a glass of something good on this merry Christmas night?"

Mrs. Pecker took her hands out of the flour; but white as they were, they were not a shade whiter than her usually rubicund face. For once in a way the landlady of the Black Bear seemed utterly at a loss for a sharp answer.

"You may come in," she gasped in a hoarse whisper,

dropping into the nearest chair as she spoke. "Betty, go upstairs, girl. I'll just hear what the man wants."

But the cook was by no means inclined to lose the conversation between her mistress and the pedlar, whatever it might be; and accustomed as she was to obey Sarah Pecker, for once in a way she ventured to hesitate.

"If it's silk or laces you're going to look at, ma'am,' she said, "I learnt a deal about 'em in my last place, for missus was always buying of Jews and pedlars; and I can tell you if they're worth what he asks for 'em."

"You're very wise, my lass, I make no doubt," answered the pedlar; "but I dare say your mistress can choose a silk gown for herself without the help of your advice. Get out of the kitchen! do you hear, girl?"

"Well, I'm sure!" exclaimed Betty, tossing her head, and not stirring from her post beside Mrs. Pecker.

"Do you hear, girl?" said the pedlar, savagely— "go!"

"Not for your tellin'" answered Betty. "I don't like leavin' you alone with such as him, ma'am," she said to her mistress. And then added in a whisper, intended for Sally's ears alone, "There's your silver watch hanging beside the chimney piece, and three teaspoons on the dresser."

"Go, Betty," said Mrs. Pecker, in almost the same hoarse whisper with which she had spoken before. 'Go, girl; I shan't be above ten minutes choosin' a gown; and if the man wants to speak to me, he must have leave to speak."

She rose with an effort from the chair into which

she had fallen when the pedlar first put his head in at the kitchen door. She followed Betty down the passage, saw her safely into the hall, and then locked the door which separated the kitchen from the body of the house.

The pedlar was standing before the fire smoking a pipe when Mrs. Pecker returned to the kitchen. He had taken off his hat, and his long sleek black hair fell in greasy curls about his neck. He wore a claret-coloured coat, shabby and weather-stained, and high jack-boots, from which there issued a steam as he warmed his wet legs before the fire. "Have you made all safe?" he asked, as Mrs. Pecker re-entered the kitchen.

"Yes."

"No chance of listeners creeping about? **No eyes** nor ears at keyholes?"

"No."

"That's comfortable. Now then, Sarah Pecker, listen to me."

Whatever the pedlar had to say, or however long he was saying it, no one but the mistress of the Black Bear could have told. Betty, the cookmaid, with her eye and her ear alternately applied to the keyhole of the door at the end of the passage, could only perceive, by the aid of the first organ, the faint glimmer of the firelight in the kitchen; while by the help of the second, strain it how she might, she heard nothing but the gruff murmur of the pedlar's voice.

By-and-by that gruff murmur ceased altogether, and Betty began to think that the man had gone; but still Mrs. Pecker did not come to unlock **the** door **and** announce the departure of her visitor.

For upwards of a quarter of an hour Betty listened, growing every moment more puzzled by this strange silence.

"The man must have gone," she thought; "and missus has forgotten to call me back to the kitchen."

She shook and rattled at the lock of the door.

"Please bring the key, ma'am," she cried through the keyhole. "The last batch of pies will be spoiled if they're not turned!" But still there was no answer.

"Missus! missus!" screamed the girl at the top of her voice. Not a sound came from the kitchen in reply to her appeal.

The girl stood still for a few minutes, with her heart beating loud and fast, wondering what this ominous silence could mean. Then a sudden terror seized her : she gave one sharp shrill scream, and hurried off as fast as her legs would carry her to look for Mr. Samuel Pecker.

Her fear was that this strange pedlar, with the barbarous rings in his ears, had made away with the ponderous Sarah, for the sake of the big watch and the silver spoons.

Samuel was seated in the wainscoted parlour, conversing with some of the Compton tradesmen, who were a little the worse for steaming punch and the influence of the season.

"Master! master!" cried the girl, thrusting her pale face in at the door, and troubling the festivity by her sudden and alarming appearance.

"What is it, Betty?" asked Samuel. Perhaps he, too, had taken some slight advantage of the season, and made himself merry, or, let us rather say, a shade less dismal than usual.

" Betty, what is it?" he repeated, drawing himself
into an erect position and looking defiantly at the girl,
as much as to say,—

" Who says I have been drinking ?"

The cookmaid stood in the doorway silently staring
at the assembly, and breathing hard.

" What is the matter, Betty ?"

" Missus, sir."

Something—surely it was not a ray of joy?—some
pale flicker of that feeble spirit-lamp, which the parson
of the parish told Samuel was his soul—illuminated
the innkeeper's countenance as he said interrogatively,—

" Taken bad, Betty?"

" No, sir; but a pedlar, sir—a strange man, dark
and fierce-like—asked to see missus, and was told to
go about his business, for there was constables, but
wouldn't, and offered missus silk gowns; and she
turned me out of the kitchen—likewise locked the
passage-door—which that's an hour ago and more,
and—please, sir, I think he must have—run away
with missus."

Another ray, scarcely so feeble as the first, lit up
the landlord's face as Betty gasped out the last of
these semi-detached sentences.

" Your missus is rather heavy, Betty," he murmured
thoughtfully; " is the pedlar a big man ?"

" He'd have made two, of you, sir," answered the
girl.

" So he might, Betty; but two of me wouldn't be
much agen Sarah."

He seemed so very much inclined to sit down and
discuss the matter philosophically, that the girl almost
lost patience with him.

H

"The passage-door is locked, sir, and I can't burst it open : hadn't we better take a lantern and go round to the kitchen t'other way?"

Samuel nodded.

"You're right, Betty," he said; "get the lantern and I'll come round with you. But if the man *has* run away with your missus, Betty," he added argumentatively, "there's such a many roads and by-roads round Compton, that it wouldn't be over much good going after them."

Betty did not wait to consider this important point. She lighted a bit of candle in an old horn lantern, and led the way into the yard.

They found Purvis the carrier standing at the back door.

"I've knocked nigh upon six times," he said, "and can't get no answer."

Betty opened the door and ran into the kitchen, followed by Samuel and the carrier.

There was no sign of the foreign pedlar; and stretched upon the hearth in a dead swoon lay Mrs. Sarah Pecker.

They lifted her up, and dashed vinegar and cold water over her face and head. There were some feathers lying at one end of the dresser, which Betty had plucked from a fat goose only an hour before. Some of these, burned under Sarah's nostrils, restored her to consciousness.

"I'll lay a crown-piece," said Betty, "that the watch and silver spoons are gone!"

Mrs. Pecker revived very slowly; but when at last she did open her eyes, and saw the meek Samuel patiently awaiting her recovery, she burst into a sudden flood of tears, and flinging her stout arms about his neck, indifferent to the presence of either Betty or the carrier, cried out passionately,—

"You've been a good husband to me, Samuel Pecker, and I haven't been an indulgent wife to you; but folks are punished for their sins in this world as well as in the next, and I'll try and make you more comfortable for the future; for I love you truly, my dear—indeed I do!"

This unwonted show of emotion almost frightened Samuel. His weak blue eyes opened to their widest extent in a watery stare, as he looked at his tearful wife

"Sarah!" he said; "good gracious, don't! I don't want you to be better to me: I'm quite happy as we are. You may be a little sharp-spoken like now and then, but I'm used to it now, Sally, and I should feel half lost with a wife that didn't contradict me."

"The spoons and tne watch is gone," exclaimed Betty, who had been inspecting the premises; "and missus's purse, I daresay. I knew that pedlar came here with a bad meaning."

"He did! he did!" cried Sarah Pecker.

It was thought a very strange thing by-and-by, in the village of Compton-on-the-Moor, that the mere fact of having been robbed of ten or fifteen pounds' worth of property by a dishonest pedlar should have worked a reformation in the temper and manners of Mrs. Sarah Pecker as regarded Samuel her husband; but so it was, nevertheless. Christmas passed away. Hard frosts succeeded drizzling rains, and the fitful February sunshine melted January's snows, releasing tender young snowdrops and crocuses from their winter bondage. Milder breezes, as the winter months fell back into the past, blew across Compton Moor; spring blossoms burst into bloom in sheltered nooks beneath the black hedges, and the hedges themselves grew green in the fickle April weather; and still Sarah was mild of speech and pleasant of manner to her astonished husband.

The meek landlord of the Black Bear walked about as one in a strange but delicious dream. He had the key of his cellars in his own possession, and was allowed to drink such portions of his own liquors as he thought fit; and Samuel did not abuse the unwonted privilege, for he was naturally a sober man. He was no longer snubbed and humiliated before the face of his best customers. His tastes were consulted, his wishes were deferred to. Nice little dinners were prepared for him by Sarah's own hands, and the same hands would even deign to mix for him a nightcap of steaming rum-punch, fragrant as the perfumed groves of Araby the blest. Mr. Pecker was almost master in his own house. Sometimes this new state of things seemed well nigh too much for him. Once he went to his wife, and said to her, imploringly,—

"Sarah, speak sharp to me, will you, please; for I feel as if I wasn't quite right in my head."

CHAPTER IX.

SIR LOVEL MORTIMER'S DRUNKEN SERVANT.

It has been said that Ringwood Markham was a milk-sop. In days when men's swords were oftener out of the scabbard than in, the young squire had little chance of winning much respect from the braggarts and roysterers who were his boon companions in the gaming-houses and taverns that he loved to frequent, except by the expenditure of those golden guineas which his father had hoarded in the quiet economical life the Markham family had led at Compton Hall before the death of the old squire. The Hall property, which was by no means inconsiderable, was so tightly tied up that Ringwood was powerless either to sell or mortgage it ; and as he saw his father's savings melting away, he felt that the time was not far distant when he must either go back to Compton, turn country gentleman, and live upon his estate, or else sink to the position of a penniless adventurer, hanging about the purlieus of the scenes in which he had once lorded it pleasantly over half-a-dozen shabby toad-eaters, and the obsequious waiters of twenty different taverns.

Ringwood Markham had never been in love. He was one of those men who, unassailed by the tempests of passion that wreck sterner souls, sink in some pitiful quicksand of folly. With no taint of profligacy in his own lymphatic nature, he was led by his vanity to ape the vices of the most profligate among his vicious companions. With an utter distaste for drinking, he had learned to become a drunkard ; without any real passion for play, he had half ruined himself at the gaming-table; but, do what he would, he was still a girlish coxcomb, and men laughed at his pretty face, his silky golden hair, and small waist.

Darrell Markham and his cousin Ringwood had met once or twice in London, but the old quarrel still rankled in the heart of the young squire; and the coolness between the two men had never been abated. Darrell felt a contempt for Millicent's brother which he took little pains to conceal; and it was only Ringwood's terror of his cousin that kept him from showing the hatred which had been engendered on the day of the one brief encounter between the kinsmen. Darrell's sphere of action lay far away from the taverns and coffeehouses in which the young squire wasted his useless life. He had, indeed, sought to drown his regrets in the whirlpool of fashionable dissipation; but had discovered very speedily that his wounds were too deep to be healed by any such treatment, and that it was a vain waste of time and substance to seek consolation in the temples of modish folly, inasmuch as his sorrow accompanied him wherever he went, and was not to be drowned by the noise of any tea-garden orchestra or the rattle of tavern dice. So, finding that memory was not to be drowned in a punch-bowl, and that the image of Millicent Duke was too deeply engraven on his heart to be put to flight by the factitious charms of any painted madam in London, Darrell reconciled himself to Sorrow, and accepted Memory as his friend and companion, and was all the better man, perhaps, for that sad companionship.

True to the memory of the past, he was true also to the duties of the present. He had ambitious dreams that consoled him in those lonely hours in which his

cousin Millicent's mournful face stole between him and
the pages of some political pamphlet. He had high hopes
for a future, which might be brilliant, even if it could
never be happy. And perhaps even when he fancied
himself most hopeless, there lurked in some secret corner
of his mind a dim foreshadowing of a day on which the
good ship Vulture should go down under a tattered
and crime-stained flag, and he and Millicent be left
high and dry upon the shore of life.

In the summer succeeding that Christmas upon the
eve of which the foreign-looking pedlar had robbed
Mrs. Sally Pecker of three silver spoons, a Tompion
watch, seven pounds twelve shillings and fourpence in
money, and her senses; while the mowers were busy
about Compton in the warm June weather, Ringwood
Markham was occupying a shabby lodging in the
neighbourhood of Bedford Street, Covent Garden. The
young squire's purse was getting hourly lower; but
though he had been obliged to leave his handsome lodgings and dismiss the man who had served him as valet
for a couple of years, flattering his weaknesses, wearing
his waistcoats, and appropriating casual handfuls of his
loose silver; though he could no longer afford to spend
a twenty-pound note upon a tavern supper, or to shatter
his wine-glass upon the wall behind him after proposing
a toast, Ringwood Markham still contrived to wear a
peach-blossom coat with glittering silver lace, and to
show his elegant person and pretty girlish face at his
favourite haunts.

He spent half the day in bed, and rose an hour or
two after noon, to lounge till dusk in a dirty satin
dressing-gown, which was variegated as much with
wine-stains as with the embroidered flowers that had

been worked by Millicent's patient fingers years before. His dinner was brought from a neighbouring tavern, together with a beer-stained copy of the *Flying Post*, in which Ringwood patiently spelt out the news, in order that he might be enabled to swagger and display his stale information to the companions of the evening. It was while the young idler was poring over this very journal, with the June sunlight streaming into his shabby chamber, where the finery worn the previous night lay side by side with the relics of the morning's breakfast in the shape of an empty chocolate-cup and the remains of a roll—it was during Ringwood's dinner-hour that he was disturbed by the slipshod servant maid of the lodging-house, who came to tell him that a gentleman, one calling himself Mr. Darrell Markham, was below, and wished to speak with him.

Ringwood glanced instinctively to the space above the mantelshelf, upon which there was a great display of pistols, rapiers, and other implements of warfare, and then, in rather a nervous tone of voice, told the servant girl to show the visitor upstairs.

Darrell's rapid step was heard upon the landing before the girl could leave the room.

"It is no time for ceremony, Ringwood," he said, dashing into the apartment, "nor for any old feeling of ill-will: I have come to talk to you about your sister."

"About Millicent?"

Mr. Ringwood Markham's countenance betrayed a powerful sense of relief as Darrell declared the object of his visit.

"Yes, about Mrs. George Duke. If your sister

were dead and buried, Ringwood Markham, I doubt if you would have heard the news."

"Millicent was always a poor correspondent," pleaded the squire, who wasted the best part of a day in scrawling a few ill-shaped characters and ill-spelt words over half a page of letter-paper ; "but what's wrong?"

"I scarce know if that which has happened may be well or ill for my poor cousin," answered Darrell. "Captain Duke has been away a year and a half, and no word of tidings of either him or his ship has reached Compton."

Mr. Ringwood Markham opened his eyes and breathed hard by way of expressing strong emotion. He was so essentially selfish that he was a bad hypocrite. He was so utterly indifferent to his fellow-men that he had never taught himself to affect an interest in other people's affairs.

Darrell Markham was walking rapidly up and down the room, his spurs clattering upon the worm-eaten boards.

"I only got the news to-day," he replied, "in a letter from Sally Pecker. I had not heard from Compton for upwards of eight months, nor had I sought for any news, for it does me little good to have the old place brought to my mind ; and to-day I got this letter from Sally, who says that the Captain's return has long ceased to be looked for in Compton, except by Millicent, who still seems to expect him."

"And what do you think of all this?" asked Ringwood.

"What do I think? Why, that Captain George Duke, and his ship the Vulture, have met the fate that all who sail under false colours deserve. I know of those

who can tell of a vessel, with the word 'Vulture'
painted on her figurehead, that has been seen off the
coast of Morocco, with the black flag flying at the fore,
and a crew of Africans chained down in the hold.   I
know of those who can tell of a wicked traffic between
the Moorish coast and the West India Islands, and who
speak of places where the coming of George Duke is
more dreaded than the yellow fever.   Good heavens!
can it be that this man has met his fate, and that
Millicent is free ? "

" Free ? "

" Yes, free to marry an honest man," cried Darrell,
his face flushing crimson with agitation.

Ringwood Markham had just intellect enough to be
spiteful.   He remembered the encounter in Farmer
Morrison's kitchen, and said maliciously,—

"Millicent will never be free till she hears certain
news of her husband's death ; and who knows that the
news would reach her if he were dead ?   If George
Duke is such a roving customer as you make him out
to be, his carcass may rot upon some foreign shore and
she be none the wiser."

" He has been away a year and a half," answered
Darrell ; " if he does not return within seven years
from the time of his first sailing, Millicent may marry
again."

" Is that the law ? "

" As I've heard it, from a boy. A year and a half
gone ; five years and a half to wait. My little Millicent, my poor Millicent, the time will seem but a day,
an hour, with such a star of hope to beckon me on to
the end."

Darrell turned from his cousin, ashamed of his

emotion. He seated himself in a chair against the open window, and buried his face in his hands.

Ringwood Markham could not resist the pleasure of inflicting another wound.

" I shouldn't wonder if the Captain is back before the summer is out," he said : " from what I know of George Duke, I think him no likely fellow to lose his life lightly either on sea or land."

Darrell took no notice of this speech. It is doubtful if he even heard it. His thoughts had wandered far away from the shabby lodging near Covent Garden, and the commonplace present, to lose themselves in the mystic regions of the Future.

" Hark ye, Ringwood," he said presently, rising and walking towards the door, " I did not come here to talk lovers' talk. If George Duke does not return, Millicent will be a lonely and helpless woman for nearly six years to come, with nothing to live upon but the interest of the two thousand pounds the squire gave her on her marriage. I am a poor man, but I claim a cousin's right to help her. Even you will easily understand that I must keep from her all knowledge of the quarter whence that help will come. You, as her brother, are bound to protect her. See that she wants for no comfort that can cheer her lonely life."

If Ringwood had not been afraid of his stalwart cousin, he would have whimpered out some petty excuse about his own poverty; but as it was, he said, with rather a long face,—

" I will do all I can, Darrell."

Darrell shook hands with him for the first time since their quarrel, and left him to his toilette and his evening's dissipation.

Ringwood dressed himself in the peach-blossom and silver suit, and cocked his hat jauntily upon his flowing locks. In an age when wigs and powdered hair were all the fashion, the young squire prided himself much upon the luxuriant natural curls which clustered about his narrow forehead. This particular evening he was especially careful of his toilette, for he had appointed to meet a gay party at Ranelagh, the chief member of which was to be a certain West-country baronet, called Sir Lovel Mortimer, and better known in two or three taverns of rather doubtful reputation than in the houses of the aristocracy.

The West-country baronet outshone Ringwood Markham both in the elegance of his costume and the languid affectation of his manners. Titled ladies glanced approvingly at Sir Lovel's slim figure as he glided through the stately contortions of a minuet, and many a bright eye responded with a friendly scintillation to the flaming glances of the young baronet's great restless orbs. This extreme restlessness of Sir Lovel's black eyes, which Darrell had perceived even in the apartment at the Reading inn, was of course a great deal more marked in a crowded assembly such as that which was gathered in the brilliant dancing-room at Ranelagh.

The West-country baronet seemed ubiquitous. His white velvet coat, upon which frosted rosebuds glittered in silk embroidery and tiny foil stones; his diamond-hilted court sword and shoebuckles; his flaxen periwig and burning black eyes, were to be seen in every direction. This incessant moving from place to place rendered it almost impossible for any but the most acute observer to discover that Sir Lovel

Mortimer had very few acquaintances amongst the aristocratic throng, and that the only persons whom he addressed familiarly were the four or five young men who had accompanied him, Ringwood Markham included.

The young squire was delighted with his good fortune in having made so distinguished an acquaintance. It was difficult for the village-bred Cumbrian to detect the difference between the foil stones upon Sir Lovel's embroidered coat and the diamonds in his shoebuckles; how impossible, then, for him to discover the nice shades and delicate distinctions wherein the West-country baronet's manners differed from those of the aristocratic fops and loungers who lifted their eye-glasses to look at him with the last fashionable stare of supercilious wonder. Ringwood followed Sir Lovel with a wide open-eyed gaze of respect and admiration; and when the place began to grow less crowded, and the baronet proposed adjourning to his lodgings in Cheyne Walk, where he could give the party a broiled bone and a few throws of the dice, the squire was the first to assent to the proposition.

The young man walked to the house where the baronet lodged. It was not in Cheyne Walk, though Sir Lovel had been pleased to say as much, but in an obscure street leading away from the river—a street in which the houses were small and gloomy.

Sir Lovel Mortimer stopped before a house the windows of which were all dark, and knocked softly with his cane upon the panel of the door.

Ringwood, who had been already drinking a great deal, caught hold of the brazen knocker and sounded a tremendous peal.

"You have no need to arouse the neighbours, Mr. Markham," said the baronet, with some vexation; "I make no doubt my servant is on the watch for us."

But it seemed as if Sir Lovel was mistaken, for the young men waited some time before the door was opened; and when at last the bolts were undone, and the party admitted into the house, they found themselves in darkness.

"Why, how's this, you lazy hound?" cried Sir Lovel; "have you been asleep?"

"Yesh," answered a thick unsteady voice; "sh'pose —I've been—'shleep."

"Why, you're drunk, you rascal!" exclaimed the baronet: "here, fetch a light, will you?"

"I'm feshin' a light," the voice answered; "I'm feelin' for tind' box."

A scrambling of hands upon a shelf, the dropping of a flint and steel, and the rattling of candlesticks, succeeded this assertion; and in a few moments a light was struck, a wax candle lighted, and the speaker's face illuminated by a feeble flicker.

Sir Lovel Mortimer's servant was drunk; his face was dirty; his wig pushed over his eyebrows, and singed by the candle in his hand; his cravat was twisted awry, and hung about his neck like a halter; his eyes were dim and watery from the effect of strong liquors; and it was with difficulty he kept himself erect by swaying slowly to and fro as he stood staring vacantly at his master and his master's guests.

But it was not the mere drunkenness of the man's aspect which startled Ringwood Markham.

Sir Lovel Mortimer's servant was Captain George Duke!

About four o'clock the next afternoon, when Ringwood awoke from his prolonged drunken sleep, the first thing he did was to find a sheet of paper, scrawl half-a-dozen words upon it, fold it, and direct it thus:

> "*Darrell Markham, Esq.*,
> "*At the Earl of C——'s,*
> "*St. James's Square.*"

The few words Ringwood scrawled were these:

"Dear Darrell,—George Duke is not ded. I saw him last nite at a hous in Chelsey.—Yours to comand,

"R. MARKHAM."

CHAPTER X.

THE HOUSE AT CHELSEA.

DARRELL MARKHAM had left London on some business for his patron when Ringwood's messenger delivered the brief lines telling of the young man's encounter with Captain George Duke.

It was a week before Darrell returned to St. James's Square, where he found the young squire's letter waiting for him. One rapid glance at the contents of Ringwood's ill-spelled epistle was enough. He crumpled the letter into his pocket, snatched up his hat, and without a moment's delay ran straight to the squire's lodging by Bedford Street.

He found Ringwood lying in bed, spelling out the grease-stained pages of one of Mr. Fielding's novels. Tavern tankards and broken glasses were scattered on the table, empty bottles lay upon the ground, and the bones of a fowl and the remnants of a loaf of bread

adorned the soiled tablecloth. Master Ringwood had
entertained a couple of friends to supper on the previous
evening.

"Ringwood Markham," said his cousin, holding out
the young man's missive, "what is the meaning of this?"

"Of which?" asked the squire, with a stupid stare.
The fumes of last night's wine and punch had not quite
cleared away from his intellect, somewhat obscure at
the best of times.

"Of this letter, in which, as I think, you tell me the
biggest lie that ever one man told another. George
Duke in England—George Duke at Chelsea—what does
it mean, man? speak!"

"Don't you be in a hurry," said Ringwood, throwing
his book into a corner of the room. The young man
rubbed his eyes, propped himself up on his pillow, took
a pinch of snuff from a box under the bolster, and looked
at Darrell with a species of half-tipsy gravity most
ludicrous to behold. "Split me, if you give a fellow
time to collect his ideas," he cried. "As to big lies,
you'd better be careful how you use such expressions
to a man of my reputation. Ask 'em round in Covent
Garden whether I didn't offer to throw a spittoon at the
sea captain who insulted me; and would have done it,
too, if the bully hadn't knocked me down first. As to
my letter, I'm prepared to stand to what I said in it.
And now what did I say in it?"

"Look at it in your own hand," answered Darrell,
giving him the letter.

Ringwood spelt out his own epistle as carefully as if
it had been some peculiar and mystic communication
written in Greek or Hebrew; and then returning it
to his cousin, he said, with a toss of his pale golden

locks that flung his silk nightcap rakishly askew on his forehead,—

"As to that letter, cousin Darrell Markham, the letter's nothing. What do you say to my finding George Duke, of the Vulture, acting as servant to my distinguished friend from Devonshire, Sir Lovel Mortimer, Baronet? What do you say to his taking Sir Lovel's orders like any low knave that ever was? What do you say to his being in so drunken a state as to be sent away to bed, with a sharp reprimand from his master, before I had the chance to speak a word to him?"

"What do I say to this?" cried Darrell, walking up and down the room in his agitation; "why, that it can't be true. It's some stupid mistake of yours."

"It can't be true, can't it? It's some stupid mistake of mine, is it? Upon my word, Mr. Darrell Markham, you're a very mannerly person to come into a gentleman's room and take advantage of his not having his sword at his side to tell him he's a fool and a liar. I tell you I saw George Duke drunk, and acting as servant to my friend Sir Lovel Mortimer."

"Did George Duke recognize you?" asked Darrell.

"Don't I tell you that he was blind drunk!" cried the young squire, very much exasperated: "how should he recognize me when he could scarcely see out of his eyes for drunkenness? I might have spoken to him; but before I could think whether 'twas best to speak or not, Sir Lovel had given him a kick and sent him about his business; and on second thoughts I reflected that it would be no great gain to expose family matters to the baronet by letting him know that my brother-in-law was serving him as a lacquey."

I

"But did you make no inquiries about this scoundrel?"

"I did. I told Sir Lovel I had a fancy that I knew the man's face, and asked who he was. But it seems the baronet knows nothing of him, except that he has served him for a twelvemonth, and is as faithful a fellow as ever breathed, Sir Lovel says, though over-fond of drink."

Darrell did not make any reply to his cousin's speech for some little time, during which pause he walked up and down the room absorbed in thought.

"Ringwood Markham," he said at last, stopping short by the side of the bed, "there's some mystery in all this that neither you nor I can penetrate. I know this Lovel Mortimer, this West-country baronet."

"Then you know my very good friend," answered Ringwood with a consequential smirk.

"I know one of the most audacious highwaymen who ever contrived to escape the Old Bailey."

"A highwayman! The Baronet — the mould of fashion and the glass of form, as Lawless the attorney called him; the most elegant beau that ever danced at Ranelagh; the owner of one of the finest estates in Devonshire! Have a care, Darrell, how you speak of my friends."

"It would be better if you had more care in choosing them," answered Darrell quietly. "My poor foolish Ringwood, I hope you have not been letting this man clean out your pockets at hazard."

"I have lost a few guineas to him at odd times," muttered Ringwood, with a very long face.

The young squire had paid dearly enough for his love of fashionable company, and he had borne his losses without a murmur; but to find that he had been made a fool of all the time was a bitter blow to his self-conceit: still more bitter, since Darrell, of all others, was the person to undeceive him.

"You mean to tell me, then," he said ruefully, "that this Sir Lovel——"

"Is no more Sir Lovel than you are," answered Darrell: "all the fashionable breeding he can pretend to is what he has picked up on the king's highway; and the only estate he will ever be master of in Devonshire or elsewhere will be enough stout timber to build him a gallows when his course comes to an abrupt termination. He is known to the knights of the road and the constables by the nickname of Captain Fanny, and there is little doubt the house in Chelsea to which he took you was a nest of highwaymen."

Ringwood had not a word to say; he sat with his nightcap in his hand and one foot out of bed, staring helplessly at his cousin, and scratching his head dubiously.

"But that is not all," continued Darrell: "there is some mystery in the connection between this man and George Duke. They might prove a dozen alibis, and they might swear me out of countenance, but prove what they may, and swear all they may, I can still declare that George Duke was the man who robbed me between Compton-on-the-Moor and Marley Water— George Duke was the man who stole my horse; and only seven months back I found that very horse, stolen from me by that very George Duke, in the custody of this man, your friend the baronet, *alias* Captain Fanny. The upshot of it is, that while we have thought George Duke was away upon the high seas, he has been hiding in London and going about the country robbing honest men. The ship Vulture is a fiction; and instead of being a merchant, a privateer, a pirate, or a slaver, George Duke is neither more nor less than a highwayman and a thief."

"I only know that I saw him one night last week at a house in Chelsea," muttered Ringwood feebly. His weak intellect could scarcely keep pace with Darrell's excitement.

"Get up and dress yourself, Ringwood, while I run to the nearest magistrate. This fellow, Captain Fanny, stole my horse and emptied my pockets on the Bath road. We'll get a warrant out, take a couple of constables with us, and you shall lead the way to the house in which you saw George Duke. Don't waste time staring at me, man, but get yourself ready against I come back to fetch you. We'll unearth the scoundrels and find a clue to this mystery before night."

"Two constables is not much," murmured Ringwood doubtfully. "Sir Lovel always had his friends about him, and there may be a small regiment in that house."

Darrell looked at his cousin with undisguised contempt.

"We don't want you to face the gang," he said; "we shall only ask you to show us the way and point out the house: you can run away and hide round the corner when you've done that, while I go in with the constables."

"As to pointing out the house," answered the crestfallen squire, "I'll give you my help and welcome; but a man may be as brave as a lion, and yet not have any great fancy for being shot from behind a door."

"I'll take the risks of any stray bullets, man," cried Darrell, laughing; "only get up and dress yourself without loss of time, while I go and fetch the constables."

The getting of a warrant was rather a long business, and sorely tried Darrell's patience. It was dusk when the matter was accomplished, and the young man returned to Ringwood's lodging with the two constables and the official document which was to secure the elegant person of Captain Fanny.

Darrell found his cousin specially equipped for the expedition, and armed to the teeth with a complicated collection of pistols, of the power to manage which he was as innocent as a baby. A formidable naval sword swung at his side, and got between his legs at every turn, while the muzzles of a tremendous pair of horse-pistols peeped out of his coat-pockets in such a manner that had they by any chance exploded, their charge must inevitably have been lodged in the elbows of the squire.

Darrell set his cousin's warlike toilette a little in order, Ringwood reluctantly consenting to content himself with one pair of pistols, and to substitute a small rapier for the tremendous cutlass he had placed so much faith in.

"It isn't the size of your weapon, but whether you're able to use it, that makes the difference, Ringwood," said Darrell. "Come along, my lad. We won't leave you in the thick of the fight, depend upon it."

Ringwood looked anxiously into the faces of the two constables, as if to see whether there were any symptoms of a disposition to run away in either of their stolid countenances; and being apparently satisfied with the inspection, consented to step into the hackney coach with his three companions.

Ringwood Markham was by no means the best of guides. The coachman who drove the party had rather a bad time of it. First Ringwood was for going to Chelsea through Tyburn turnpike, and could scarcely be persuaded that Ranelagh and Cheyne Walk did not lie somewhere in that direction. Then the young squire harassed and persecuted his unfortunate charioteer by suddenly commanding him to take abrupt turnings to the left, and to follow intricate windings to the right, and to keep scrupulously out of the high road which would have taken him straight to his direction. He grew fidgetty the moment they passed Hyde Park Corner, and was for driving direct to the Marshes about Westminster, assuring his companions that it was necessary to pass the Abbey in order to get to Chelsea, for he had passed it on the night in question; and at last, when Darrell fairly lost patience with him, and bade the coachman to go his own way to Cheyne Walk without further waste of time, Millicent's brother threw himself back in a fit of the sulks, declaring that they had made a fool of him by bringing him as their guide and then forbidding him to speak.

When they reached Cheyne Walk, where they left the coach against Don Saltero's tavern, and set out on foot to find the house occupied by Captain Fanny, Ringwood Markham was of very little more use than before. In the first place, he had never known the name of the street to which his friend had taken him; in the second place, he had gone to it from Ranelagh, and not from London, and that made all the difference in the finding of it, as he urged, when Darrell grew

Impatient of his stupidity; and then again, he had been with a merry party on that particular night, and had therefore taken little notice of the way. At last Darrell hit upon the plan of leading his cousin quietly through all the small streets at the back of Cheyne Walk, in hopes by that means of arriving at the desired end. Nor was he disappointed; for, after twenty false alarms, and just as he was beginning to give up the matter for a bad job, Ringwood suddenly came to a dead stop before the door of a substantial looking house, and cried triumphantly,—

"That's the knocker!"

But the young squire had given Darrell and the constable so much trouble for the last hour and a half by stopping every now and then, under the impression that he recognized a door-step or a shutter, a lion's head in stone over the doorway, a brass bell-handle, a scraper, a peculiarly shaped paving-stone, or some other object, and then, after a few moments' deliberation, confessing himself to be mistaken, that, in spite of his triumphant tone, his cousin felt rather doubtful about the matter.

"You're sure it is the house, Ringwood?" he said.

"Sure! Don't I tell you I know the knocker? Am I likely to be mistaken, do you think?" asked the squire indignantly, quite forgetting that he had confessed himself mistaken about twenty times in the last hour.

"Don't I tell you that I know the knocker? I now it because I gave a sturdy knock with it, and Sir Lov—— he——the Captain, said I was a fool for rousing the neighbours. It's a dragon's-head knocker in brass. I remember it well."

" A dragon's head is a common enough pattern for a knocker," said Darrell, rather hopelessly.

"Yes; but all dragon's heads are not beaten flat on one side, as this is, are they ? " cried Ringwood. " I remember taking notice how the brass had been battered by some constable's cudgel or roysterer's loaded cane. I tell you this is the house, cousin; and if you want to see George Duke, you'd. better knock at the door. As I was a friend of Sir Lovel's, and have received civilities from him, I'd rather not be seen in the matter; so I'll just step round the corner.

With which expression of gentlemanly feeling, Mr. Ringwood Markham retired, leaving his cousin and the constables upon the door-step. It had long been dark, and the night was dull and moonless, with a heavy fog rising from the river.

Darrell Markham directed the two men to conceal themselves behind a projecting doorway a few paces down the street, while he knocked and reconnoitred the place. His summons was answered by a servant girl, who carried a candle in her hand, and who told him that the West-country baronet, Sir Lovel Mortimer, had indeed occupied a part of the house, with his servant and two or three of his friends; but that he had left three days before, and the lodgings were now to be let.

Did the girl know where Sir Lovel had gone? Darrell asked.

She believed he had gone back to Devonshire ; but she would ask her mistress if the gentleman wished.

But the gentleman did not wish to trouble her mistress, he said. The girl's manner convinced him that she was telling the truth, and that Captain Fanny had indeed quitted the Chelsea lodging-house. He was so disappointed at the result of his expedition that he scarcely cared even to make an attempt at putting it to some trifling use.

But, as he was turning to leave the door-step, he stopped to ask the girl one more question.

" This servant of Sir Lovel's," he said, " what sort of a person was he ? "

" A nasty grumpy disagreeable creature," the girl answered decisively.

" Did you know his name ? "

" His master always called him Jeremiah, sir ; and some of the other gentlemen called him sulky Jeremiah, because he was always grumbling and growling, except when he was tipsy."

" Can you tell me what he was like ? " asked Darrell. " Was he a good-looking fellow ? "

" O, as for that," answered the servant girl, " he was well enough to look at, but too surly for the company of decent folks."

Darrell dropped a piece of silver into the girl's hand, and wished her good night. The constables emerged from their lurking-place as the young man left the door-step.

" Is it the right house, sir ? " asked one of them.

" Yes," replied Darrell ; " we've found the nest, sure enough, but the birds have flown. We must even make the best of it, my friends, and go home, for our warrant is but waste paper to-night."

They found Ringwood Markham waiting patiently enough round the corner. He chuckled rather maliciously when he heard of his cousin's disappointment.

" You'll believe me, though, anyhow," he said, " since you found that it was the right house."

" Yes, it was the right house," answered Darrell, moodily ; " but there's little satisfaction in that.   How do I know that this sulky servant of the highwayman's was really George Duke, and that you were not deceived by some fancied likeness ?"

CHAPTER XI.

AFTER SEVEN YEARS.

THE star of the young squire, Ringwood Markham, shone for a very little longer in the metropolitan hemisphere. His purse was empty, his credit exhausted, his health impaired, his spirits gone, and himself altogether so much the worse for his few brief years of London life, that there was nothing better for him to do than to go quietly back to Compton-on-the-Moor and take up his abode at the Hall, with an old woman as his housekeeper, and a couple of farm labourers for the rest of his establishment. This old woman had lived at Compton Hall while the shutters were closed before the principal windows, the heavy bolts remained undrawn on the chief doors, and the dust gathering fast and thick upon the portraits of those dead-and-gone Markhams whose poor painted images looked out with wan and ghastly simpers from the oaken wainscoting. The old housekeeper had led a very easy life in the dreary darkened house while Ringwood, its master, was roystering in the taverns about Covent Garden; and she was by no means too well pleased when, in the dusk of a misty

October evening, the young squire rode quietly up the deserted avenue, dismounted from his horse in the stable-yard, walked in at the back door leading into the servants' regions, and, standing upon the broad hearth in the raftered kitchen, told her rather sulkily that he had come to live there.

His coming made very little change in the domestic arrangements of the Hall. He established himself in the oak parlour, in which his father had smoked and drunk and sworn himself into his coffin; and after giving strict orders that only the shutters of those rooms used by himself should be opened, he determinedly set his face against the outraged inhabitants of Compton. Now these simple people, not being aware that Ringwood Markham had spent every guinea that he was free to spend, took great umbrage at his eccentric and solitary manner of living, and forthwith solved the enigma of his existence by setting him down a miser.

Sometimes in the dusk of the evening the squire crept out of the Hall gates, and strolled up the village street to honest Sally Pecker's hospitable mansion, where he took his glass of punch in the best parlour, and made himself tolerably agreeable to the company assembled there. The honest Compton folks were glad to welcome the returned prodigal, and paid their homage to him as they had done to his father, when that obstinate-tempered and violent old gentleman had been pleased to hold his court at the Bear. Ringwood felt that, simple as the Cumbrian villagers were, they were wiser then the Londoners who had emptied his purse for him while they laughed in their sleeves at his dignity. Yes, on the whole, he was certainly happier at Compton than in his Bedford Street lodgings, or **with** his old tavern companions, in whose society he had been tormented sometimes by a vague idea that he was only a dupe and a fool. He had been used to lead a very narrow life at the best, and the dull monotony of this new existence gave him no pain.

Millicent saw very little of her brother. He would sometimes drop into the cottage at dusk on his way to the Black Bear, and sit with her for a few minutes, talking of the village, or the farm, or some other of the everyday matters of life ; but his sister's simple society only wearied him ; and after about a quarter of an hour he would begin to yawn drearily behind his hand, and then, after kissing her upon the forehead as he bade her good night, he would stroll away to Sarah Pecker's, switching his light riding-whip as he walked, and pleased by the sensation his embroidered coat created amongst the urchins and the idle women gossiping at their doors. It had been agreed between Darrell and Ringwood that Millicent was to know nothing of the house in Chelsea and the young squire's mysterious rencontre with George Duke or his double.

People in Compton—who knew of Darrell's encounter with the highwayman upon the moor, and of Mrs. Duke's meeting with the ghost upon Marley Pier—said that the Captain of the Vulture was cursed with the attendance of a shadow which appeared sometimes to those belonging to him, and whose appearance was no doubt a sign of trouble and calamity to the Captain himself. Such things had been before, they whispered, let the parson of the parish say what he would ; and there were some ghosts that all the Latin that worthy gentleman knew would never lay in the Red Sea.

.. quiet years rolled slowly by, unmarked by change
either at the Hall, the Black Bear, or the little cottage
in which Millicent spent her tranquil days. No tidings
came to Compton of the Vulture or its captain; and
though Millicent refused to wear a widow's dress, the
feeling gradually crept upon her that she was indeed a
widow, and that the tie knotted for her by others, and
so bitter to bear, was broken by the mighty hand which
severs so many tender links, and seems so slow sometimes to loosen the chains of a cruel bondage.

For the first year or two after Ringwood Markham's
return, it was thought that he would most likely marry
and take his place in the village as his father had done
before him. The Hall estate was considered to be a
very comfortable fortune in the neighbourhood of Compton-on-the-Moor, and many a rich farmer's daughter
sported her finest ribbons, and pinned her jauntily
trimmed hat coquettishly aslant upon her roll of glossy
hair, in hopes of charming the young squire. But
Ringwood's heart was a fortress by no means easy to
be stormed. Selfishness held her court therein, and a
complete indifference to all simple pleasures, and a
certain weariness of life, had succeeded the young
man's brief career of dissipation.

As his fortune mended with the first few years of
his new and steady life, something of the miser's feeling
took possession of his cold nature. He had spent
his money upon ungrateful boon companions, who had
laughed at him for his pains, and refused him the loan
of a guinea when his purse was low. He would be
warned by the past, he thought, and would learn to be
wiser in the future. Small tenants on the Compton
Hall estate began to murmur to each other that Master

Ringwood Markham was a hard landlord, and that times
were even worse now for poor folks than in the old
squire's day.   These poor people spoke nothing but the
truth.   As Ringwood's empty purse filled once more,
the young man felt a greedy eagerness to save money;
for what purpose he scarcely gave himself the trouble
to think.   Perhaps when he did think very seriously, a
shuddering fear came over him that his impaired constitution was not to be easily mended—that even the fine
north-country air sweeping across broad expanses of
brown moorland, and blowing in at the open windows of
the oak parlour, could never bring a healthy glow back
to his flushed cheeks;   and that it might be that he
inherited with his mother's fair face something of his
mother's feebleness of constitution.   But it was rarely
that he suffered his mind to dwell upon these things.
He found plenty of employment for himself in protecting
his own interests.   He was his own steward, and rode
a grey pony about the farm, watching the men at their
work, and gloating over the progress of the crops as
the changing seasons did their bounteous work, and the
bright face of Plenty met him in his way.

Northern harvests are late, and that harvest was
especially late which was garnered in the seventh
autumn succeeding the last sailing of the good ship
Vulture from the harbour at Marley Water.   Septem-
ber had been wet and cold, and October set in with a
gloomy aspect, as of an unwelcome winter come before
his due time.   In the early days of this chill and cheerless October they were still stacking the corn upon the
Compton Hall farm, while Ringwood, on his grey pony,
rode from field to field to watch the men at their

labours, and to grumble at their laziness. The young squire was cautious and suspicious, and rarely thought that work was well done unless he was at the heels of those who did it.

He paid dearly enough for this want of faith in those who served him, for it was in one of these rides that he caught a chill which settled on his lungs, and threw him on a bed of sickness.

At the first hint of his illness Millicent was by his side, patient and loving, eager to soothe and comfort, to tend and to restore. Like all creatures of his class, weak alike in physical and mental qualities, the young man peculiarly felt the helplessness of his state. He clung to his sister as if he had been a sick child and she his mother. In the dead of the night he would awake, with the cold drops standing on his brow, and cry aloud to her to come to him. Then, comforted and reassured on finding her watching by his side, he would fall into a peaceful slumber with her hand clasped in his, and his fair head pillowed upon her shoulder.

The Compton doctor shook his head ominously when he looked at the young squire's hectic cheeks and sounded his narrow chest. Not satisfied with the village surgeon's decision, Millicent sent to Marley Water for a physician to look at her sinking brother; but the physician only confirmed what his colleague had already said. There was no hope for Ringwood. Little matter whether they called it a violent cold, or a spasmodic cough, inflammation of the lungs, or low fever. All that need be told about him would have been better told in one word—consumption. His mother had died of the same disease before him, fading quietly away as he was fading now.

In the dismal silences of those long winter nights in
which the sick man awoke so often—always to see
Millicent's fair face, lighted by the faint glimmer of the
night-lamp or the glow of the embers in the grate—
Ringwood began to think of his past life—a brief life,
which had been spent to no useful end whatever; a
selfish life, which had been passed in stolid indifference
to the good of others—perhaps, from this terrible use-
lessness, almost a wicked life.

A few nights before that upon which the young squire
died, he lay awake a long time counting the chiming of
the quarters from the turret of Compton church, listening
to the embers falling on the broad stone hearth, and
the ivy-leaves flapping and scraping against the window-
panes, with something like the sound of skeleton fingers
tapping for admittance.   And from this he fell to
watching his sister's face as she sat in a low chair
by the hearth, with her large thoughtful blue eyes fixed
upon the hollow fire, and the unread volume half
dropping from her loose hand.

How pretty she was, he thought; but what a pensive
beauty!   How little of the light of joy had ever beamed
from those melancholy eyes since the old days when
Darrell and she had been friends and playfellows,
before Captain George Duke had ever shown his handsome face at the Hall!   Thinking thus, it was only
natural for the sick man to remember his own share in
forcing on this unhappy marriage; how he had persuaded his father to hear no girlish prayers, and to heed
neither tears nor lamentations.   Remembering this, he
could but remember also the mean motive which had
urged him to this course; the contemptible spite against
his cousin Darrell, which had made him eager even for

the shipwreck of his sister's happiness, so that her lover might suffer. He was dying now, and the world, with all that was in it, was of so little use to him that he was ready enough to forgive his cousin all the old grudges between them, and to wish him well for the future.

"Millicent!" he said by-and-by.

"Yes, dear," answered his sister, creeping to his side. "I thought you were asleep. Have you been awake long, Ringwood?"

"Yes, a long time."

"A long time! my poor boy!"

"Perhaps it's better to be awake, sometimes," murmured the sick man. "I don't want to slip out of life in one long sleep. I've been thinking, Millicent."

"Thinking, dear?"

"Yes, thinking what a bad brother I've been to you."

"A bad brother, Ringwood! No, no, no!" She fell on her knees by the bedside as she spoke, and wound her loving arms about his wasted frame.

"Yes, Millicent, a bad brother. I helped to urge on your marriage with a man you hated. I helped to part you from the man you loved, and to make your young life miserable. You know that, and yet you're here, night after night, nursing me as tenderly as if I'd never thought but of your happiness."

"The past is all forgiven long ago, dear Ringwood," said his sister earnestly; "it would be ill for brother and sister if the love between them could not outlive old injuries, and be the brighter and the truer for old sorrows. You did not know what a cruel wrong you were doing me when you advised that wretched marriage. I have outlived the memory of my misery long

K

ago. Ringwood, dear, I have led a tranquil life for years past, and it seems as if it had pleased God to set me free from the ties that seemed so heavy to bear."

"You will be almost a rich woman after my death, Milly," said her brother, with a more cheerful tone. "I have done a good deal in these last five years to improve the property, and you will find a bag full of guineas in the brass-handled bureau, where I keep all my papers and accounts. I think you may trust John Martin, the bailiff, and Lawson, and Thomas, and they will keep an eye upon the farm for your interest. You'll have to grow a woman of business when I am gone, Milly, and it will be a fine change for you from yonder cottage in Compton High Street to this big house."

"Ringwood, Ringwood, don't speak of this!"

"But I must, Milly. It's time to speak of these things when a man feels he has not an hour upon this side of the grave that he can call his own. I want you to promise me something, Millicent, before I die; for a promise made to a dying man is always binding."

"Ringwood, dear, what is there I would not do for you?"

"I knew you wouldn't refuse. Now listen. How long has Captain Duke been away?"

She thought by this sudden mention of her husband's name that Ringwood's mind was wandering.

"Seven years, dear, next January."

"I thought so. Now, Milly, listen to me. When the month of January is nearly out, I want you to take a journey to London, and carry a letter from me to Darrell Markham."

"I'll do it, dear Ringwood, and would do more than

that, if you wish. But why in January? Why not sooner?"

"Because it's a fancy I have; a sick man's fancy, perhaps. The letter is not written yet, but I'll write it before I fall asleep again. Get me the pen and ink, Milly."

"To-morrow, dearest, not to-night," she pleaded; "you've been fatiguing yourself already with talking so much: write the letter to-morrow."

"No, to-night," he said impatiently; "this very night, this very hour. I shall fall into a fever of anxiety if I don't write without a moment's delay. It is but a few lines."

His loving nurse thought it better to comply with his wishes than to irritate him by a refusal. She brought paper, pens, ink, sealing-wax, and seals, and a lighted candle, and arranged them on the little table by his bedside. She propped him up with pillows, so as to make his task as easy to him as possible, and then quietly withdrew to her seat by the hearth.

The reader knows how difficult penmanship was to Ringwood Markham even when in good health. It was a very hard task to him to-night. He laboured long and painfully with the spluttering quill pen, and wrote but a few lines after all. These he read and re-read with evident satisfaction; and then folding the big sheet of foolscap very carefully, he sealed it with a great splash of red wax and a weak impression of the Markham arms, and addressed it, in a feeble sprawling hand, with many blots, to "*Darrell Markham, Esq. to be delivered to him by Millicent Duke at the close of January*, 17—."

"I have done Darrell many a wrong," he said, as he

handed the letter to his sister; " but I think that this may repair all. It is my last will and testament, Milly; I shall make no other, for there is none to claim the property but you."

"And you have left Darrell something, then ?" she asked.

"Nothing but that letter. I trust to you to deliver it faithfully, and I know that Darrell will be content."

*   *   *   *   *

Mrs. Sarah Pecker came to the Hall whenever she had a spare moment, to help Millicent in her task of nursing the dying man. She was with her at that last trying moment when the faint straws of life to which the young squire had clung floated one by one out of his feeble hands, and he sank into the unknown depths of Death's pitiless ocean.

Friendly and loving faces were the last to fade away from the dying man's eyes; soothing voices were the last to grow faint and strange upon his dull ears; gentle hands supported the fainting frame; cool fingers laid their touch upon the burning brow. It was better to die thus than to spill his blood on a sanded floor in a tavern brawl, though he had been the most distinguished buck, duellist, bully, and swaggerer between Covent Garden and Pall Mall.

CHAPTER XII.

CAPTAIN FANNY.

Six years had passed since that Christmas-eve upon which the foreign-looking pedlar had robbed Mrs. Sarah

Pecker, and worked such a wonderful change for the
better in the fortunes and social status of her husband
Samuel. Six years had passed away, and it was Christmas time once more. Again Betty the cookmaid was
busy plucking geese and turkeys; and again Mrs. Sarah
stood at her ample dresser rolling out the paste for
Christmas pies; again the mighty coal fire roared half-
way up the chimney, and the capacious oven was like
a furnace, and only to be approached with due precaution,—a mysterious cavern out of which good things
seemed for ever issuing—big sprawling crusty golden-
brown loaves, steaming batches of pies, small regiments
of flat cakes of so little account as to be flung without
ceremony upon the bare hearth to grow cool at their
leisure, and other cates and confections too numerous
to mention. Again was the loitering carrier expected
with groceries from the market town; again did rich
streams of a certain spicy perfume unknown to court
perfumers, and commonly known as the odour of rum-
punch, issue from the half-open doors of the parlour
and the innermost sanctuary of the bar.

But although these Christmas preparations differed
in no manner from those of a Christmas six years
before, there were changes at the Bear—changes which
the reader has already been told of. Mrs. Pecker
had grown wondrously subdued in voice and manner.
Something almost of timidity mingled with this new
manner of the portly Sarah's—something of a perpetual uneasiness, a continual dread, no one knew of
what. So changed, indeed, was she in this respect,
that Samuel had sometimes need to cheer her and
console her when she was what he called "low," and
was fain to administer modest glasses of punch or

comfortable hot suppers as restoratives to her sinking
spirits.

While things were thus with Sarah, her worthy
husband had very much improved under his better-
half's new manner of treatment.

He was no longer afraid of his own customers nor
of his own voice. He no longer trembled or blushed
when suddenly addressed in conversation. He could
venture to draw himself a mug of his own ale without
looking nervously across his shoulder all the while,
after the manner of a dishonest waiter who tampers
with his master's tap. Samuel Pecker was a new man;
still a little given to believe in ghosts, perhaps, and to
shake his head and groan ominously when coffin-shaped
cinders flew out of the fire; still a little doubtful as to
going anywhere alone in the dark; but for all that a
very lion of courage and audacity compared to what he
had been before the foreign-looking pedlar threw Mrs.
Pecker into a swoon.

The Bear was especially gay this Christmas-eve, for
a party of gentlemen had ridden over from York, and
were dining in the white parlour, a state apartment
on the first floor. They were to sleep that night and
spend their Christmas-day at the inn, and the turkey
lying limp and helpless in Betty's lap was intended for
them.

"And isn't one of 'em a handsome one too?" said
the cook, pulling vigorously at the biggest feathers.
"You should go in and have a look at un, missus,—
such black eyes, that pierce you through and through
like a streak of lightning! and little white hands, just
for all the world like Mrs. Duke's, and all covered with
diamonds and such likes. And ain't he a saucy one, too?

and ain't the others afraid of him? The other two were for leaving here after dinner; and when he said he should stay, one of 'em asked if the place was—something, 1 couldn't catch the word; but the dark-eyed gentleman burst out laughing, and told him he was a lily-livered rascal, and not fit company for gentlemen; and the other rattled his glass on the table, and said the Captain was right—only he swore awful!" added Betty, with solemn horror.

While the cook was amusing her mistress with these details, Samuel put his head in at the kitchen door.

"Them bloods in the white parlour are rare noisy ones," he said; "they want half-a-dozen of the old port, and there's only three of 'em, and they've had Madeira and claret already. I wish you'd go up to 'em, Sarah, and give 'em a hint that they might be a little quieter. I'll go down for the wine, if you'll put yourself straight while I'm getting it."

Sarah complied, wiped the flour from her hands, smoothed her cap-ribbons, drew on her mittens, and adjusted her ample stomacher, by the time Samuel emerged from the cellar with two cobweb-shrouded black bottles under each arm.

"I've brought four, Sally," he said, as he landed the precious burden on the kitchen table. "I'll carry them up for you, and you can bring a few glasses."

The trio in the white parlour was certainly rather a riotous one. A pair of massive wax candles burned in solid silver candlesticks upon the polished oaken table, which was strewed with nut-shells, raisin-stalks, orange-peel, and nut-crackers, and amply garnished with empty bottles and glittering diamond-cut wine glasses. One of the party had flung himself back on his chair, and had

planted his spurred heels upon this very dessert **table**,
while he amused himself by peeling an orange and
throwing the rind at his opposite neighbour, who, more
than half tipsy, sat with his elbows on the table and
his chin in his hands, staring vacantly at his tormentor
The third member of the little party, and he who seemed
far the most sober of the three, lounged with his back
to the fire and his elbow leaning on the mantelpiece,
and paused in the midst of some anecdote which he
had been telling as Mrs. Pecker entered the room. His
flashing black eyes, and his small white teeth, **which**
glittered as he spoke, lit up his face, which, in spite of
his evident youth, was wan and haggard—the face of a
man prematurely old from excitement and dissipation;
for the hand of Time during the last six years had
drawn many a wrinkle about the restless eyes and
determined mouth of Sir Lovel Mortimer, Baronet,
alias Captain Fanny, highwayman, and, on occasion,
housebreaker.

Heaven knows what there was in the appearance of
any one of the party in the white parlour to overawe or
agitate the worthy mistress of the Black Bear, but it is
a sure thing that a faint and dusky pallor crept over
Sarah Pecker's face as she set the wine and glasses
upon the table. She seemed nervous and uneasy under
the strange dazzle of Captain Fanny's black eyes. It
has been said that they were not ordinary eyes; indeed,
there was something in them which the physiognomists
of to-day would no doubt have set themselves indus-
triously at work to define and explain. They were not
restless only. There was a look in them almost of
terror—not of a terror of to-day or yesterday, but
of some dim far-away time too remote for memory—

the trace of some shock to the nervous system received long before the mind had power to note its force, but which had left its lasting seal upon one feature of the face.

Sarah Pecker dropped and broke one of her best wine glasses under the strange influence of these restless eyes. They fixed her gaze as if they had possessed some magnetic power. She followed every motion of them earnestly, almost inquiringly, till the highwayman addressed her.

"We have the extreme honour of being waited upon by the landlady of the Bear in her own gracious person, have we not?" he said gallantly, admiring his small jewelled hand as he spoke. He was but a puny wasted stripling this dashing captain, and it was only the extreme vitality in himself that preserved him from insignificance.

Now, at any other time, Sarah Pecker would have dropped a curtsey, smoothed her muslin apron, and asked the guests whether their dinner had been to their liking; if their rooms were comfortable; the wine agreeable to their taste, and some other such hospitable questions; but to-night she seemed tongue-tied, as if the restless light in the Captain's eyes had almost magnetized her into silence.

"Yes," she murmured, "I am Sarah Pecker." *

"And a very comfortable and friendly creature you look, Mrs. Pecker," answered Captain Fanny, with a sublime air of patronage. "A recommendation in your own person to the hospitable shelter of the Bear. And, egad, madam! Compton-on-the-Moor has need of some pleasant place of entertainment for the unlucky traveller who finds himself by mischance in its dreary neighbourhood. Was there ever such a place, lads?" he added, turning to his two companions.

But Mrs. Sarah Pecker had been born in the village of Compton, and was by no means disposed to stand by and hear her native place so contemptuously spoken of. Turning her face a little away from the dashing knight of the road, as if it were easier to her to speak when out of the radius of those unquiet eyes, she said with some dignity,—

"Compton-on-the-Moor may be a retired place, gentlemen, being nigh upon a week's journey from London, but it is a pleasant village in summer time, and there are a great many noble families about."

"Ah! by the bye," replied Captain Fanny, "we took notice of a big redbrick square-built house, standing amongst some fine timber upon a bit of rising ground half a mile on the other side of the village. A dull old dungeon enough it looked, with half the windows shut up. Who does that belong to?"

"It is called Compton Hall, sir," answered Sarah, "and it did belong to young Squire Ringwood Markham."

"Ringwood Markham! A fair-faced lad with blue eyes and a small waist?"

"The same, sir."

"I knew him six years ago in London."

"Very likely, sir. Poor Master Ringwood had his fling of London life, and very little he got by it, poor boy. He's gone now, sir. He was only buried three weeks ago."

"Dead!" murmured Captain Fanny. "Poor Markham! I didn't think to hear such news as that of him. But he and a good many of us have had a fancy for burning

the candle at both ends, and I suppose we've no right
to grumble if it burns out quickly."

The young man said this in a musing tone that was
not without a touch of melancholy. But he roused himself from this meditative mood in the next moment, and
addressed Mrs. Pecker with his accustomed vivacity.
"And Compton Hall belonged to Ringwood Markham?"
he said.

"Yes, sir; and Compton Hall estate, which brings
in an income of six or seven hundred a year."

"And who does the Hall belong to now, then?"
asked Captain Fanny.

"To his sister, sir, Mistress Millicent that was. Mrs.
Duke."

"Mrs. Duke! The wife of a sailor—one George
Duke?"

"The widow of Captain George Duke, sir."

"The widow! What, is George Duke dead?"

"Little doubt of that, sir. The Captain sailed from
Marley Water seven years ago come January, and
neither he nor his ship, the Vulture, have ever been
heard of since."

"And the widow of George Duke has come into a
property worth six or seven hundred a year?"

"Yes, sir; the Hall estate must be worth that, if it's
worth a farthing."

"And the only proof she has ever had of George
Duke's death is his seven years' absence from Compton-
on-the-Moor?"

"She could scarcely need a stronger proof, I should
think, sir."

"Couldn't she!" exclaimed the young man with a
laugh. "Why, Mrs. Sarah Pecker, I have seen so much

of the strange chances and changes of this world, that
I seldom believe a man is dead unless I see him put into
his coffin, the lid screwed down upon him, and the earth
shovelled into his grave : and even then there are some
folks such slippery customers that I should scarcely be
surprised to meet them at the gate of the churchyard.
The world is wide enough outside Compton-on-the-
Moor ; and your sailor is a roving blade, who is apt to
take his own pleasure abroad, forgetful of any one who
may be waiting for him at home. Who knows that
Captain Duke may not come back to-morrow to claim
his wife and her fortune ? "

"The Lord forbid!" said Mrs. Pecker earnestly; "I
would rather not be wishing ill to any one : but sooner
than poor Miss Millicent should see him come back to
break her heart and waste her money, I would pray that
the Captain of the Vulture may lie drowned and dead
under the foreign seas."

"A pious wish!" cried Captain Fanny, laughing.
"However, as I don't know the gentleman, Mrs. Pecker,
I don't mind saying, Amen. But as to seven years'
absence being proof enough to make a woman a widow,
that's a common mistake and a vulgar one, Mrs. Sarah,
which I scarcely expected to hear of from a woman of
your sense. Seven years—why, husbands have come
back after seventeen ! "

Mrs. Pecker made no answer to this. If her face
was paler even than it had been before, it was concealed
from observation as she bent over the dessert table
collecting the used glasses upon her tray.

When she had left the room, and the three young
men were once more alone, Captain Fanny burst into a
peal of ringing laughter.

"Here's news!" he cried: "split me, lads, here's a joke! George Duke dead and gone, and George Duke's widow with an estate that produces seven hundred a year. If that fool, Sulky Jeremiah, hadn't quarrelled with his best friends, and given us the slip in that cursed ungrateful manner, here would have been a chance for him!"

CHAPTER XIII.

THE END OF JANUARY.

CAPTAIN FANNY, otherwise Sir Lovel Mortimer, did not leave the Black Bear until the morning after Christmas-day, when he and his two companions rode blithely off through the frosty December sunlight, after expressing much content with the festive fare provided by Mrs. Pecker; after paying the bill without so much as casting a glance at the items; after remembering the ostler, the chambermaid, the boots, and every other member of the comfortable establishment who had any claim to advance upon the generosity of the West-country baronet.

A noble gentleman, they said, in the kitchen at the Black Bear, handsome and free-spoken, reckless as a prince with his golden guineas and broad crown pieces—comfortable and substantial coins, sadly out of fashion now, but much affected in those homely days. A perfect gentleman, with charmingly lackadaisical, and no doubt high-bred manners, such as were of course common to the nobility alone. And then his eyes—those

large shining black restless eyes, unquiet as midnight
stars reflected on a storm-tossed ocean, and almost as
wonderful.   I do not mean that they said exactly these
words in the kitchen at the Bear, but they said a great
deal more or less to this effect about Captain Fanny's
lustrous orbs.   Betty the cook made one remark, the
utter inanity of which drew upon her the reprobation
and ridicule of her fellow-servants.   This foolish woman
declared that Sir Lovel Mortimer's eyes reminded her
of the night on which the strange pedlar stole the
spoons. She grew alarmingly obscure and unintelligible when asked if the baronet's eyes reminded her
of the spoons or the pedlar; and could only vaguely
protest that they brought it all back to her mind
somehow.

So entirely occupied were the domestics of the Black
Bear in discussing their late distinguished visitor, that
the news of a desperate highway robbery, accompanied
by much violence, that had taken place near Carlisle
on the night of December the twenty-third, made
scarcely any impression upon them.   Nor were they
even very seriously affected by an attack upon the
York mail, the tidings of which reached them two
days after the departure of Sir Lovel and his companions.

The sojourn of a handsome young baronet at the
Black Bear was a rare event, to be remembered and
talked of for a twelvemonth at least; while violence,
outrage, robbery, and murder upon the king's highway
were of everyday occurrence.   London kept holiday
every Monday morning, and went gipsying and sight-
seeing Tyburnwards.   Thieves, retired from business,
made goodly fortunes by hunting down old comrades.

Children were hung without mercy for the stealing of three halfpence on that *via sacra*, the king's highway; because the law — poor well-intentioned blundering monster as it was—could frame a statute, but could not make a distinction, and could only hang by the letter, where it might have pardoned according to the spirit.

So, in the kitchen at the Black Bear Mrs. Pecker's retainers spent the few remaining December evenings in talking of the gay young visitors who had lately enlivened the hostelry by their presence; while Millicent Duke, looking fairer and paler than ever in her mourning gown, sat alone in the oak parlour at Compton Hall, with the brass-handled bureau open before her, trying to understand some farming accounts rendered by her bailiff.

Mrs. George Duke found faithful Sarah Pecker an inestimable comfort to her in her bereavement and accession to fortune. 1 think but for the help of that sturdy creature poor Millicent would have made Compton Hall and Compton farm a present to the stalwart Cumbrian bailiff, and would have gone quietly back to her cottage in the High Street, to wait for the coming of death or Captain George Duke, or any other calamity which was the predestined close of her joyless life. But Sarah Pecker was worth a dozen lawyers and half-a-dozen stewards. She attended at the reading of the will, in which her own name was recorded with a bequest of " fifty golden guineas, and a mourning ring containing my hair, in remembrance of much love and kindness, to cost ten guineas and no less." She mastered all the bearings of that intricate document, in spite of the " aforesaids," and " hereinafter mentioneds," and all the dreary technicalities which obscured its meaning, and knew more of it after one reading than even the lawyer who had drawn it up. She talked to Millicent about quarters of wheat, and hay, and turnips, till poor Mrs. Duke's brain reeled, and she could only meditate with admiration on Sarah's prodigious learning. The stalwart bailiff trembled before the mistress of the Black Bear, and went into long stammering explanations to account for a missing truss of hay that had been twisted into bands, lest he should be suspected of dishonesty in the transaction.

When all was duly settled and adjusted, Millicent Duke found herself almost a rich woman. She was rich enough, at any rate, to be considered a very wealthy person by the simple inhabitants of Compton-on-the-Moor.

The Hall was hers—the stout red-brick edifice, with its handsome heavy-framed windows, dating from the days of the Tudors, lighted by small diamond-shaped panes of glass, and bordered by flapping wreaths of ivy —ivy so old that its stems had grown gnarled and massive as the trunks of trees; the noble building, with its square stone-flagged entrance-hall and broad oaken staircase, up which you might have driven your coach and pair, had you been so foolishly inclined; the faded pictures and mouldering tapestry; the oak-panelled rooms, with their low ceilings, black oak like the wainscot, and their wide hearths and square open chimneys, built surely for traitors to hide in; the roomy rickety tumble - down, ivy - covered stables, crowned with weathercocks and dovecotes; the gardens and the shrubberies, with damp walks half choked with rank overgrowth, and tenanted by bold rabbits, who stared at you as an intruder if you ventured within their domain; the broad acres of meadow and arable land, not over rich, it is true, but sufficiently profitable withal—all these were the property of Millicent Duke, to have and to hold for herself alone; unless, indeed, the long missing husband, Captain George Duke, of the good ship Vulture, should return to claim a share in his wife's newly acquired fortune.

The thought that there was a remote possibility, a shadowy chance of this, would send a cold chill to Millicent's heart, and seem almost to stop its beating.

If he should come home! If, after all these years of fearful watching and waiting, these years of terror and suspense, in which she had trembled at the sound of every manly footstep, and shuddered at the sound of every voice which bore the faintest resemblance to that one voice which she dreaded to hear; if, after all, now that she had completely given him up—now that she was rich, and might perhaps by-and-by be happy—if, at this time of all others, the man who had been the scourge of her young life should return and claim her once more as his, to hold and to torture by the laws of God and man! A kind of distraction would take possession of her at the thought. She would deliver herself up to the horrible fancy until she could call up the image of the Captain of the Vulture standing on the threshold of the door, with the wicked vengeful light in his brown eyes, and the faint far-off breezy perfume of the ocean hovering about his chestnut hair. Then casting herself upon her knees, she would call upon Heaven to spare her from this terrible anguish—

to strike her dead before that dreaded husband could return to claim her.

The diamond earring, the fellow of which Captain Duke had taken from his wife on the night of their parting at Marley Water, had been religiously kept by her in a little red morocco-covered jewel-box. She was too simple and conscientious a creature to dream of disobeying her husband's commands. She looked sometimes at the solitary trinket, and seldom looked at it without praying that she might never see its fellow. She wished George Duke no harm. Her only wish was that she and he might never meet again. She would willingly have sold the Compton property, and would have sent him every farthing yielded by its sale, had she known him to be living, so that he had but remained away from her.

Millicent was the only person in Compton who entertained any doubt of Captain Duke's decease. The seven years which had elapsed since his departure —years of absence, unbroken by a single line from himself, or by the smallest news of him from any accidental source; the common occurrence of wreck and disaster upon the seas; the suspicions entertained by many as to the Captain's unlawful mode of life, all pointed to one conclusion—he was dead. He had gone to the bottom of the sea with his own vessel, or had been hewn down by the cutlass of a Frenchman or the scimitar of a Moorish pirate. The story of Millicent's meeting with her husband's shadow upon the pier at Marley Water had never been forgotten, and the recollection of that story confirmed the inhabitants of Compton in their opinion as to the fate of George Duke.

Of course Millicent told her faithful friend Sarah Pecker of the letter written by Ringwood a few nights before his death, and to be delivered by her to Darrell Markham.

The two women looked long and inquisitively at the folded sheet of foolscap, with its sprawling red seal, wondering what mysterious lines were written on the paper : but the wishes of Millicent's dead brother were sacred; and early in January Mrs. Duke began to think of her formidable journey to London.

She had never been farther away from home than on the occasion of a brief visit to the city of York, and the thought of finding her way to the great metropolis filled her with something almost approaching terror. I doubt if an Englishwoman of this present year of grace would think as much of a voyage to Calcutta as poor Millicent thought of this southward journey ; but her staunch friend Sarah was ready to stand by her in this as in every other crisis of life.

"You don't suppose you're going to find Mr. Darrell Markham all by yourself, do you, Miss Millicent ?" asked Sarah, when the business was discussed.

" Why, who should go with me, Sally dear ?"

"Ah, who indeed ?" answered Sarah, rather sarcas-tically; " who but Sally Pecker, of the Black Bear, that nursed you when you was a baby ; who else, I should like to know ?"

" You, Sally ? "

" Yes, me. I'd send Samuel with you, Miss Millicent dear—for there's something respectable in the looks of a man, and we could put him into one of the old Markham liveries, and call him your servant; but, Lord have mercy on us ! what a lost baby that poor husband

of mine would be in the city of London! I cannot
send him to the market town for a few groceries without knowing before the time comes that he'll bring
raisins instead of sugar, or have his pocket picked
while he stands staring at some merry-andrew. No,
Miss Millicent; Samuel Pecker's the best of men, but
the best of men may be a blessed baby in the way of
business; and you don't want a helpless infant to put
you in the right way for finding Mr. Darrell. So you
must take me with you, my dear, and make the best of
a bad bargain."

"My dear good kind faithful Sally! But what will
they do without you at the Bear? It will be near upon
a fortnight's journey to London and back, allowing for
some loss of time in town. What will they do without
you, Sally?"

"Why, do their best, Miss Millicent, to be sure; and
a pretty muddle I shall find the place in when I come
back, I dare say. But don't let the thought of that
worry you, Miss Milly; I shan't mind it a bit. I sometimes fancy things go too smooth at the Bear, and I
think the servants do their work well for sheer provo-
cation."

Sarah Pecker was so thoroughly determined upon
accompanying Millicent, that Mrs. George Duke yielded
with a good grace, thanked her stout protectress, and
set to work to trim a mourning hat with ruches and
streamers of black crape. It was Sarah who devised
the trimmings for this coquettish little hat, and it was
Sarah who found some jet ornaments amongst a chest-
ful of clothes which had belonged to Millicent's mother,
wherewith to adorn Mrs. Duke's fair neck and arms.

"There is no need for Mr. Darrell to find you

changed for the worse in these seven years, Miss
Milly," Sarah remarked, as she fastened the jet necklace round Millicent's slender throat. "These black
clothes are vastly becoming to your fair skin; and I
scarce think that our Darrell will be ashamed of his
country cousin, for all the fine London madams he may
have seen since he left Compton."

Mrs. Sarah Pecker had a natural and almost religious
horror of the fair inhabitants of the metropolis, whom
she dignified with the generic appellation of "London
madams." She firmly believed the feminine portion of
the population of that unknown city to be, without
exception, frivolous, dissipated, faro-playing, pug-dog
worshipping, play-going, masquerade-haunting, painted,
patched, and bedizened creatures, whose sole end and
aim was to lure honest young country squires from
legitimate attachments to rosy-checked kinswomen at
home.

It was a cheerless and foggy morning that welcomed
Millicent and her sturdy protectress to the great metropolis. Mrs. Pecker, putting her head out of the coach
window at the village of Islington, saw a thick mass of
blackness and cloud looming in a valley before her, and
was told by a travelled passenger that it (the blackness
and the cloud) was London. It was at a ponderous
roomy rambling old inn, in the heart of the City, that
Millicent Duke and Sarah were deposited, with the one
small trunk that formed all their luggage. Mrs. Pecker
entered into conversation with a smart-looking chambermaid, who brought the travellers a very indifferent
breakfast. She asked a few questions about the town,
while Millicent, worn out with the fatigue of the night
journey, fell asleep on a hard uncomfortable-looking

sofa, and in the course of conversation took care to inform the chambermaid that the pretty fair-faced lady in mourning, who looked so girlish and innocent as she lay asleep, was one of the richest women in all Cumberland, and might have travelled post all the way from Compton to Snow Hill, had she been pleased so to spend her money. Mrs. Pecker, who had at first rather inclined towards the chambermaid, as a simple plain-spoken young person, took offence at the cool way in which she received this information, and classed her forthwith amongst the "London madams."

"Cumbrian gentry count for little with you, I make no doubt," Sarah remarked, with ironical humility; "but there are many in Cumberland who could buy up your fine town folks, and leave enough for themselves after they'd made the bargain."

After having administered this dignified reproof to the chambermaid, who (no doubt penetrated and abashed) seemed in a great hurry to get out of the room, Sarah condescended to ask the way to St. James's Square, which she evidently expected to find somewhere in the immediate neighbourhood.

She was told that a coach or a chair would take her to the desired locality, which was at the Court end of London, and much too far for her to walk, more especially as she was a stranger, and not likely to find her way thither.

Mrs. Pecker stared hard at the chambermaid, as if she would very much have liked to convict her of giving a false direction; but being unable to do so, submitted to be advised, and ordered a coach to be ready in an hour.

The " London madams " Mrs. Pecker saw from the coach window, as she and her fair charge were driven from the City to St. James's, looked rather pinched and blue-nosed in the bitter January morning. The snow upon the pavement was a black compound unknown at Compton, and the darkness of the foggy atmosphere rendered the worthy Sarah rather uneasy as to the possible speedy advent of an earthquake.

The hostess of the Black Bear had neither read Mr. Creech's translation from Horace, nor Mr. Alexander Pope's quotation from the same, but she had resolutely determined on this her visit to London to preserve her dignity by a stolid and unmoved demeanour. Not to admire was all the art she knew! She resolved that, from the whispering gallery of St. Paul's Cathedral to the merry-andrews in Bartholomew Fair, from the wax-works in Westminster Abbey to the wild beasts in the Tower, nothing she beheld should wring an exclamation of surprise from her tightly compressed lips. Although the distance between Eastcheap and Pall Mall appeared to her almost illimitable, she scrupulously preserved her equanimity, and looked from the coach window at the crowded London streets with as calm and critical an eye as that with which she would have examined a field of wheat in her native Cumberland.

All the busy panorama of the metropolis passed before the eyes of Millicent Duke as a dim and cloudy picture, in which no figure was distinct or palpable. She might have been driven close beside a raging fire, and yet have never beheld the flames ; or across a cata-ract, without hearing the roar of the boisterous waters. One thought and one image filled her heart and brain, and she had neither eyes nor ears for the busy world outside the coach windows, or for Sarah Pecker on the seat opposite to her.

She was going to see Darrell Markham.

For the first time after seven years—for the first time since she stood beside the bed upon which he lay insensible, with blood-bedabbed hair and pale lips that only uttered wandering words—she was to see him again—to see him—and perhaps to find him changed! So changed in that long·lapse of time, that it would seem as if the old Darrell was dead and gone, and only a stranger, with some trick of his face, left in his stead.

And amongst all the other changes time had worked in this dear cousin, it might be that the old hopeless love had faded out, and that a newer and brighter image had replaced Millicent's own pale face in Darrell Markham's heart. He was still unmarried. She knew as much as that by his letters to Sarah Pecker, which always came at intervals of about three months to tell of his own whereabouts, and to ask for tidings of Compton. Perhaps it was·his poverty that had kept him so long a bachelor! A sudden crimson rushed to Mrs. Duke's face as she thought of this. If this were indeed so, would it be more than cousinly—would it be more than her duty to share her own ample fortune with her dearest friend and nearest of kin, and to bid him marry the woman of his choice and be happy?

She made a picture of herself, with her pale face and mourning gown, bestowing her blessing and half of her estate upon Darrell and some defiant brunette beauty, with glowing cheeks and lustrous eyes altogether unlike her own. She acted over the imaginary scene, and composed a pretty self-abnegating, appropriate little

speech with which to address the happy bride and
bridegroom. It was so affecting a picture that Mrs.
Duke wept quietly for five minutes with her face turned
towards the opposite window to that out of which Mrs.
Pecker was looking.

The tears were still in her eyes when the coach
stopped before the big town mansion of Darrell Markham's Scottish patron. That old feeling at her heart
seemed to stop its beating, as the coachman's loud rap
resounded from the massive brazen knocker. The
blinds were all down, and wisps of loose straw lay
about the doorsteps.

"My lord is out of town, perhaps," said Mrs. Pecker,
"and Mr. Darrell with him. O, Miss Milly, if we have
had our journey for nothing!"

Millicent Duke had no power to reply. The doubt
suggested by Mrs. Pecker was unspeakably painful to
her. She was prepared for sudden death, but not for
slow torture. For seven years she had lived in com-
parative contentment without seeing Darrell Markham;
she felt now that she could scarcely exist seven minutes
without looking at that familiar face.

An old woman opened the door. My lord was evidently out of town. Mrs. Pecker directed the coachman to inquire for Mr. Darrell Markham. The great
carved doorway, the iron extinguishers upon the rail-
ings, the attenuated iron lamp-frame, the figure of the
old woman standing on the threshold, all reeled before
Millicent's eyes, and she did not hear a word that was
said. She only knew that the coach door was opened,
and that Sarah Pecker told her to alight; that she
tottered up the steps, across the threshold of the door,
and into a noble stone-flagged hall, at the end of which

a feeble handful of burning coals struggled for life in a grate wide enough to have held well nigh half a ton.

A stout gentleman, wrapped to the chin in a furred coat, and wearing high leather boots bespattered with mud and snow, was standing against this fire, with his back to Millicent, reading a letter. His hat, gloves, riding-whip, and half-a-dozen unopened letters lay on a table near him.

Millicent Duke only saw a blurred and indistinct figure of a man, who seemed one wavy mass of coat and boats; and a fire that resolved itself into a circle of lurid brightness, like the red eye of a demon. Sarah Pecker had not alighted from the coach; the old woman stood curtsying to Mrs. Duke, and pointing to the gentleman by the fireplace. Millicent had a confused idea that she was to ask this gentleman to conduct her to Darrell Markham. His head was bent over a letter, the contents of which he could scarcely decipher in the dim light from the dirty window-panes and the struggling fire. Millicent was almost afraid to interrupt him in the midst of this occupation.

While she stood for a moment deliberating how she might best address him, he crumpled the letter into his pocket, and, turning suddenly, stood face to face with her.

The **stout gentleman was** Darrell Markham.

CHAPTER XIV.

RINGWOOD'S LEGACY.

OF all the changes Millicent had ever dreamed of, none had come about. But this one change, of which she had never dreamed, had certainly come to pass. Darrel Markham had grown stouter within the past seven years; not unbecomingly so, of course. He had only changed from a stripling into a stalwart broad-chested, and soldierly-looking fellow, whose very presence inspired poor helpless Millicent with a feeling of safety. He clasped his poor little shivering cousin to his breast, and covered her cold forehead with kisses.

Yet I doubt, if even George Duke's handsome sinister face could have peeped in at the half-open hall-door at that very moment, whether the Captain of the Vulture would have had just cause for either anger or alarm.

It was a brotherly embrace which drew Millicent's slender form to that manly heart—it was a brother's protecting affection that showered kisses thick and fast upon her blushing face; and a brother's sheltering arm that crushed the pretty mourning hat which Mrs. Pecker had been at so much pains to trim.

Poor Sally Pecker! if she could only have known how little Darrell Markham saw of the crape ruches and streamers, the jet necklace and bracelets, and all the little coquetries she had prepared for his admiration! He only saw the soft blue eyes, with the old pleading look he remembered long ago, when Ringwood and he were apt to fall to quarrelling with each other at Compton Hall, and the anxious trembling girl would creep between them to make peace. Millicent's eyes were tearless now, and such a mist was before Darrell's sight that he could scarcely distinguish the happy face looking up at him from under the crushed mourning hat.

"Bless you, my darling! bless you!" he said again and again, seeming indeed to have little more to say than this; but a great deal of inarticulate language in the way of kisses to supply his want of words.

"Bless you, bless you, my own precious Milly!"

Nor did Mrs. George Duke do very much on this occasion to establish a character for eloquence, for, after a great deal of blushing and trembling, she could only look shyly up at her cousin, and say,—

"Why, Darrell, how stout you have grown!"

Only a moment before Mr. Markham had felt a very great inclination to cry, but as these simple faltering words dropped from his cousin's lips, he laughed aloud, and opening a door near at hand led her into my Lord C——'s library, where the dust lay thick upon furniture and books, and the oaken window-shutters were only half open.

"My Millicent," he said, "my dearest girl! what a happy chance that I should have ridden into town on this snowy morning to fetch some letters of too great importance to be trusted to an ordinary messenger! I have spent Christmas with my lord in Buckinghamshire, and it was but an accident my coming here to-day."

He took the mourning hat from Millicent's head, and cast it ignominiously on the floor. Then smoothing his cousin's pale golden ringlets with gentle caressing hands, he looked long and earnestly at her face.

"My darling," he said, "all these weary years have not made an hour's change in you!"

"And in you, Darrell——"

"In me! why, I am stouter, you say, Milly."

"Yes, yes, a little stouter; but I don't mean that!" She hesitated, and stood twisting one of the buttons of his furred coat round and round with her slender fingers, her head bent, and the dim light from the half-opened shutters slanting upon her golden-tinted hair. Innocent and confiding, a pale saint crowned with a pale aureole, she looked too celestial a creature for foggy London and St. James's Square.

"What then, Millicent?" said Darrell.

"I mean that you must be changed in other things—changed in yourself. I have dawdled away my quiet life at Compton, with no event to break these seven years but the death of my poor brother; but you have lived in the world, Darrell, the gay and great world, where, as I have always read, all is action, and the sufferings or pleasures of a lifetime are often crowded into a few brief months. You must have seen so many changes that you must needs be changed yourself. I fancy that we country people fall into the fashion of imitating the nature about us. Our souls copy the slow growth of the trees that shelter us, and our hearts are changeless as the quiet rivers that flow past our villages. That must be the reason why we change so little. But you, in this busy turbulent London—you, who must have made so many acquaintances, so many friends—noble and brilliant men—amiable and beautiful women——"

As in a lady's letter a few brief words in the postscript generally contain the whole gist of the epistle, so, perhaps, in this long speech of Mrs. George Duke's the drift of the exordium lay in the very last sentence.

At any rate it was to this sentence that Darrell Markham replied:

"The loveliest woman in all London has had little charm for me, Millicent; there is but one beautiful face in all the world that Darrell Markham ever cared to look upon, and that he sees to-day for the first time after seven years."

"Darrell, Darrell!"

The joy welling up to her heart shone out from under the shelter of her drooping lashes. He was unchanged, then, and there was no dark town-bred beauty to claim her old lover. She was a married woman herself, and George Duke might return to-morrow; but it seemed happiness enough to know that she was not to hear Darrell Markham's wedding bells yet awhile.

"I was coming to Compton at the beginning of next month to see you, Milly."

"To see me?"

"Yes; to remind you of an old promise, broken once but not forgotten. To claim you as my wife."

"Me, Darrell—a married woman?"

"A married woman!" he cried passionately; "no, Millicent, a widow by every evidence of common sense. Free to marry by the law of the land. But tell me, dearest, what brought you to town?"

"This, Darrell."

She took her dead brother's letter from her pocket, and gave it to him.

"Three nights before his death, my poor brother Ringwood wrote this," she said, "and at the same time bade me put it with my own hand into yours. I hope, Darrell, it contains some legacy, even though it were to set aside Ringwood's will, and leave you the best part of the fortune. It is more fitting that you should be the owner of it than I."

Darrell Markham stood with the letter in his hand, looking thoughtfully at the superscription.

Yes, there it was, the sprawling straggling penman-ship which he had so often laughed at; the ill-shaped letters and the ill-spelt words, all were there; but the hand was cold that had held the pen, and the sanctity of death was about poor Ringwood's letter, and changed the scrawl into a holy relic.

" He wrote to me before he died, Millicent? He forgot all our old quarrels, then ?"

" Yes, he spoke of you most tenderly. You will find loving words in the poor boy's letter, I know, Darrell, and I hope some mention of a legacy."

" I have neither need nor wish for that, Milly; but I am happy that Ringwood remembered me kindly upon his death-bed."

Darrell Markham broke the seal, and read the brief epistle. As he did so a joyous light broke suddenly out upon his handsome face.

" Millicent, Millicent !" he said; " do you know the contents of this letter ?"

" Not one word, Darrell."

" It was noble and generous of my cousin Ringwood to write this to me. O, Milly, Milly ! he has left me the most precious legacy that ever mortal man received from the will of another."

" I am so glad of that, Darrell. Glad, ay, more than glad, if he has left you every acre of the Compton estate. My little cottage is big enough for me; and I should be so happy to see you master of the old Hall."

"But it is not the Compton estate, Milly darling. The legacy is something dearer and more valuable than all the lands and houses in merry England."

"Not the Compton estate?"

"No: the legacy is—you."

He caught her in his arms, and clasped her once more to his heart. This time it was scarcely so brotherly an embrace with which he encircled the slender form, and this time, had the Captain of the Vulture been peeping in at the library door, he might have felt himself called upon to interfere.

"Darrell, Darrell, what do you mean?" cried Millicent, as soon as she could extricate herself, with flushed cheeks and tangled curls, from her cousin's arms.

"What do I mean? Read poor Ringwood's letter, Milly."

Mrs. George Duke opened her blue eyes in an innocent stare of wonder as she took the foolscap sheet from her cousin's hand. In sober earnest she began very much to fear that Darrell Markham had become suddenly distracted.

"Read, Milly, read!"

Bespattered with unsightly blots, smudges, erasures, and feeble half-formed characters, this poor scrawl, written by the weak hand of the sick man, was no such easy matter to decipher; but to the eye of Millicent Duke every syllable seemed burnt upon the paper in letters of fire.

It was thus that poor Ringwood had written:

"Cousen Darrel,

"When you gett this, Capten Duk will hav bin away sevin years. I cauot lieve you a legasy, but I lieve you my sister Mily, who after my deth will be a ritch woman, for your tru and lovyng wife. Forgett all past ill blud betwixt us, and cherish her for the sake of

"Ringwood Markham."

With her pale face dyed unnaturally red with crimson blushes, and her blue eyes bent upon the Turkey carpet in my lord's library, Mrs. Duke stood, holding her brother's letter in her trembling hands.

Darrell Markham dropped on his knees at her feet.

"You cannot refuse me now, my own dear love," he said, with unutterable fondness; "for even if you could find the heart to be so cruel, I would not take the harsh word No from those beloved lips. You are mine, Mrs. Duke—mine to have and to hold. You are the legacy left me by my poor cousin."

"Am I free to wed, Darrell?" she faltered; "am I free?"

"As free as you were, Millicent, before ever the shadow of George Duke darkened your father's door."

While Darrell Markham was still upon his knees on my lord's Turkey carpet, and while Millicent Duke was still looking down at him with a glance in which love, terror, and perplexity had equal share, the library door was burst open, and Mrs. Sarah Pecker dashed in upon the unconscious pair.

"So, Mrs. George Duke and Mr. Darrell Markham," she said, "this is mighty pretty treatment upon my first visit to London! Here have I been sitting in that blessed coach for the space of an hour by your town clocks, and neither of you have had so much civility as to ask me to come in and warm my fingers' ends at your wretched fires."

Darrell Markham had risen from his knees on the advent of Mrs. Pecker; and it is to be recorded to her credit that the discreet Sally had evinced no surprise whatever at the abnormal attitude in which she had discovered Millicent's cousin; and furthermore that, although expressing much indignation at the treatment she had received, Sarah appeared altogether in very high spirits and amazing good humour.

"You've been rather a long time giving Master Darrell the letter, Miss Milly," she said slyly.

"That won't surprise you, Sally, when you hear the contents of the letter," answered Darrell; and then he planted Mrs. Pecker in a high-backed leather-covered chair by the fireplace, and told her the whole story of Ringwood's epistle.

It is doubtful if Millicent Duke would ever have freely given her consent to the step which appeared to her such a desperate one; but between Darrell Markham and Sarah Pecker she was utterly powerless; and when her cousin handed her back to the coach that had been so long in waiting, she had promised to become his wedded wife without an hour's unnecessary delay.

"I will make all arrangements for the ceremony, dearest," Darrell said, as he lingered at the coach door, loth to bid his cousin good-bye. "That done, I must ride into Buckinghamshire with my lord's letters, and wish him farewell for a time. I will breakfast with you to-morrow morning at your inn, and escort you and

Sally to see some of the lions of this big city. Good-
bye, darling; God bless you!"

The blue-nosed coachman smacked his whip, and
the coach drove away, leaving Darrell Markham standing on the doorsteps looking after his cousin.

"O, Sally, Sally, what have I done?" cried Millicent
as soon as the coach had left St. James's Square.

"What have you done, Miss Milly!" exclaimed Mrs.
Pecker; "why, only what was right and proper, and
according to your poor brother's wishes. You wouldn't
have gone against them, miss, would you, knowing
what a wickedness it is to thwart those that are dead
and gone?" ejaculated Sarah, with pious horror.

For the rest of that day Millicent Duke was as one
in a dream. She seemed to lose all power of volition,
and to submit quietly to be carried hither and thither at
the behest of stout Sarah Pecker. As for the worthy
mistress of the Black Bear, this suddenly devised wedding between the two young people, whom she had
known as little children, was so deep a delight to her,
that she could scarcely contain herself and her importance within the limits of a hired coach.

"Shall I bid the man stop at a silk mercer's, Miss
Milly?" she asked, as the vehicle drove citywards.

"What for, Sally?"

"For you to choose a wedding-dress, miss. You'll
never be married in mourning?"

"Why not, Sally? Do you think I mourn less for
my brother because I am going to marry Darrell Markham? It would be paying ill respect to his memory
to cast off my black clothes before he has been three
months in his grave."

"But only for your wedding-day, Miss Millicent!

Think what a bad omen it would be to wear black on your wedding-day."

Mrs. Duke smiled gravely. "If it please Heaven to bless my marriage, Sally," she said, "I do not think the colour of my dress would come between me and Providence."

Sarah Pecker shook her head ominously. "There's such things as tempting Providence, and flying in the face of good fortune, Miss Milly," she said; and without waiting for leave from Millicent, she ordered the coachman to stop at a mercer's on Ludgate hill, a very shabby dingy little shop compared to the splendid emporiums of to-day, but grander than anything Mrs. Pecker had ever seen at Carlisle.

Mrs. Duke did not oppose her protectress; but when the shopman brought his rolls of glistening silks and brocade, and cast them in voluminous folds upon the narrow counter, Millicent took care to choose a pale lavender-coloured fabric, arabesqued with flowers worked in black floss silk.

"You seem determined to bring bad luck upon your wedding, Mrs. Duke," Sarah said sharply, as Millicent made this sombre choice. "Who ever heard of black roses and lilies?"

But Millicent was determined; and they drove back to the big gloomy hostelry in the heart of the City, where Mrs. Pecker seated herself at once to her task of making the wedding dress.

The fortnight that must needs elapse before the marriage could take place seemed only one long bewildering dream to Millicent Duke. She gave herself up into the hands of Sarah and Darrell, and let them do as they pleased with her. It was Darrell's delight to make that first visit to London a pleasant holiday for his beloved cousin. He removed the two women from the busy City hostelry to a quiet lodging near Covent Garden; and here he spent much of his time with them, taking them to see all the grandest sights in London —to Westminster Abbey and St. Paul's, to the Tower, and to Kensington Gardens, where they had the honour of beholding their Majesties King George and Queen Charlotte, to say nothing of a whole bevy of Court beauties, whose costumes Mrs. Pecker contemplated with unbounded curiosity and admiration, but whom she condemned *en masse* as "London madams." Darrell conducted his cousin and her faithful companion to Ranelagh, and to the two great theatres, where Mrs. Duke was delighted with *Artaxerxes*, and was moved to pity for hapless Mistress Shore. It would have been altogether a most delightful period for Millicent if she had not been tormented by vague doubts and shadowy fears, which she tried in vain to banish from her mind, but which grew and multiplied as the day appointed for her marriage drew nigh.

CHAPTER XV.

MILLICENT'S WEDDING.

VERY little breakfast was eaten upon the wedding morning by any one of the trio assembled in the cheerful little sitting-room in Soho. The weather had been cold and rainy during the past fortnight; but to-day there was neither rain nor sleet falling from the leaden sky. There was that blackness in the air and in the heavens which predicts the coming of a tremendous fall of snow. The mud of the day before had frozen in the gutters, and the pavements were hard and dry in the bitter frosty morning—so bitter a morning that Mrs. Pecker's numbed fingers could scarcely adjust the brocade wedding-dress, and all the feminine furbelows which it had been her delight to prepare. A cheerless, black, and hopeless frost—black alike upon the broad moors around Compton and in the dark London streets, where the breath of half-frozen foot-passengers and shivering horses made a perpetual mist. A dismal wedding morning this, for the second nuptials of Squire Markham's daughter.

Sally Pecker was the only member of the little party who took any especial notice of the weather. Darrell's cheeks glowed with the crimson flush of pleasant excitement, his eyes shone with the light of hope and love; and if Millicent trembled and grew pale, she knew not whether it was from the bitter cold without, or that icy shuddering terror which filled her heart, and over which she had no control.

The coach was waiting before the door of the lodging-house, and Mrs. Pecker was putting the last finishing touches to the festooned bunches of Millicent's brocaded gown, and the soft folds of the quilted petticoat beneath, when this feeling broke forth into words; and Mrs. George Duke, falling on her knees at Darrell's feet, lifted up her clasped hands and appealed to him thus:—

" O, Darrell, Darrell, I feel as if this was a wicked thing that we are going to do! What evidence have I that George Duke is dead? and what right have I to give my hand to you, not knowing whether it may not

still belong to another ? Delay this marriage. Wait,
wait, and more certain news may reach us; for something tells me that we have no justification for the vows
we are going to take to-day."

She spoke with such a solemn fervour, with such an
earnestness in every word, with a light that seemed
almost the radiance of inspiration shining in her blue
eyes, that Darrell Markham would have been led to
listen to her almost as seriously as she had spoken, but
for the interference of Mrs. Sarah Pecker. That ag-
grieved matron, however, showered forth a whole volley
of indignant exclamations, such as " Stuff and nonsense,
child ! " and " Who ever heard such a pother about
nothing ? " and " I call it a'most ingratitude to me, after
my sitting at work at the wedding dress till my fingers
froze upon my hands," and a great deal more to the
same effect. And then having talked herself breathless,
the excited Sarah hustled Millicent and Darrell down
the staircase, and into the coach, before either of them
had time to remonstrate.

St. Mary's church in the Strand—called at this time
the new church in the Strand—had been selected by
Darrell for the performance of the ceremony; and on
the way thither Mrs. Pecker devoted herself to lamentations on the performance of this London wedding.

" Not so much as a bell ringing," she said; " and
if it had been at Compton, they'd have made the
old steeple rock again, to do honour to the squire's
daughter."

It was a brief drive from the lodging near Covent
Garden to St. Mary's church in the Strand. The
broad stone flags before the sacred edifice were slippery
with frozen sleet and mud, and Darrell had to support

his cousin's steps, half carrying her from the coach to the door. The church was dark in the wintry morning; and Romeo, breaking into the tomb of the Capulets, could scarcely have found himself in a gloomier building than that which Darrell entered with his shivering bride.

Mrs. Sarah Pecker lingered behind to give some directions to the coachman; having done which, she was about to follow the young people, when she was violently jostled by a stout porter, laden with parcels, who ran against her, and nearly knocked her down.

Indeed, the pavement being slippery, it is a question whether the dignified hostess of the Black Bear would not have entirely lost her footing but for the friendly interposition of a muscular though slender arm in a claret-coloured velvet coat-sleeve, which was thrust out to save her, while a foppish voice drawled a reproof to the porter.

Poor Sally Pecker, saved from the collision, was once more like to fall at the sound of this effeminate voice, for it was the very same which she had heard a month before in her best room at the Black Bear, and the arm which had saved her from falling was that of Sir Lovel Mortimer, the West-country baronet.

Mrs. Sarah would scarcely have recognized him had she not heard his voice, for he was wrapped in great woollen mufflers, which half buried the lower part of his face, and, instead of the flowing flaxen wig he usually affected, he wore to-day a brown George, which was by no means so becoming. But under his slouched beaver hat, and above the many folds of his woollen mufflers, shone the restless black eyes which, once seen, were not easily to be forgotten.

" Sir Lovel Mortimer!" exclaimed Mrs. Pecker, clasping her broad hands about the young man's arm, and staring at him as one aghast.

" Hush, my good soul; you've no need to be so ready with my name," he said, looking round him suspiciously as he spoke. " Why, what ails the woman?" he cried presently, as Sarah still stood staring at her deliverer's face with the same uneasy bewildered wondering expression with which she had regarded him on his visit to Compton.

" O, sir, forgive a poor childless woman for looking over-hard at you. I've never been able to get your honour's face out of my head since last Christmas night."

Captain Fanny laughed gaily.

" I'm pretty well used to making an impression upon the fair sex," he said ; " and there are many who have taken care to get the pattern of my face by heart before this. Why, strike me blind, if it is not our worthy hostess of the Cumbrian village, where we ate such a glorious Christmas dinner. Now, what in the name of all that's wonderful has brought you to London, ma'am ? "

" A wedding, your honour."

" A wedding!—your own, of course ? Then I'm just in time to salute the bride."

" The wedding of Mrs. George Duke with her first cousin, Mr. Darrell Markham."

" Mrs. George Duke, the widow, whose husband is away at sea ? "

" The same, sir."

Captain Fanny pursed up his lips and gave a low but prolonged whistle. " So, so, Mrs. Pecker, that is the

business which has brought you all the way from
Cumberland to the Strand. A strange business, Mrs
Pecker, a very strange business—but no affair of mine
as you'll say, perhaps. Pray present my best compliments to the bride and bridegroom, and good-day to
you."

He bowed gallantly to the innkeeper's wife, and
hurried off. Sarah Pecker stood looking after him
with an eager yearning gaze; but his slender figure
was soon lost amidst the crowd of pedestrians.

A shivering parson in a tumbled surplice read the
marriage service, and a grim beadle gave Millicent to
" this man," in consideration of a crown-piece which
Darrell gave him for his trouble. The trembling girl
could not but glance behind her as the clergyman read
that preliminary passage which called on any one knowing any just cause or impediment why these two
persons should not be joined together, to come forward
and declare the same. She looked back with a foolish
fear that she might see George Duke advance with his
hand raised to arrest the ceremony.

One of the ponderous doors of the church was
ajar, and a biting frozen wind blew in from the open
street; but there was no Captain George Duke lurking in the shadow of the doorway, or hiding behind
a pillar, ready to come forth and protest against the
marriage.

Had the Captain of the Vulture been in waiting for
this purpose, he must have lost no time in carrying
it into effect; for the shivering parson gave brief
opportunity for interference, and rattled through the
solemn service at such a rate that Darrell and Millicent
were man and wife before Mrs. Pecker had recovered

from the surprise of her unexpected encounter with
Captain Fanny.

The snow was falling in real earnest when Millicent,
Darrell, and Sarah took their seats that night in the
comfortable interior of the York mail, and the chilly
winter dawn broke next morning upon whitened fields
and hedges, and far-off distances and hill-tops that
shone out white against the blackness of the sky. All
the air seemed thick with snow-flakes throughout that
long homeward journey; but Darrell and Millicent
might have been travelling through an atmosphere of
melted sapphires and under a cloudless Italian heaven
for aught they knew to the contrary; for the sometime
wife and widow of George Duke had forgotten all old
sorrows in the absorbing thought, that she and Darrell
were to go henceforth and for ever side by side in life's
journey. This being so, it mattered little whether they
went northward through the bleak January weather,
or travelled some rose-bestrewn path under the impossible azure of the brightest skies that were ever painted
on a fire-screen or a tea-board.

So Millicent abandoned herself to the delight of
Darrell's presence, and had well-nigh forgotten that
she had ever lived away from him. She was with him,
sheltered and protected by his love, and all the vague
doubts and terrors of the wedding morning had
vanished out of her mind. It seemed as if she had
left her fears in the stony London Church from which
she had emerged as Darrell Markham's wife. She had
felt a shadowy apprehension of some shapeless trouble
hovering near at hand, some unknown sorrow ready to
fall upon her and crush her; but she felt this apprehension no longer. Nothing had occurred to interrupt

the marriage. It seemed to her, therefore, as if the
marriage, being permitted by Providence, must needs
be happy.

The travellers reached York on the third day from
that of the wedding; and here it was decided that they
should finish the journey in a postchaise, instead of
waiting for the lumbering branch coach that travelled
between York and Compton.

It was twilight when the four horses of the last
relay swept across the white moorland and dashed into
the narrow Compton High Street. Past the forge and
the little cottage Millicent had lived in so long—past
the village shop, the one great emporium where all the
requirements of Compton civilization were to be pur-
chased—past groups of idle children, who whooped and
hallooed at the postchaise for no special reason, but
from a vague conviction that any persons travelling in.
such a vehicle must be necessarily magnates of the
land, and bent upon some errand of festivity and re-
joicing—past every familiar object in the old place,
until the horses drew up, with a suddenness that sent
the lumbering chaise rocking from side to side, before
the door of the Black Bear, and under the windows
of that very room in which Darrell Markham had
lain so long a weary invalid, pining for one glance
of the beloved eyes, one tender touch from the beloved
hand.

The reason of this arrangement was that Mrs.
Pecker, knowing the scanty accommodation to be obtained at Compton Hall, had sent on an express from
York to bid Samuel prepare the best dinner that had
ever been eaten within the walls of the Black Bear, to
do honour to Mr. and Mrs Darrell Markham.

In her eagerness to ascertain if this message had been duly acted upon, Sarah was the first to spring from the postchaise, leaving Darrell and Millicent to alight at their leisure.

She found Samuel upon the door-step; not the easy self-assured, brisk and cheerful Samuel of late years, but the pale-faced vacillating feeble-minded being of the old dispensation; an unhappy creature, who looked at his ponderous better-half with a deprecating glance, which seemed to say, "Don't be violent, Sarah; it is not my fault."

But Mrs. Pecker was in too great a hurry to notice these changes. She dashed past her husband into the spacious hall, and glanced with considerable satisfaction towards an open door, through which was to be seen the oak parlour, where, on a snowy table-cloth, glittered the well-polished plate of the Pecker family, under the light of half-a-dozen wax candles.

"The dinner's ready, Samuel?" she said.

"Done to a turn, Sarah," he replied dolefully. "A turkey, bigger than the one we cooked at Christmas; a sirloin; a pair of capons, boiled; a plum pudding, and a dish of Christmas pies. I hope, poor things, they may enjoy it!" added Mr. Pecker, in a tone that was positively funereal.

Mrs. Sarah Pecker turned sharply round upon her husband, and stared with something of her old glance of contempt at his pale scared face.

"Enjoy it!" she said; "I should think they would enjoy it, indeed, after the cold journey they've had since breakfast-time this morning. Why, Samuel Pecker," she added, looking at her dismal spouse more earnestly than before, "what on earth is the matter

with you? When I want you to be most brisk and
cheerful, and to have everything bright and joyful
about the place to do honour to Miss Milly and her
loving husband, my own handsome Master Darrell,
here you are quaking and quavering, and seemingly
took with one of your old fits of the doldrums.
What's the matter with you, man? and why don't
you go out and bring Mrs. Markham and her husband
in, and offer your congratulations?"

Samuel shook his head mournfully.

"Wait a bit, Sarah," he said, in a voice scarcely
above a whisper, "wait a bit! It will all come in good
time, and I dare say it's all for the best; but I was took
aback at first by it, and it threw me a little backward
with the cooking, for it seemed as if neither me nor
Betty could put any heart into the basting or the
gravies afterwards. It seemed hard, you know, Sarah,
when it first came upon me all of a sudden; and the
more I think of it the harder it seems."

"What seems hard?—What! what!" cried Sarah,
some indistinct terror chilling her very blood; "what
is it, Samuel?—have you lost your speech?"

It seemed indeed for a moment as if Mr. Pecker had
been suddenly deprived of the use of that faculty. He
shook his head from side to side, swallowed and gasped
alternately, and then grasping Sarah by the arm,
pointed with his disengaged hand to another half-open
door exactly opposite to that of the room in which the
dinner-table was laid.

"Look there!" he ejaculated in a hoarse whisper
close to Sarah's ear.

Following the direction of Samuel's extended hand,
Mrs. Pecker looked into a room which was generally

devoted to the ordinary customers at the Bear, but which on this winter's evening had but one occupant.

This solitary individual was a man wearing a dark-blue travel-stained coat, jack-boots, and loose brown curling hair tied with a ribbon. His back was turned to Sarah and her husband, and he was bending over the sea-coal fire with his elbows on his knees and his chin resting in his hands. While Mrs. Sarah Pecker stood as if transfixed, staring silently at this traveller, Darrell followed Millicent into the hall, and thence into the oak parlour, closing the door behind him.

"O, Samuel, Samuel! how shall I ever tell her?" exclaimed Mrs. Pecker.

She turned towards the oak parlour, as if she would have gone straight to Millicent; but Samuel caught her by the arm.

"Let 'em have their dinner first, Sarah," he said pleadingly. "It'll seem hard enough whenever it comes; but it might seem harder if it came upon an empty stomach."

CHAPTER XVI.

THE THIRD APPEARANCE OF THE CAPTAIN'S DOUBLE.

WHILE the wedding-dinner was being eaten in the oak parlour, Mrs. Sarah Pecker and her husband sat looking at each other with pale anxious faces within the sacred precincts of the bar.

In vain had Millicent and Darrell implored their old and faithful friend to sit down and partake of the good cheer which had been prepared at her expense.

"No, Miss Milly dear," she said, "it isn't for me to

sit at the same table with Squire Markham's daughter and—and—her—cousin. In trouble and sorrow, dear—and surely trouble and sorrow seem to be the lot of all of us—I'll be true to you to the end of life ; and if I could save your young life from one grief, dear, I think I'd throw away my own to do it."

She took Millicent in her stout arms as she spoke, and covered the fair head with passionate tears and kisses.

"O, Miss Milly, Miss Milly," she cried, "it seems as if I was strong enough to save you from anything ; but I'm not, my dear—I'm not ! "

It was Millicent's turn to chide and comfort the stout-hearted Sarah. She had completely forgotten all her own doubts and fears, and was so happy in this return to Compton with the devoted lover of her youth, the fond protector of her childhood. The past, with all its sorrow, seemed to have faded from her like a forgotten dream, and the fair horizon of the future shone upon her bright and cloudless as a summer morning. She looked at Sarah with wondering eyes, astonished at the honest creature's unwonted emotion.

"Why, Sally dear," she said, "you seem quite out of spirits this evening."

"I *am* a little worn and harassed, Miss Milly ; but never you mind that—never you think of me, dear ; only remember that if I could save you from grief and trouble, I'd give my life to do it."

Mrs. Pecker hurried from the room before Millicent could question her further ; but her ominous words had left a vague sense of apprehension in the breast of Darrell's loving wife. The bright look of perfect happiness had faded from her face when she seated herself opposite her husband, at the table which Samuel had caused to be loaded with such substantial fare as might have served to regale a party of stalwart farmers at an audit dinner.

The traveller sitting over the fire in the common parlour was still alone. He had been served with a bowl of rum-punch; but Mr. Samuel Pecker had not waited upon him in person.

"You haven't spoke to him, then, Samuel?" asked Mrs. Pecker.

"No, Sarah, no; nor he to me. I saw him a-comin' in at the door like a evil spirit, as I've half a mind he is; but I hadn't the courage to face him, so I crept into the passage quietly and listened agen the door, while he was askin' all sorts of questions about Compton Hall, and poor Miss Milly, and one thing and another. And at first I was in hopes it was my brain as was unsettled, and that it was me as was in a dream like, and not him as was come back; and then he ordered a bowl of rum-punch, and then I knew it was him, for you know, Sarah, rum-punch was always his liquor."

"How long was it before we got home, Samuel?"

"When he came?"

"Yes."

"Nigh upon an hour."

"Only an hour—only an hour," groaned Sarah: "if it had pleased Providence to have taken his life before that hour, what a happy release for them two poor innocent creatures in yonder room!"

"Ah, what a release indeed!" echoed Samuel. "He's sittin' with his back to the door: if somebody could go behind him sudden with a kitchen poker," added the innkeeper, looking thoughtfully at Sarah's stout arm;

N

"but then," he continued, reflectively, "there'd be the body; and that would be against it. If you come to think of it, the leading inconvenience of a murder is that there's generally a body. But I suppose it's only right it should be so; for if it wasn't for bodies, murders would be uncommon easy."

Sarah did not appear particularly struck by the brilliancy of her husband's discourse; she sat in her own particular arm-chair before the old-fashioned fireplace, with her hands clasped upon her knees, rocking herself to and fro, and repeating mournfully,—

"O, if it had but pleased Providence to take him before that hour!—if it had but pleased Providence!"

She remembered afterwards that as she said these words there was a feeling in her heart tantamount to an inarticulate prayer that some species of sudden death might overtake the traveller in the common parlour.

Neither Sarah nor her husband waited upon the newly-married pair. The chambermaid took in the dishes, and brought them out again almost untouched. Mr. and Mrs. Pecker sat in the bar, and the few customers who came to the Black Bear that night were sent into a little sitting-room next to the oak parlour, and on the opposite side of the hall to that chamber in which the solitary traveller drank his rum-punch.

It was striking eight by Compton church, and by the celebrated eight-day oaken clock that had belonged to Samuel Pecker's mother, when this traveller came out of the common parlour, and after paying his score and wrapping a thick cashmere shawl about his neck, strode out into the snowy night.

He paid his score to the girl who had taken him the punch, and he did not approach the bar, in the innermost recesses of which Sarah Pecker sat with her knitting-needles lying idle in her lap, and her husband staring hopelessly at her from the other side of the fire-place.

"He's gone to the Hall, Samuel," said Mrs. Pecker, as the inn-door closed with a sonorous bang, and shut the traveller out into the night. "Who's to tell her, poor dear?—who's to tell her?"

Samuel shook his head vaguely.

"How pleasant it would be if he could lose himself in the snow any way between this and Compton Hall!" he said thoughtfully. "I've read somewheres in a book of somewheres in foreign parts, where there's travellers and dogs, and where they're always a-doin' it, only the dogs save 'em; besides which there was the old woman hat left Winstell market late on a Christmas night, that year as we had so many snowstorms, and was never heard of again."

Mrs. Pecker not appearing to take any special comfort from these rather obscure remarks, Samuel relapsed into melancholy silence.

Sarah sat in her old position, rocking herself to and fro, only murmuring now and then,—

"Who's to tell her? Poor innocent child! she was against marrying Master Darrell from the first to the last; and it was me that helped to drive her to it."

Half an hour after the departure of the traveller, Darrell Markham opened the door of the oak parlour, and Millicent came out into the hall equipped for walking.

Her new husband's loving hands had adjusted the wrappers that were to protect her from the piercing cold; her husband's strong arm was to support her in the homeward walk, and guide her footsteps through the snow. To walk home through the winter night with him was better than to ride in the grandest carriage that ever was built for a queen. No more loneliness—no more patient endurance of a dull and joyless life. A happy future stretched before her, as fair to look upon as a long flower-begemmed vista in the wood she had played in when she was a child.

Sarah took up her knitting-needles, and made a show of being busy, as Millicent and Darrell came out into the hall, but she was not to escape so easily.

" Sally dear, you'll bid me good night, won't you?" Millicent said tenderly.

Mrs. Pecker came out of her retreat in the bar, and once more took her old master's daughter in her arms.

" O, Miss Milly, Miss Milly," she cried, " I'm a little dull and a little cast down like to-night, and I'm all of a tremble, dear. I haven't strength to talk to you : only remember in any trouble, my darling, always remember to send for Sally Pecker, and she'll stand by you to the last."

" Sally, Sally, what is it?" asked Millicent tenderly; " I know something is wrong. Is it anything that has happened to you, Sally?"

" No, no, no, dear."

" Or to any one connected with you?"

" No, no."

" Then what is it, Sally?"

" O, don't ask me ; don't, for pity's sake, ask me, Miss Millicent;" and, without another word, Sarah Pecker broke from the embrace of the soft arms which were locked lovingly about her neck, and ran back into the bar for shelter.

" I couldn't tell her, Samuel," she whispered in her
husband's ear—" I couldn't tell her though I tried.
The words was on my lips, but something rose in
my throat and choked all the voice I had to say 'em
with. Now, look you here, Samuel, and mind you do
what I tell you faithful, without making any stupid
mistakes."

" I will, Sarah ; I'll do it faithful, if it's to walk
through fire and water ; though that ain't likely, fire
and water not often coming together, as I can see."

" You'll get the lantern, Samuel, and you'll go with
Mr. Darrell and Miss Millicent to light them to the
Hall ; and when you get there you won't come away
immediately, but you'll wait and see what happens, and
bring me back word, especially——"

" Especially what, Sarah ? "

" If they find *him* there."

" I'll do it faithful, Sarah. I often bring you the
wrong groceries from market, and I know I'm trying
to the mildest temper ; but I'll do this faithful, for my
heart's in it."

So Millicent and Darrell went out into the snowy
night, as the traveller had gone before them.

Samuel Pecker attended with the lantern, always
dexterously contriving to throw a patch of light exactly
on that one spot in the road where it was most unlikely
for Darrell and Millicent to tread. A very will-o'-the-
wisp was the light from Samuel's lantern ; now shining
on the topmost twig of a leafless hedge, now glimmering at the bottom of a ditch, now far ahead, now shoot-
ing off to the left, now darting suddenly to the extreme
right, but never shedding one ray upon the way that
he and his companions had to go. The feathery snow-

flakes drifting on the moors shut out the winter sky till all the atmosphere seemed blind and thick with woolly cloud. The snow lay deep on every object in the landscape—house-top and window-ledge, chimney and porch, hedge and ditch, tree and gate-post, village street and country road, all melted and blotted away in one mass of unsullied whiteness; so that each familiar spot seemed changed, and a new world just sprung out of chaos could hardly have been more strange to the inhabitants of the old one.

Compton Hall was situated about half a mile from the village street, and lay back from the high road, with a waste of neglected shrubbery and garden before it. The winding carriage-way, leading from the great wooden entrance-gates to the house, was half choked by the straggling and unshorn branches of the shrubs that grew on either side of it. There were few carriage folks about Compton-on-the-Moor, and the road had been little used save by foot-passengers.

At the gate Darrell Markham stopped and took the lantern from Mr. Pecker's hand.

"The path is rather troublesome here," he said; "perhaps I'd better light the way myself, Samuel."

It was thus that the light of the lantern being cast upon the pathway straight before them, Millicent happened to perceive footsteps upon the snow.

These footsteps were those of a man, and led from the gates towards the house: the feet could but just have trodden the path, for the falling snow was fast filling in the traces of them.

"Who can have come to the Hall so late?" exclaimed Millicent.

She happened to look at Samuel Pecker as she spoke.

The innkeeper stood staring helplessly at her, his teeth audibly chattering in the quiet night.

Darrell Markham laughed at his wife's alarm.

"Why, Milly," he said, "the poor little hand rest-ing on my arm trembles as if you were looking at the footmarks of a ghost—though I suppose, by the bye, that ghostly feet scarce leave any impression behind them. Come, Milly, come, I see the light of a fire in your father's favourite parlour. Come, dearest, this cold night is chilling you to the heart."

Something had indeed chilled her to the heart, but it was no external influence of the January weather. Some indefinable instinctive terror had taken possession of her on seeing those footmarks in the snow. Darrell led her to the house. A terrace built of honest red brick, and surmounted by grim stone vases of hideous shape, ran along the façade of the mansion in front of the windows on the ground floor. Darrell and Millicent ascended some side steps leading to this terrace, followed by Mr. Pecker.

To reach the front door they had to pass several windows; amongst others that window from which the fire-light shone. Passing this it was but natural they should look for a moment at the chamber within.

The light from a newly kindled fire was flickering upon the sombre oaken panelling; and close beside the hearth, with his back to the window, sat the same traveller whom Samuel Pecker had last seen beneath his own roof. The uncertain flame of the fire, shoot-ing up for a moment in a vivid blaze, only to sink back and leave all in shadow, revealed nothing but the mere outline of this man's figure, and revealed even that but dimly, yet at the very first glance through

the uncurtained window Millicent Duke uttered a
great cry, and falling on her knees in the snow, sobbed
aloud,—

"My husband! My husband, returned alive to make
me the guiltiest and most miserable of women!"

She grovelled on the snowy ground, hiding her face
in her hands and wailing piteously.

Darrell lifted her in his arms and carried her into
the house. The traveller had heard the cry, and stood
upon the hearth, with his back to the fire, facing the
open door; and the traveller was in sorry truth ·the
Captain of the Vulture—that person of all others upon
earth whose presence was most terrible to Darrell and
Millicent.

In the dusky shadow of that fire-lit room there was
little change to be seen in the face or person of George
Duke. The same curls of reddish auburn fell about
his shoulders, escaped from the careless ribbon that had
knotted them behind; the same steady light burned in
the hazel-brown eyes, and menaced mischief as of old.
Seen by this half-light, seven years seemed to have
made no change whatever in the Captain of the Vulture.

"What's this, what's the meaning of all this?" he
exclaimed, as Darrell Markham carried his helpless burden into the oak parlour. "What does it mean?"

Darrell laid his cousin on a couch beside the hearth
on which the Captain stood, before he answered this
question.

"It means this, George Duke," he said at last; "it
means, that if ever you were pitiful in your life, you
should be pitiful to this poor girl to-night."

The Captain of the Vulture laughed aloud. "Pitiful,"

he cried; " I never yet heard that a woman needed any great pity on having her husband restored to her after upwards of seven years' separation."

Darrell looked at him half contemptuously, half com-passionately.

" Can you guess nothing ? " he said.

" No."

" Can you imagine no fatal result of your long absence from this place ; many people—every one—thinking you dead ? "

" No."

" Can you think of nothing likely to have happened —remembering, as you must, that this poor girl married you in obedience to her father's commands, and against her own wishes ? "

" No."

" Can you guess nothing ? "

" How if I don't choose to guess, Master Darrell Markham ?   How if I say that whatever you want me to know you must speak out word for word, however much cause you and my lady there may have to be ashamed to tell it.   I'll help you by no guesses, I can tell you. Speak out ! what is it ? "

He stirred the fire with the toe of his boot, striking the coals into a blaze, in order that the light might shine upon his rival's face, and that whatever trouble or humiliation Darrell Markham might have to· undergo might not be lost to him.

" What is it ? " he repeated savagely.

" It is this, George Duke :—but before I speak another word, remember that whatever has been done was done in opposition to—your wife."

The acute pain he suffered in calling the woman he

loved by this name was not lost on Captain Duke. Darrell could see his anguish reflected in the malicious sparkle of those cruel brown eyes, and nerved himself against affording another triumph to his rival.

"Remember," he said, "through all, that she is blameless."

"Suppose we leave her and her blamelessness out of the question, and drop sentiment, Mr. Markham," answered the Captain, "until you've told me what has been done."

"Millicent Duke, being persuaded by her brother in a letter written on his dying bed, being further persuaded by every creature in this place, all believing you to be dead, being persuaded by her old nurse and by me, who used every prayer I knew to win her consent, against her own wish and in opposition to her own better judgment, was married to me three days ago in London."

"O, that's what you wanted me to guess, is it?" exclaimed the Captain; "by the heaven above me, I thought as much! Now you come here and listen to me, Mistress Millicent Markham, Mrs. George Duke, Mrs. Darrell Markham, or whatever you may please to call yourself. Come here, I say."

She had been lying on the sofa, never blest by one moment's unconsciousness, but acutely sensible of every word that had been said. Her husband caught hold of her wrist with a rough jerk, and lifted her from the sofa.

"Listen to me, will you," he said, "my very dutiful and blameless wife! I am going to ask you a few questions. Do you hear?"

"Yes."

She neither addressed him by his name nor looked at him as he spoke. Gentle as she was, tender and loving as she was to every animate thing, she made no show of gentleness to him, nor any effort to conceal her shuddering abhorrence of him.

"When your brother died he left you this property, did he not?"

"He did."

"And he left nothing to your cousin, Mr. Darrell, yonder?"

"Nothing—but his dear love."

"Never mind his dear love. He didn't leave an acre of land or a golden guinea, eh?"

"He did not."

"Good! Now, as I don't choose to hold any communication with a gentleman who persuades another man's wife to marry him in her husband's absence, against her own wish, and in opposition to her better judgment, I use his own words, mark you—you will be so good as to tell your fine cousin, Mr. Darrell Markham, this: Tell him that, as your husband, I claim a share in your fortune, whatever it may be; and that as to this little matter of a marriage, in which you have been so blameless, I shall know how to settle accounts with you upon that point, without any interference from him. Tell him this, and tell him also that the sooner he takes himself out of this house the pleasanter it will be for all parties."

Millicent stood with her hands clasped tightly together, and her fixed eyes staring into vacancy, while he spoke, and it seemed as if she neither heard nor comprehended him. When he had done speaking, she turned round, and, looking him full in the face, cried out,

" George Duke, did you stay away these seven years on purpose to destroy me, body and soul ? "

" I stayed away seven years, because ten months after I sailed from Marley Water I was cast away upon a desert island in the Pacific," he answered doggedly.

" Captain Duke," said Darrell, " since my presence here can only cause pain to your unhappy wife, I leave this house. I shall call upon you to-morrow to account for your words ; but in the mean time, remember that I am yonder poor girl's sole surviving kinsman, and, by the heaven above me, if you hurt but a hair of her head, you had better have left your bones to rot on one of the islands of the Pacific, than have come back here to account to Darrell Markham ! "

" I'm not afraid of you, Mr. Markham. I know how to treat that innocent lady there, without taking a lesson from you or any one else. Good night to you."

He nodded with an insolent gesture in the direction of the door.

" To-morrow," said Darrell.

" To-morrow, at your service," answered the Captain.

" Stop ! " cried Millicent, as her cousin was leaving the room ; " my husband took an earring from me when we parted at Marley, and bade me ask him for it on his return. Have you that trinket? " she asked the Captain.

She looked him in the face with an earnest, half-terrified gaze. She remembered the double of George Duke, seen by her upon Marley pier, in the winter moonlight.

The sailor took a small canvas bag from his waist-coat pocket. The bag contained a few pieces of gold and silver money, and the diamond earring which Millicent had given George Duke on the night of their parting.

" Will that satisfy you, my lady? " he asked, hand-ing her the gem.

" Yes," she answered, with a long heavy sigh; and then going straight to her cousin, she put her two icy hands into his, and addressed him thus:

" Farewell, Darrell Markham, we must never, never meet again. Heaven forgive us both for our sin; for Heaven knows we were innocent of evil intent. I will obey this man in all reasonable things, and will share my fortune with him and do my duty to him to my dying day; but I can never again be what I was to him before he left this place seven years ago; I can never be his wife again. Good night."

She put her cousin from her with a solemn gesture, which, with the simple words that she had spoken, seemed to him like a dissolution of their marriage.

He took her in his arms, and pressed his lips with a despairing fondness to her forehead. And then he led her back to George Duke, and said,—

" Be merciful to her, as you hope for God's mercy."

In the hall without Darrell Markham found Mr. Samuel Pecker, who had been crouching against the half-open door, listening patiently to the foregoing scene.

" It was according to the directions of Sarah," he said, apologetically, as Darrell emerged from the parlour and surprised the delinquent. " I was to be

sure and take her word of all that happened. Poor
young thing, poor young thing! It seems such a pity
that when Providence casts folks on desert islands, it
don't leave 'em there snug and comfortable, and no
inconvenience to themselves or anybody else."

Upon this particular night Mr. Pecker was doomed
to meet with inattentive listeners. Darrell Markham
strode past him on to the terrace, and from the terrace
to the pathway leading to the high road, without being
conscious of his existence.

The young man walked so fast that Samuel had
some difficulty in trotting after him.

"Excuse the liberty, Mr. Markham, but where
might you be going?" he said, when at last he over-
took Darrell, just as the latter dashed out on to the
high road, and halted for a moment, as if uncertain
which way to turn; "humbly begging your pardon, sir,
where might you be going?"

"Ay, where indeed?" said Darrell, looking back at
the lighted window. "I don't like to leave the neighbourhood of this house to-night. I want to be near
her. My poor, poor girl!"

"But, you see, Mr. Darrell," urged Samuel, inter-
rupting himself every now and then to shift the lantern
from his right hand to his left, and to blow upon his
disengaged fingers, "as it don't happen to be particular
mild weather, I don't see how you can spend the night
hereabout very well: so I hope, sir, you'll kindly make
the Black Bear your home for such time as you may
please to stay in Compton; only adding that, the longer
the better for me and Sarah."

There was an affectionate earnestness in Samuel's
address which could not fail to touch Darrell, even

in the midst of his utter misery and distraction of mind.

"You're a good fellow, Pecker," he said, "and I'll follow your advice. I'll stay at the Bear to-night, and I'll stay there till I see how that man means to treat my unfortunate cousin."

Samuel led the way, lantern in hand. It was close upon eleven o'clock, and scarcely a lighted window glimmered upon the deserted village street; but half-way between the Hall and the Black Bear, the two pedestrians met a man wearing a horseman's cloak, and muffled to the chin, with the snow-flakes lying white upon his hat and shoulders.

Samuel Pecker gave this man a friendly though feeble good-night, but the man seemed a surly fellow, and made no answer. The snow lay so deep upon the ground that the three men passed one another as noise-lessly as shadows.

"Have you ever taken notice, Mr. Darrell," said Samuel, some time afterwards, "that folks in snowy weather looks very much like ghosts; quiet, and white, and solemn?"

    *   *   *   *   *   *

Left alone in the solitude of the bar, Mrs. Pecker, lost in dreamy reflection, suffered the fire to burn low and the candles to remain unsnuffed, until the long wicks grew red and topheavy, smouldering rather than burning, and giving scarcely any light.

The half-hour after ten struck from the eight-day clock on the stairs. It was half an hour before Darrell Markham and Samuel Pecker left the Hall, and the Black Bear gave signs of shutting up for the night.

The few customers, who had been drinking and

talking together since six or seven o'clock, strolled out into the snow, leaving the house together for the sake of one another's company, and the business of the inn was done. The one waiter, or Jack-of-all-trades of the establishment, prepared to shut up the house ; and, as the first step towards doing so, opened the front door and peered out into the darkness to see what sort of night it was.

As he did so, the biting winter breeze blew in upon him, extinguishing the candle in his hand, and also putting out the two lights in the bar.

" What are you doing there, Joseph ?" Mrs. Pecker exclaimed sharply. " Come in, and shut up the place."

Joseph was about to obey, when a horseman galloped up to the door, and springing from his horse, looked into the dimly lighted hall.

" Why, you're all in the dark here, good people," he said, stamping his feet and shaking the snow from his shoulders. " What's the matter ? "

Mrs. Sarah Pecker was stooping over the red embers, trying to relight one of the candles.

" Can you tell me the way to Compton Hall, my good friend ? " said the traveller to Joseph the waiter.

" Squire Markham's that was ? "

" Ay, Squire Markham's that was."

" The waiter gave the necessary directions, which were simple enough.

" Good," said the stranger ; " I shall go on foot ; so do you fetch the ostler and give him charge of my horse. The animal's dead beat, and wants rest and a good feed of corn."

The waiter hurried off to find the ostler, who was asleep in a loft over the stables. The stranger strode up to the bar, in the interior of which Mrs. Pecker was still struggling with the refractory wick of the tallow candle.

"You seem to have a difficult job with that light, ma'am," he said; "but perhaps you'll make as short work of it as you can, and give me a glass of brandy, for my very vitals are frozen with a twenty-mile ride through the snow."

There was something in the stranger's voice which reminded Sarah Pecker of some other voice that she knew; only that it was deeper and gruffer than that other voice.

She succeeded at last in lighting the candle, and, placing it in front of the bar between herself and the traveller, took up a wine glass for the brandy.

"A tumbler, a tumbler, ma'am," remonstrated the stranger; "this is no weather for drinking spirits out of a thimble."

The man's face was so shaded by his slouched hat, and further concealed by the thick neckerchief muffled about his throat, that it was utterly irrecognizable in the dim light of Sarah Pecker's one tallow candle; but as he took the glass of brandy from Sally's hand, he pushed his hat off his forehead, and lowered his neckerchief in order to drink.

He threw back his head as he swallowed the last drop of the fiery liquor, then throwing Mrs. Pecker the price of the brandy, he bade her a hasty good-night, and strode out of the house.

The empty glass dropped from Sarah's hand, and shivered into fragments on the floor. Her white and terror-stricken face frightened the waiter when he returned from his errand to the stables.

The man she had served with brandy could not surely be George Duke, for the Captain had an hour before set out for the Hall; but if not George Duke himself, this man was most certainly some unearthly shadow or double of the Captain of the Vulture.

Sarah Pecker was a woman of strong sense; but she was human, and when questioned about her pale face and evident agitation, she told Joseph the waiter, Betty the cook, and Phœbe Price the pretty chambermaid, the whole story of Millicent's fatal marriage, Captain Duke's return, and the ghost that had followed him back to Compton-on-the-Moor.

"When Miss Millicent parted from her husband seven years ago, she met the same shadow upon Marley pier, and now that he's come back the shadow has come back too. There's more than flesh and blood in all that, you may take my word for it."

The household of the Black Bear had enough to talk of that night. What was the excitement of a West-country baronet, generous and handsome as he might be, to that caused by the visit of a ghost, which called for a tumbler of brandy, drank it, and paid for it like a Christian?

Samuel and Sarah sat up late in the little bar talking of the apparition, but they wisely kept the secret from Darrell Markham, thinking that he had trouble enough without the knowledge.

CHAPTER XVII.

CAPTAIN DUKE AT HOME.

GEORGE DUKE sat by the fire, staring moodily at the burning coals, and never so much as casting a look in the direction of his wretched wife, who stood upon the spot where Darrell had left her, with her hands clasped about her heart, and her blue eyes dilated in a fixed and vacant gaze, almost terrible to look upon.

The sole domestic at the Hall was the same old woman who had succeeded Sally Masterson as the squire's housekeeper, and had since kept house for Ringwood and his sister. She was half blind and hopelessly deaf, and seemed to have only a vague consciousness of external things. She took the return of Captain Duke as quietly as if the sailor had not been away seven weeks.

How long she stood in the same attitude, seeing nothing, thinking of nothing, in a kind of stupor which was almost too dull for despair, how long Captain George Duke sat brooding over the hearth, with the red blaze upon his cruel face, Millicent never knew. She only knew that by-and-by he addressed her, still without looking at her:

" Is there anything to drink—any wine or spirits in 'his dull old hole ? " he asked.

She told him that she did not know, but that she would go and find Mrs. Meggis (the deaf woman), and ascertain.

In the overwrought state of her brain, it was a relief to her to have to do her husband's bidding; a relief to her to go outside into the chilly hall and breathe

another atmosphere than that which George Duke
respired.

It was a long time before she could make Mrs. Meggis
understand what was wanted ; but when at last the state
of the case dawned upon the old woman, she nodded
several times triumphantly, took a key from a great
bunch that hung over the dresser, opened a narrow door
in one corner of the large stone-flagged kitchen, and,
candle in hand, descended a flight of steps leading into
the cellar.

After a considerable period she emerged with a dusty
cobweb-shrouded bottle under each arm. She held each
of these bottles before the light for Millicent to see the
liquid they contained. That in one was of a bright
amethyst colour, the other a golden brown. The first
was claret, the second brandy.

Millicent was preparing to leave the kitchen, followed
by the old housekeeper carrying the bottles and a couple
of glasses, when she was startled by a knocking at
the hall-door. When Mrs. Meggis became aware of
this summons, she put down her tray of bottles and
glasses, and went once more to the bunch of keys ; for
on the departure of Darrell and Samuel Pecker the
door had been locked for the night. It was now past
eleven. An unusual hour for visitors anywhere ; an
unearthly hour at this lonely Cumbrian mansion. Millicent had but one thought. It must be Darrell
Markham.

She took the tray in her own hands, and followed
Mrs. Meggis, who carried the light and the keys. When
they reached the hall, Millicent left the old woman to
open the door, and went straight into the parlour to
carry George Duke the liquor he had asked for.

"That's right," he said, "my throat's as hot as fire. So, so! no corkscrew? Heaven bless these pretty novel-reading wives, theyr'e so good at looking after a man's comfort!"

He took a pistol from his breast, and knocked off the necks of the two bottles with the butt-end of it, spilling the wine and spirit upon the polished parlour table.

He filled a glass from each and drained them one after the other.

"Good," he said; "the claret first, and the brandy afterwards. We don't get such liquor as this in—in the Pacific. I shall leave no heel-taps to-night, Mrs. Duke. What's that?"

He looked up to ask the question, after draining his glass for the third time.

That which had attracted his attention was the sound of voices in the hall without—the shrill treble pipe of Mrs. Meggis, and the deep voice of a man.

"What is it?" repeated George Duke. "Go and see, can't you?"

Millicent opened the parlour door and looked out into the hall. Mrs. Meggis was standing with the heavy door in her hand, parleying with some strange man who stood in the snow upon the threshold.

The same bitter winter wind which had extinguished the lights at the Black Bear had blown out the guttering tallow candle carried by Mrs. Meggis, and the hall was quite dark.

"What is it?" Millicent asked.

"Why, it is merely this, ma'am," answered the man upon the threshold: "this good woman here is rather hard of hearing, and not over easy to understand; but from what she tells me, it seems that Captain Duke has come home. Is that true?"

The man spoke from behind the thick folds of a woollen handkerchief, which muffled and disguised his voice as much as it concealed his face. Even in the obscurity he seemed jealous of being seen, for he drew himself further back into the shadow of the doorway as he spoke to Mrs. Duke.

"It is quite true," answered Millicent; "Captain Duke has returned."

The man muttered an angry oath.

"Returned," he said; "returned. Surely he must have come back very lately?"

"He came back to-night."

"To-night! to-night! Not half-a-dozen hours ago, I suppose?"

"Not three hours ago."

"That's good," muttered the man with another imprecation; "that's like my luck. Down once, down always: that's the way of the world. Good-night, ma'am!"

He left the threshold without another word, and went away; his footsteps noiseless in the depth of snow.

"Who was it?" asked George Duke when Millicent had returned to the parlour.

"Some man who wanted to know if you had returned."

"Where is he?" cried the Captain, starting from his seat, and going towards the hall.

"Gone."

"Gone without my seeing him?"

"He did not ask to see you."

The Captain of the Vulture clenched his fist with

a savage frown, looking at Millicent as if in some sudden burst of purposeless fury he could fain have struck her.

"Gone! gone!" he said; "d—— him, whoever he is. On the very night of my return, too!"

He began to pace up and down the room, his arms folded upon his breast, and his head bent gloomily downwards.

"The garden room has been prepared for you, Captain Duke," said Millicent, walking towards the door, and pausing upon the threshold to speak to him; "it is the best room in the house, and has been kept well aired, for it was poor Ringwood's favourite chamber. Mrs. Meggis has lighted a good fire there."

"Ay," said the Captain, looking up with a malicious laugh, "it would be clever to give me damp sheets to sleep upon, and give me my death of cold on the night of my return. Folks could scarcely call that murder, and it might be so easily done."

She did not condescend to notice this speech.

"Good-night, Captain Duke," she said.

"Good-night, my kind dutiful wife, good-night. I am to have the garden room, am I? well and good! May I ask in what part of the house it may please your ladyship to rest?"

"In the room my poor mother slept in," she said. "Good-night."

Left to himself, the Captain of the Vulture drew the table close to the hearth, seating himself in old Squire Markham's high-backed arm-chair, stretched out his legs before the blaze, filled his glass, and made himself thoroughly comfortable.

The broad light of the fire shining full upon his face

brought out the changes worked in his seven years' absence. Wrinkles and hard lines, invisible before, seemed to grow and gather round his eyes and mouth as he sat gloating over the blaze, and the strong drink, and the comfort about him. With his distorted shadow cast upon the panelling behind his chair, darkening all the wall with its exaggerated shape, he looked like some evil genius brooding over that solitary hearth, and plotting mischief against the roof that sheltered him.

Every now and then he looked up from the blaze to the bottles upon the table, the fire-lit walls, the antique bureau, the oaken sideboard, adorned with massive tankards of tarnished silver and Indian china punch-bowls, the quaint silver candlesticks, and all other evidences of solid countrified prosperity around him, and rubbed his hands softly, breaking out into a low triumphant chuckle as he did so.

"Better than over yonder," he said with a backward gesture of his head—" better than over yonder, anyhow. Thunder and fury! better than that, George Duke. You've not changed your quarters for the worse, since you bade good-bye to old comrades over there."

He filled his glass again, and burst into some fragment of a French song, with a jingling chorus of meaningless syllables.

"To think," he said, "only to fancy that this Ringwood Markham, a younger man than myself, should have died within a few months of my coming home! Egad, they've said that George Duke was one of those fellows who always fall on their feet. I've had a hard time of it for the last seven years, but I've dropped into good luck after all—dropped into my old luck—a fortune, and a poor frightened wife that can't say bo to a goose—a poor trembling novel-reading pale-faced baby, that——"

He broke off to fill himself another glass of claret. He had nearly finished the bottle by this time, and his voice was growing thick and unsteady. Presently he fell into a half-doze, with his elbows on his knees, and his head bent over the fire. Sitting thus, nodding forward every now and then, as if he would have fallen upon the burning coals, he woke presently with a sudden jerk.

"The chain," he cried, "the chain! D—— you, you French thief! bear your own share of the weight."

He looked down at his feet. One of the heavy fire-irons had fallen across his ankles. Captain Duke laughed aloud, and looked round the room, this time with a drunken half-bewildered stare.

"A change," he said, "a change for the better."

The bottles were both nearly empty, and the fire had burned low. Midnight had sounded some time before from the distant church-clock—the strokes dull and muffled in a snowy weather. The Captain of the Vulture rubbed his eyes drowsily.

"My head is as light as a feather," he muttered indistinctly; "I've not been over-used to a bottle of good wine lately. I'm tired and worn out, too, with three days' coach-travelling and a week's tossing about in stormy weather. So now for the garden room; and to-morrow, Mrs. George Duke and Mr. Darrell Markham, for you."

He shook his fist at the low fire as if he had seen the images of his wife and her kinsman looking at him out

of the hollow coals ; then rising with an effort, he took
one candle from the table, blew out the other, and
staggered off to find his way to the room in which he
was to sleep.

The house had been so familiar to him in the old
squire's lifetime, that, drunk as he was, he had no fear
of losing himself in the gloomy corridors on the upper
floor.

The garden room was a large chamber, which had
been added to the house about a hundred years before,
for the accommodation of a certain whimsical lady of
fortune, who had married old Squire Markham's grandfather. It was a large apartment, with small diamond-
paned windows overlooking a flower-garden, which had
been laid out immediately after the accession of William
the Third, and was called the Dutch garden—a stiff un-
picturesque parterre with flower-beds cut in geometrical
forms, trimly cut box borders, quaintly-shaped shrubs,
and a fountain that had long been dry. A half-glass
door opened on to a flight of stone steps, leading down
into this garden; which advantage, in conjunction with
the superior size and furniture of the apartment, had
long made the garden room the state chamber at
Compton Hall. A great square bed, with gilded
framework, mouldering tapestry curtains, faced the
casement windows and the half-glass door, which was
shrouded in winter by a curtain of tapestry like the
hangings of the bed.

George Duke set his candle on a table near the fire
and looked about him.

Millicent had spoken the truth when she said that
Mrs. Meggis had made a good fire, for long as it was
since the chamber had been prepared for its inhabitant,

the wood and coal burned brightly behind the bars of the wide grate. The Captain replenished the fire, flung himself into a comfortable tapestried arm-chair near the hearth, and kicked off his damp worn boots.

"There isn't a shred about me that would have held out a week longer," he said, as he looked at his patched and threadbare blue coat, the tarnished lace on which hung in frayed fragments here and there. "So it's no bad fortune that brought me back to look for Mistress Millicent."

There are some men upon whose nature good wine has a softening and even elevating influence. There are some topers so generous in their drunkenness that they would give away kingdoms if they had them to bestow; some so tender that they weep maudlin tears over the friend of the hour, and would fain clasp all creation in one tipsy embrace; some so exalted and inspired by rich wines that grand and noble sentiments and bright poetic fancies will flow like water from their feverish lips, until those who listen must needs believe that the gods have returned to earth, and that Bacchus himself discourses from the mouth of his votaries. But the finest vintages of sunny Burgundy were wasted on George Duke. For any genial influence which the wine exercised upon him, the Captain might as well have been drinking vinegar. Even in his drunkenness he took a malicious delight in the idea that he had returned to cheat and outwit his wife. He laughed aloud —a tipsy brutal laugh; and the eyes that had grown dull under the influence of strong drink lighted up once more with that red glimmer which the Captain's enemies declared was like the diabolical brightness in the eyes of a fiend.

He took off his coat and waistcoat, put a pair of pistols under the pillow, and threw back the counter-pane of the bed. Then, without further preparation, he flung himself down, half burying himself in the luxurious bed which the chatelaines of Compton had counted amongst their treasures for upwards of a century.

"I wonder whether yonder glass door is bolted," he muttered, as he dropped off to sleep; "of course it is, though—and little matter if it wasn't: I'm not much afraid of the honest villagers of Compton-on-the-Moor. Folks who come from the place I have just left don't often carry much to be robbed of."

Mechanically his wandering right hand sought the butt-end of the pistol beneath the pillow, and so with his fingers resting on the familiar weapon, George Duke dropped off to sleep.

It is doubtful if he had ever said a prayer in his life. He said none that night.

———

CHAPTER XVIII.

WHAT WAS DONE IN THE GARDEN ROOM.

For Millicent Duke there was no sleep that wretched hopeless night. She did not undress, but sat still and rigid, with her hands locked together, and her eyes staring straight before her, thinking. Thinking of what?

What was she? It was that question which some weary monotonous piece of mechanism in her brain was for ever asking, and never answering. What was she,

and what had she done? What was the degree of guilt
involved in this fatal marriage, and for how much of
that guilt was she responsible?

She had opposed the marriage, it is true. She had
striven hard against the tender pleadings of every
memory of her youth and its one undying affection;
but she had yielded. She had yielded, as Darrell had
but truly said, against her better judgment; or rather
against some instinctive dread, some shapeless terror,
in defiance of the warning accents of a mystic voice,
which had whispered to her that she was not free to
wed.

What was the extent of her guilt?

She had been simply and piously educated. She had
been educated by people whose honest minds knew no
degrees of right or wrong; whose creed was made up
of hard unassailable doctrines; and who set up the Ten
Commandments as so many stone boundaries about the
Christian's feet, and left him without one gap or loop-
hole by which he might escape their full significance.

What would the curate of Compton say to her the
next day when she went to him to fall at his feet and
tell her miserable story? Strange weakness of poor
human nature! It was of the Compton curate she
thought rather than of his Divine Master. She dreaded
that the priest would be pitiless, and forgot the illimitable tenderness, the inexhaustible compassion of Him
whose example the priest was bound to follow. Her
intellect was not strong enough to support her in this
terrible crisis of her life. She exaggerated the enor-
mity of her sin. She fancied herself the victim of some
hideous fatality. Not Œdipus, in the hour when the
revelation of his unconscious guilt burst fully on his

tortured spirit, could have felt a deeper horror of his crime, than this poor frail fair-haired woman, who cast herself upon the ground, and lay grovelling there and tearing her pale golden hair, crying out again and again that she was a guilty and a miserable creature.

Then, above even the thought of her sin, more horrible even than this consciousness of guilt, arose the black shadow of her future life—her future life, which was to be spent with *him*—with this hated and dreaded being, who now had a good excuse for the full exercise of his jealous spite against her, suppressed before, but never hidden. She tried to think of what her life would be—the light of Heaven blotted out, the angry hand of offended Providence stretched forth against her, and the cruel eyes of George Duke watching and gloating upon her anguish, till her miseries wore her life away, and she dropped into her grave and went to meet the eternal punishment of her sins.

The thought of these things maddened her. She went to a bureau opposite the empty fireplace and opened a drawer. She was in the room which had once been occupied by her dead father and mother, and she remembered that in this drawer there were some razors that had belonged to the old squire. She found the case containing them, and taking one of them in her hand looked at the shining blade. For one desperate moment she had thought that she would put an end to her wretched life, and thus cheat George Duke of his victim; but this gentle pious patient creature was not of the stuff out of which suicides are made.

"O, no," she cried piteously; "no, no, no, I cannot die with my sins unrepented of."

In her terror of herself and eagerness to escape temptation, she was awkward in shutting the razor; so awkward, that before she could succeed in doing it, the blade slipped between the old-fashioned handle and cut her across the inside of her hand. It was not a dangerous cut, nor yet a very deep one, but deep enough to send the blood spattering over the razor-blade and handle, the oak flooring, the open drawer of the bureau, and the skirt of Millicent's mourning dress.

She thrust the razor back into the case, and the case into the drawer, bound up her hand with a cambric handkerchief, and sat down again by the empty hearth.

"O, if Sally were here—my good faithful Sally—what a comfort she would be to me!" said Mrs. Duke.

The stillness and loneliness of the house oppressed her. She opened the window and looked out at the snow-covered garden below. The feathery flakes still falling, always falling, thick and silently from the starless sky, shut out the world and closed about the old house like a vast white winding-sheet. The casement whence Millicent looked was at that angle of the house which was most remote from the garden room; but she could see at the further end of the terrace the reflection of the fire-light shining through one uncurtained window red upon the snow.

The red reflection made a luminous patch upon the ground, peculiarly bright when contrasted with the surrounding darkness.

As Millicent looked at this illuminated spot, some dark object crossed it rapidly, blotting out the light for a moment.

It was such a night of wretchedness and misery, that this circumstance, which at another time might have alarmed her, made no impression upon Mrs. Duke's bewildered mind. She closed the casement, and returned to the fireplace, where she sat down again, in the same listless attitude, and with the same sad despairing face staring blankly at the cheerless hearth.

But the silence and solitude became utterly intolerable to her: she took the candle in her hand, opened her chamber door, went out upon the landing-place, and listened. Listened, she knew not for what—listened, perhaps hoping for some sound to break that intolerable stillness.

She could hear the ticking of the clock in the hall below. Beyond that, nothing. Not a sound, not a breath, not a murmur, not a whisper throughout the house.

Suddenly—to her dying day she never knew how the idea took possession of her—she thought that she would go straight to the garden room, awake George Duke, make him an offer of every guinea she had or was likely to have in the world, and entreat him to leave her and Compton for ever.

She would appeal to his mercy—no, rather to his avarice and self-interest; she knew of old how little mercy she need expect from him. She turned into the long corridor leading to the other end of the house, and walked rapidly towards her husband's chamber. The door of the garden room was shut, and Mrs. Duke's right hand being wounded, and muffled in a handkerchief, she was some time trying to turn the handle of the lock. The blood from the cut across her hand had oozed through the bandage, and left red smears upon the old-fashioned brass knob.

Millicent was perhaps rather more than two minutes trying to open the door.

All was still within the garden chamber. The fire-light shone in fitful flashes upon the faded tapestry and the dim pictures on the walls. Millicent crept softly round to the side of the bed upon which Captain Duke had thrown himself. The sleeper lay with his face turned towards the fire, and his hand still resting on the butt-end of his pistol—exactly as he had lain an hour before, when he fell asleep.

Millicent remembered how her brother Ringwood had lain in this very room, dead and tranquil, but three months before. Awe-stricken by the stillness, terrified by the thought of the desperate proposition she was about to make, Millicent paused between the foot of the bed and the fireplace, wondering how she should awake her husband.

The firelight, changeful and capricious, now played upon the sleeper's ringlets, lying in golden-brown tangles upon the pillow, now glanced upon the white fingers resting on the pistol, now flashed upon the tarnished gilding of the bed-posts, now glimmered on the ceiling, now lit up the wall; while Millicent's weary eyes followed the light, as a traveller, astray on a dark night, follows a will-o'-the-wisp.

She followed the light wherever it pleased to lead her. From the golden ringlets on the pillow to the hand upon the pistol, from the gilded bed-posts to the ceiling and the wall, lower and lower down the wall, creeping stealthily downwards, to the oaken floor beside the bed, and to a black pool

which lay there, slowly saturating the time-blackened
wood.

The black pool was blood—a pool that grew wider
every second, fed by a stream which was silently pouring from a hideous gash across the throat of Captain
George Duke, of the good ship Vulture.

With one long cry of horror, Millicent Duke turned
and fled.

Even in her blind unreasoning terror she remembered that it was easier to escape from that horrible
house by the glass door leading to the garden than by
the staircase and the hall. This half-glass door was in
a recess, before which hung the tapestry curtains. Millicent dashed aside the drapery, opened the door, which
was only fastened by one bolt, and rushed down the
stone steps, across the garden, along the neglected
pathways, and out on to the high road.

The snow was knee-deep as she tottered through it
onward towards the village street. She never knew
how she dragged her weary limbs over the painful
distance; but she knew that the clocks were striking three when she knocked at the door of the Black
Bear.

The door was opened by Samuel Pecker, whose
limited intellect had sustained a severe shock from the
events of the day, and who was yet more terrified by
this unwonted knocking, which had aroused him from
a muddled dream in which innumerable Captain Dukes
and roast turkeys had gibbered at and mocked him in
bewildering confusion. Pale as ashes, and with his
garments flung upon him in picturesque disorder, Mr.
Pecker came to attend this mysterious summons. Millicent had been knocking some time when he opened

the door a few inches wide, and, candle in hand, looked out of the aperture.

So had he opened that very door for the same visitor more than seven years ago, upon a certain autumn night, when Darrell Markham lay above stairs in the blue room, prostrate and delirious.

"Who is it?" he asked, shivering in every limb.

"It is I—Millicent. Let me in, let me in; for the love of God, let me in!"

There was such terror in her voice as made the inn-keeper forgetful of any alarm of his own. He gave way before this terrified woman as all men must yield to the might of such intense emotion, and opening the door wide, let her pass by him unquestioned.

The hall was all ablaze with light. Darrell Markham, Mrs. Pecker, and the servants had come down half dressed, each carrying a lighted candle. The night had been one of agitation and excitement; none had slept well, and all had been aroused by the knocking.

No unearthly shadow of the dead, or unholy double of the living, no ghost newly arisen in the grave-clothes of the long-buried, could have struck more horror to these people's minds than did the figure of Millicent Duke, standing amidst them, her pale dishevelled hair damp with the melted snow, her disordered garments trailing about her, wet and blood-stained, her eyes dilated in the same fixed gaze of horrified astonishment with which she had looked upon the murdered man, and her wounded hand, from which the handkerchief had dropped, dyed red with hideous smears.

She stood amongst them for some moments, neither speaking to them nor looking at them, but with her eyes still fixed in that horror-stricken stare, and her wounded hand wandering about her forehead till her brow and hair were disfigured with the same red smears.

His own face blanched to the ghastly hue of hers, as Darrell Markham looked at his cousin. Some horrible dread—shapeless but unspeakably terrible—took possession of him, and for the moment he was powerless to question her. Sarah Pecker was the first to recover her presence of mind.

"Miss Milly," she said, trying to take the distracted girl in her arms; "what is it? What has happened? Tell me, dear."

At the sound of this familiar voice the fixed eyes turned towards the speaker, and Millicent Duke burst into a long hysterical laugh.

"My God," cried Darrell, "that man has driven her mad!"

"Yes, mad!" answered Millicent, "mad! Who can wonder? He is murdered. I saw it with my own eyes. His throat cut from ear to ear, and the red blood bubbling slowly from the wound to join that black pool upon the floor. O, Darrell! Sarah! have pity upon me, have pity upon me, and never let me enter that dreadful house again!"

She fell on her knees at their feet and held up her clasped hands.

"Be calm, dear, be calm," said Mrs. Pecker, trying to lift her from the ground. "See, darling, you are with those who love you—with Master Darrell, and with your faithful old Sally, and with all friends about you. What is it, dear? who is murdered?"

"George Duke."

"The Captain murdered! But who could have done it, Miss Milly? Who could have done such a dreadful deed?"

She shook her head piteously, but made no reply.

It was now for the first time that Darrell interfered.

"Take her upstairs," he said to Mrs. Pecker, in an undertone. "For God's sake, take her away! Ask her no questions, but get her away from all these people, if you love her."

Sarah obeyed; and between them they carried Millicent to the room in which Darrell had been sleeping. A few embers still burned in the grate, and the bed was scarcely disturbed, for the young man had thrown himself dressed upon the outside of the counterpane. On this bed Sarah Pecker laid Millicent, while Darrell with his own hands relighted the fire.

On entering the room he had taken the precaution of locking the door, so that they were sure of being undisturbed; but they could hear the voices of the agitated servants and the innkeeper loud and confused below.

Mrs. Pecker occupied herself in taking off Millicent's wet shoes, and bathing her forehead with water and some reviving essence.

"Blood on her forehead!" she said, "blood on her hand, blood on her clothes! Poor dear, poor dear! what can they have been doing to her?"

Darrell Markham laid his hand upon her shoulder, and the innkeeper's wife could feel that the strong man trembled violently.

"Listen to me, Sarah," he said; "something horrible has happened at the Hall. Heaven only knows what; for this poor distracted girl can tell but little.

I must go down with Samuel to see what is wrong. Remember this, that not a creature but yourself **must** come into this room while I am gone. **Not a creature** but yourself must **come near** Millicent Duke. You understand? "

" Yes, yes ! "

" You will yourself keep watch over my unhappy cousin, and not allow another mortal to see her ?"

" I will not, Master Darrell."

" And you yourself will refrain from questioning her; and should she attempt to talk, you will check her as much as possible ? "

" I will—I will, poor dear," answered Sarah, bending tenderly over the prostrate figure on the bed.

Darrell Markham lingered for a moment to look at his cousin. It was difficult to say whether she was conscious or not; her eyes were half open, but they had a lustreless unseeing look which bespoke no sense of that which passed before them. Her head lay back upon the pillow, her arms had fallen powerless at her sides, and she made no attempt to stir when Darrell turned away from the bed to leave the room.

" You will come back when you have found out——"

" What has happened yonder ? Yes, Sarah, I will."

He went downstairs, and in the hall found one of the village constables, who lived near at hand, and who had been aroused by an officious ostler, anxious to distinguish himself in the emergency.

" Do you know anything of this business, Master Darrell ?" asked this man.

" Nothing more than what these people about here can tell you," answered Darrell. " I was just going down to the Hall to see what had happened."

"Then I'll go with your honour, if it's agreeable. Fetch a lantern, somebody."

The appeal to "somebody" being rather vague, everybody responded to it; and all the lanterns to be found in the establishment were speedily placed at the disposal of the constable.

That functionary selected one for himself, and handed another to Darrell.

"Now then, Master Markham," he said, "the sooner we start the better."

But the officious ostler who had fetched the constable, and the other servants of the Black Bear, had no idea of being deprived of any further share in the business. They were forming themselves into a species of impromptu procession, armed with a couple of rusty blunderbusses and a kitchen poker, with a view to accompanying Darrell and the constable, when the latter personage turned sharply round upon them, and addressed them thus:

"Now you look here," he said; "we don't want all of you straggling through the village with your fire-arms and your fire-irons, a-going direct against the Riot Act. Whatever's wrong down yonder, me and Mr. Markham is strong enough and big enough to see into it, without the help of any of you." With which unceremonious remarks the constable shut the door of the Black Bear upon its master and his servants, and strode forth into the snow, followed by Darrell Markham.

Neither of the two men spoke to each other on the way to the Hall, except once when the constable again asked Darrell if he knew anything of this business, whereupon Darrell again answered, as he had answered before, that he knew nothing of it whatever. The light shining from the shutterless window of the garden room showed them the house far off. This light came from Millicent's candle, which still burned where she had set it down before she discovered the murder.

"We shall have difficulty enough to get in," said Darrell, as they groped their way towards the terrace; "for the only servant I saw in the house was a deaf old woman, and I doubt if Mrs. Duke aroused her."

"Then Mrs. Duke ran straight out of the house when the deed was done, and came to the Black Bear?"

"I believe so."

"Strange that she did not run to nearer neighbours for assistance. The Bear is upwards of a mile and a half from here, and there are houses within a quarter of a mile."

Darrell Markham made no reply.

"See yonder," said the constable; "we shall have no difficulty about getting in—there is a door open at the top of those steps."

He pointed to the half-glass door of the garden room, which Millicent had left ajar when she fled. The light, streaming through the aperture, threw a zigzag streak upon the snow-covered steps.

The snow still falling, perpetually falling, through that long night, blotted out all footprints almost as soon as they were made.

"Do you know in which room the murder was committed, Master Darrell?" asked the constable as they went up the steps.

"I know nothing but what you know yourself."

The constable pushed open the half-glass door and the two men entered the room.

The candle, burned down to the socket of the quaint old silver candlestick, stood where Millicent had left it on a table near the window. The tapestry curtain, flung aside from the door as she had flung it in her terror, hung in a heap of heavy folds. That hideous pool between the bed and the fireplace had widened and spread itself; but the hearth was cold and black, and the bed upon which George Duke had lain was empty.

It was empty. The pillow on which his head had rested was there, stained a horrible red with his blood. The butt-end of the pistol, on which his fingers had lain when he fell asleep was still visible beneath the pillow. Red ragged stains and streaks of blood, and one long gory line which marked what way the stream had flowed towards the dark pool on the floor, disfigured the bedclothes; but beyond this there was nothing.

"He must have got off the bed and dragged himself into another room after his wife left him for dead," said the constable, taking the candle from his lantern and thrusting it into the candlestick left by Millicent; "we must search the house, Mr. Markham."

Before leaving the garden room, the rustic official bolted the half-glass door, and then, followed by Darrell, went out into the corridor.

They searched every room in the great dreary house, but found no trace of Captain George Duke, of the good ship Vulture. The sharp eyes of the constable took note of everything, and amongst other things of the half-open drawer in the bureau in the room which Millicent had last occupied. In this half-open drawer he found nothing but the razor-case, which he put into his pocket, after having examined its contents.

" What do you want with those ?" Darrell asked.

" There's bloodstains upon one of them, Mr. Markham. They may be wanted when this business comes to be looked into," the man answered quietly.

In one of the smaller rooms Darrell and the constable came upon the old woman, Mrs. Meggis, snoring peacefully, happily ignorant of all that had passed, and as there seemed little good to be obtained from awakening her, they left her to her slumbers.

The empty broken-necked bottles and the high silver candlestick stood on the oaken table in the parlour, as Captain Duke had left them when he went to bed. On the sideboard the tarnished silver tankards, ranged in a prim row, stood undisturbed as they had stood in the old squire's lifetime ; the hall door, fastened with heavy bolts, remained as it had been left by the deaf-housekeeper. Throughout the house there was no sign of plunder nor of violence, save the pool of blood in the garden chamber.

" Whoever has done this business," said the constable, looking gravely about him and pointing to the plate upon the sideboard, " is no common burglar."

" You mean——"

" I mean that it hasn't been done for gain. There's something more than plunder at the bottom of this."

They went once more to the garden room, and the constable walked slowly round the chamber, looking at everything in his way.

"What 's come of the Captain's clothes, I wonder?"

ho said, rubbing his chin, and staring thoughtfully at the bed.

It was noticeable that no vestige of clothing belonging to Captain George Duke was left in the apartment.

CHAPTER XIX.

AFTER THE MURDER.

THE grey January morning dawned late and cold upon Compton-on-the-Moor. The snow still falling, for ever falling through the night, had done strange work in the darkness. It had buried the old village, and left a new one in its stead. An indistinct heap of buildings, with roof-tops and gable-ends so laden with snow, that the inhabitants of Compton scarcely knew the altered outlines of their own houses.

The coach that passed through Compton, on its way northward to Marley Water, had been stopped miles away by the snow. Waggons and carriers' carts, that had been used to come blundering through the village, were weatherbound in distant market towns. Horsemen were few and far between upon the dangerous roads; and those who were hardy enough to brave the perils of the way paid dearly for their temerity. Compton was cut off from the outer world, and cast upon its own resources, on the clear cold morning which succeeded that night of ceaseless snow; but Comptom had enough to talk about, and enough to think about, within its own narrow limits—so much, indeed, that

the coach itself was hardly missed, save inasmuch as it
would have afforded the inhabitants a kind of solemn
and ghastly pleasure to tell the passengers of the dire
event, and to watch their scared faces as they received
the intelligence.

A murder had been done at Compton-on-the-Moor.
At that simple Cumbrian village, whose annals until
now had been unstained with this the foulest of crimes,
a murder had been done in the silence of the long
winter's night, beneath that white and shroud-like
curtain of thick-falling snow—a murder so wrapped
in mystery, that the wisest in Compton were baffled in
their attempts to understand its meaning.

With the winter dawn every creature in Compton
knew of the deed that had been done. People scarcely
knew how they heard of it, or who told them; but
every lip was busy with conjecture, and every face was
charged with solemn import, as who should say, " I am
the sole individual in the place who knows the real
story, but I have my instructions from higher autho-
rities, and I am dumb."

Every creature in Compton, with the exception of
an old woman who had been bedridden since Millicent
Duke's babyhood, and the curate's wife, who couldn't
leave her seven children, went to look at the Hall in
the course of the morning. It seemed the prevailing
impression that some great change would have taken
place in the building itself, and there was considerable
disappointment felt by the young and sanguine on
finding the brick and mortar in its normal condition.
Again, everybody went with a view of exploring the
interior of the house and looking for the body of
Captain Duke, which they all individually conceived

themselves destined to find. It was no small mortification, therefore, to discover that the house, and even the gates leading to the grounds, were strongly barricaded, and that no creature, save a few happy semi-officials, in the employ of that mighty being, the constable, were to be admitted on any pretence whatever.

The constable had taken up his abode at the Hall for the time being, and sat in the little oaken parlour in solemn state, holding conference now and again with the semi-officials in his employ, who were busy, according to the current belief of Compton, looking for the body.

Under this prevailing impression, the semi-officials had rather a hard time of it, as whenever they emerged from the Hall gates they were waylaid and seized upon by some anxious Comptonian, eager to know "if they had found it."

The one all-absorbing idea in the mind of every Comptonian was the idea of the missing body of Captain George Duke. Busy volunteers made unauthorized search for it in every unlikely direction. In chimney-corners and cupboards of unoccupied houses, in out-buildings, pigsties, and stables ; in far-away fields, where they went waist-deep in snow, and were in imminent peril of altogether disappearing in unlooked-for pitfalls; in the churchyard ; nay, some of the most sanguine spirits went so far as to request being favoured with the keys of the church itself, in order that they might look for Captain Duke in the vestry cupboard, where a skilful assassin might have hidden him behind the curate's surplice.

The all-pervading idea of the body, which was only a pleasant excitement by daylight, and in mixed com-

pany, grew very awful as dusky evening darkened
into moonless night, and the Comptonians sat in little
groups of two or three before their cottage fires. There
were shadowy corners in the dimly lighted chambers,
corners in which it would have seemed only a natural
thing to find some special image of the murdered man
lurking, blood-stained and ghastly. There were corkscrew staircases provided with niches that seemed specially intended for the reception of that horrible thing
which *must* be hidden somewhere in the village.

Perhaps the only person in Compton who was quite
indifferent to the terrible event which had occurred was
the deaf old housekeeper, Mrs. Meggis. The constable
made some feeble attempt to acquaint her with the
catastrophe which had happened, when he awoke her
at daybreak, with a view to cross-questioning her as to
the events of the previous night; but it was evident
that the tidings never reached the dim obscurities of
her inner consciousness, for she only replied, "That it
wasn't to be wondered at at this time of the year, and
that it was seasonable, sir, very seasonable, though uncommon bad for old folks as was a'most crippled by
chilblains, and was subject to the rheumatics," by which
the constable inferred that she had imagined him to be
talking all the time of the snowy weather. Whatever
hope he might have had of obtaining information from
this quarter was therefore very quickly dispelled; so,
having locked the door of that garden chamber, where
the gory pool was scarcely dry, he bade Mrs. Meggis
go about her daily business, and light a fire for him in
the oak parlour.

He had been at the Black Bear early that morning to
ask for an interview with Mrs. George Duke, in order

to hear her statement about the murder; but Sarah kept watch and ward over Millicent, and she and Dar- rell and the village surgeon all protested against the unhappy girl being questioned until she had somewhat recovered from the mental shock which had prostrated her. So the constable was fain to withdraw, after whispering some directions to one of the semi-officials, who, red-nosed, blue-lipped, and shivering, hung about the Black Bear all that day, consuming numerous mugs of ale, and regarded with reverential curiosity by all the servants of the establishment.

Millicent was indeed in no state to be questioned. She lay in the same dull stupor into which she had fallen between three and four o'clock that morning. Sarah Pecker and Darrell Markham, watching her ten- derly through the day, could not tell whether she was conscious of their presence. She never spoke, but some- times tossed her head from side to side upon the pillow, moaning wearily. It was a cruel and a bitter day of trial for Darrell Markham. He never stirred from his place by the bedside, only looking up every now and then—when Sarah returned after having left the room to ascertain what was going on downstairs—to ask anxiously if anything had been discovered about the murder—if they had found the assassin or the body.

Whatever gloomy thought was in his mind, as he sat pale and watchful by the bedside, from the first grey glimmer of dawn till the sombre shadows, gathering on the white expanse of moorland, shut out the open country before the windows and crept into the corners of the room — whatever thought was in his mind throughout that patient watch, he kept it to himself, and made no confidant even of the faithful mistress of

the Black Bear.   Watch him closely as she might, tormented by her own vague fears, she could not penetrate
the gloom that shrouded his face, or guess the bent of
his thoughts in that long reverie.

Below stairs all was confusion and bewilderment;
for only the presence of strong-minded Sarah could
have preserved order and tranquillity during a period
of such excitement.   But business was very brisk, and
Samuel and his retainers had as much as they could
do in supplying the wants of thirsty Comptonians, who
were eager to discuss the event of the previous night,
and greedy of information as to the mental and physical
state of Mrs. Duke, whose strange conduct on the previous night was by this time known to all Compton.

Samuel Pecker, always of a morbid turn of mind,
was in his element during this crisis.   The absence of
the body of the supposed murdered man was a source
of never-ending wonder and bewilderment to his simple
mind.   He demanded over and over again how there
could possibly be a murder without a body, when the
leading feature of a murder always was the body?

This led to much discussion of a belief very prevalent
in Compton, namely, that the Captain of the Vulture
had cut his own throat, and quietly walked away to a
certain cross-road where the Carlisle mail was to be
met at about half-past three o'clock every morning, and
had laid himself down there in the snow, ready for the
unholy stake of the *felo-de-se*.   Others contended that
it was but likely that the unknown assassin had only
half done his work, and that the Captain, with a great
gash in his throat, and speechless from loss of blood,
was hiding somewhere within call of all Compton ; and
nervous people were afraid to go into solitary chambers

lest they should come suddenly upon the ghastly figure of George Duke crouching in some dark corner.

The shadows gathered black and dense upon the moorland, and Compton Hall, wrapt in snow from the basement to the gabled roof, looked like some phantom habitation glimmering dimly through the dusk. The semi-officials made their report in the oaken parlour, where the constable sat over a blazing sea-coal fire, taking pencil notes in a plethoric and greasy leathern pocket-book; but they could bring no report which in any way tended to throw light upon the whereabouts of the Captain of the Vulture, alive or dead.

It was quite dark when the constable, after locking the doors of the principal rooms in the old house, and putting the keys in his pockets, gave strict directions to Mrs. Meggis to admit no one, and to keep the place securely barricaded. By dint of considerable perseverance he contrived to make the old woman understand him to this extent, and then nodding good-naturedly to her, left her for the night, happily ignorant of what had been so lately done beneath the roof that sheltered her.

From the Hall Hugh Martin, the constable, walked straight to a mansion about half-a-mile distant, which was inhabited by a certain worthy gentleman and county magistrate, called Montague Bowers. A very different man from that magistrate before whom Darrell Markham had charged Captain Duke with highway robbery seven years before.

In the private sitting-room, study, or *sanctum sanc-torum* of this Mr. Bowers, Hugh Martin, the constable, made his report, detailing every particular of his day's work. "I've done according as was agreed upon

Q

between you and me this morning, sir," he said. " **I've** waited out the day, and kept all dark, taking care to keep my eye upon 'em up yonder; but I can't see any way out of it but one, and I don't think we've any course but to do as we said then."

Hugh Martin was closeted with the justice for a considerable time after this; and when he left the residence of Mr. Bowers, he hurried off at a brisk pace in the direction of the village and through the High Street to the door of the Black Bear. In the wide open space before that hostelry he came upon a man lounging in the bitter night, as if it had been some pleasant summer's evening, whose very atmosphere was a temptation to idleness. This man was no other than the red-nosed and blue-lipped semi-official, who had been drinking at the bar, and loitering about the neighbourhood of the inn all that day. He was a constable himself, but so inferior in position to the worthy Mr. Hugh Martin, that he was only looked upon as an assistant or satellite of that gentleman; useful in a fray with poachers, to be knocked down with the butt-end of a gun before the real business of the encounter began; good enough to chase a refractory youngster who had thrown pebbles at the geese in the village pond; to convey an erratic donkey to safe keeping in the pound; or to induct a drunken brawler in the stocks; but fit for nothing of a higher character.

" All right, Bob?" asked Mr. Hugh Martin of this gentleman.

" Quite right."

" Anybody left the inn ?"

" Why Pecker himself has been in and out, up and down, and here and there, gabbling and chattering like

an old magpie; but that's all, and he's safe enough in
the bar now."

"Nobody else has left the place?"

"Nobody."

" That's all right. Keep on the look-out down here,
and if I open one of those windows overhead and
whistle, you'll know you are wanted."

The appearance of the constable created intense excitement amongst the loungers at the bar of the Black
Bear. They gathered round him, so eager for information, that amongst them they very nearly knocked him
down.

What had he discovered? Who had done it? What
had been the motive? Had he found the weapon? Had
he found the body? Had he found the murderer?

Mr. Hugh Martin pushed all these eager questioners
aside without any wonderful ceremony, and walked
straight to the bar, where he addressed himself to the
worthy Samuel Pecker.

"Mr. Markham is upstairs, is he not?" he asked.

"He is in the blue room, poor dear gentleman."

"With the lady—his cousin?"

"Yes."

" Then I'll just step upstairs, Pecker, for I've a few
words to say to him about this business."

The bystanders had gathered about Mr. Martin, and
had contrived to hear every syllable of this brief dialogue.

"He has found out all about it," they said, when the
constable went upstairs, "and he's gone to tell Mr.
Markham—very proper, very right, of course."

Feeling that it was not unlikely they would have a
reversionary interest in the information that the constable had just taken up to the blue room, the excited

Comptonians lingered patiently about the foot of the stairs, waiting for Hugh Martin's return.

In the blue room Millicent Duke sat with her fair head resting on Sarah Pecker's ample shoulder, her frail form supported by the strong arm of that faithful friend. The two women were seated on a great roomy sofa drawn close up to the fire, against which stood a table, with a tea-tray on which Mrs. Pecker's choicest old dragon china cups and saucers were set forth. On the opposite side of the fireplace sat Darrell Markham, his eyes still fixed upon his cousin, with the same look of anxious watchfulness which had marked his face all that day. Millicent had recovered from that terrible stupor. She had recognized Darrell and Mrs. Pecker, and had been soothed and tranquillized by their presence. She had told them the brief story of the night before. How she had gone to George Duke's chamber, with the intention of making an appeal to his mercy, and how she had found him with his throat cut from ea to car—dead!

Sarah had taken off Mrs. Duke's blood-stained dress, and wrapped her in some garments of her own, which hung about her slender figure in thick clumsy folds. The hideous stains had been removed from her hands and forehead, and there was nothing now about her to tell of the horrors through which she had passed.

Mrs. Pecker was holding a tea-cup to Millicent's lips, imploring her to drink, when Darrell Markham started from his chair, and went to the door, where he stood with his head bent, listening to some sound without.

" What's that ? " he exclaimed.

It was the tramp of a man's footstep upon the stair, the footstep of Mr. Hugh Martin, the constable.

Darrell's face grew even paler than it had been al; that day; he drew back, holding his breath, terribly calm and white to ;ook upon. The constable tapped at the door, and without waiting for an answer, walked in.

Hugh Martin carried a certain official-looking document in his hand. Armed with this, he walked straight across the room to the sofa upon which Millicent sat.

" Mrs. Millicent Duke," he said, " in the King's name I arrest you for the wilful murder of your husband, George Duke."

Darrell Markham flung himself between his cousin and the constable.

" Arrest her !" he cried ; " arrest this weak girl, who was the first to bring the tidings of the murder ! "

" Softly, Mr. Markham, softly, sir," answered the constable, opening the nearest window, and whistling to the watcher beneath. "I am sorry this business ever fell to my lot; but I must do my duty. My warrant obliges me to arrest you as well as Mrs. Duke."

CHAPTER XX.

COMMITTED FOR TRIAL.

MILLICENT and Darrell were taken to a dreary dilapidated building called the lock-up, very rarely tenanted, save by some wandering vagrant, who had been found guilty of the offence of having nothing to eat and no place of shelter; or some more troublesome delinquent, in the shape of a poacher, who had been taken in the act of appropriating the hares and pheasants on a neighbouring preserve.

To this place Hugh Martin the constable, and his
assistant, Bob, conducted gentle and delicately nurtured Mrs. George Duke; and the only one privilege
which the entreaties of Darrell Markham and Sarah
Pecker could obtain for her was the constable's permis-
sion to Sally to stop all night in the cell with the female
prisoner.

Darrell prayed Hugh Martin to take them straight
to the house of Mr. Montague Bowers, in order that any
examination which had to be made might take place
that very night; but the constable shook his head
gravely, and said that Mr. Bowers had made up his
mind to wait till morning.   So, in a dilapidated chamber, which had been divided across the centre by a thin
wooden partition, for the accommodation of an occa-
sional press of prisoners, Millicent and Sarah spent that ·
long and dismal night.   A dirty casement window,
secured by bars of rusty iron, was their only separation
from the village street.   They could see the feeble
lights in cottage windows, blurred and dim through the
discoloured glass; and could hear every now and then
the footsteps of a passer-by, crunching the crisp snow
beneath his tread.

Millicent, lying on a truckle-bed close to this window
and listening to those passing footsteps, remembered how
often she had gone by that dismal building, and how
utterly unmindful she had been of those within.   She
shuddered as she looked at the ragged stains of damp
and mildew on the plaster walls—which transformed
themselves into grotesque and goblin faces in the uncertain flicker of a rushlight—remembering how many helpless creatures must have lain there through long winter
nights like this, conjuring hideous faces from the same

crooked lines and blotches, and counting the cobwebs hanging from the roof.

It was strange that since her arrest and removal to this dreary lock-up Millicent Duke had seemed to recover the quiet gentleness which was so much a part of her nature. She had been incoherent before, but she was now perfectly calm and collected. Hers was one of those natures which rise with the occasion; and though a shrinking timid soul at ordinary times, she might on emergency have become a heroine. Not a Joan of Arc nor a Charlotte Corday, nor any such energetic creature; but a gentle saintly martyr of the old Roman Catholic days, quietly going forth to meet her death without a murmur.

She put her arms about Mrs. Pecker's neck, and tenderly embraced the outraged matron.

"All will be right in the end, dear," she said; "they never, never, never can think me guilty of this dreadful deed. They are searching for the real murderer, perhaps this very night, while I lie here. God, who knows that I am innocent, will never permit me to suffer."

"Permit you to suffer! No, no, no, darling, no," cried Sarah, clinging about Millicent, and bursting into a passion of tears.

She remembered, with a shudder, how many hapless wretches suffered in those days, and how scarcely a week went by unmarked by an execution at Carlisle; for every Monday was black Monday a hundred years ago, and Mr. Ketch had his hands full in every part of the country. To-night Mrs. Pecker thought of these things with unutterable horror. How did she know that all who died that ignominious death were guilty of the crimes whose penalty they paid? She had never thought of it till now;

taking it always for granted that judges and juries knew best; and that these cold-blooded judicial murders were done in the cause of morality, and for the protection of honest people.

"O, Miss Milly, Miss Milly, if I had only been with you last night!" she said: "I had half a mind to have come down to the Hall after Mr. Darrell left you; but I knew I was no favourite with Captain Duke, and I thought my coming might only make him angry against you."

The last footfall died away upon the snow, the last dim light faded out in the village street; and the two women kept silence, waiting patiently for the dawn. To those weary watchers the long winter night seemed almost eternal: but it wore itself out at last, and the cheerless daybreak showed a wan and ghastly face at the barred casements of Compton gaol.

A coach, hired from the Black Bear, carried the two prisoners to the magistrate's house. The family was at breakfast when the little party arrived, and the prisoners heard the prattle of children's voices as they were ushered through the hall into the magistrate's study. A grim chamber, this hall of audience, lighted by two narrow windows, and furnished with stiff high-backed oaken chairs, ponderous tables, and a solemn-faced eight-day clock, which was subject to those internal snortings and groanings common to eight-day clocks, and altogether calculated to strike terror to the heart of a criminal.

Here Millicent and Darrell, with Hugh Martin the constable, and Sarah Pecker, waited for Mr. Montague Bowers, justice of the peace, to make his appearance.

Hanging about the hall and gathered round the door

of this chamber were several people who had persuaded themselves into the idea that they knew something of the disappearance of Captain Duke, and were eager to serve the State by giving evidence to that effect. The ostler who had aroused the constable; half-a-dozen men who had helped in the ineffectual search for the body; a woman who had assisted in conveying Mrs. Meggis, the deaf housekeeper, to the spot that morning, and many others equally unconnected with the case, were amongst these. There was therefore a general sensation of disappointment and injury when Mr. Montague Bowers, coming away from his breakfast, selected Samuel Pecker from amongst this group of outsiders, and bidding the innkeeper follow him, walked into the chamber of justice, and closed the door upon the rest.

"Now, Mr. Pecker," said the justice, seating himself at the oaken table, and dipping a pen into the ink, after having duly sworn the timid Samuel, "what have you to say about this business?"

Taken at a disadvantage thus, Samuel Pecker had very little indeed to say about it. He could only breathe hard, fidget nervously with his plaited ruffles (he had put on his Sunday clothes in honour of the occasion), and stare at the justice's clerk, who sat, pen in hand, waiting to take down the innkeeper's deposition.

"Come, Mr. Pecker," said the justice, "what have you to state respecting the missing man?"

Samuel scratched his head vaguely, and looked appealingly at his wife Sarah, who sat by the side of Mrs. Duke, weeping audibly.

"Meaning him as was murdered?" suggested Mr. Pecker

"Meaning Captain George Duke," replied the justice.

"Ah, but there it is," exclaimed the bewildered Samuel; "that's just where it is. Captain George Duke. Very good; but which of them? Him as asked me the way to Marley Water seven years ago on horseback last October? you remember, Master Darrell, for you was by at the time," said the innkeeper, addressing himself to one of the accused. "Him as Miss Millicent saw on Marley pier by moonlight, when the clocks was a-striking twelve? Him as came to the Black Bear the day before yesterday at three o'clock in the afternoon? or him as drank and paid for a glass of brandy between eight and nine the same night, and left a horse in our stables, which has never been fetched away?"

Mr. Montague Bowers stared hopelessly at the witness.

"What is this?" he demanded, looking at Sarah and the two prisoners in his despair; "what, in Heaven's name, does it all mean?"

Whereupon Mr. Samuel Pecker entered into a detailed account of all that had happened at Compton-on-the-Moor for the last seven years, not forgetting even the foreign-looking pedlar, who stole the spoons; and, indeed, throwing out a feeble suggestion that the itinerant might be in some way connected with the murder of Captain George Duke. When urged to come to the point, after rambling over nearly three sides of foolscap, he became so bewilderingly obscure that it was only by means of brief and direct questioning that the justice approached any nearer to the object of the examination.

"Now, suppose you tell me, Mr. Pecker, at what

hour Captain Duke left your house on the night before last."

" Between eight and nine."

" Good; and you next saw him——"

" Between nine and ten, when I went to the Hall with Miss Millicent and Mr. Darrell."

" Did Mrs. Duke and her husband appear to be on friendly terms ?"

To this question Samuel Pecker made a very discursive answer, setting out by protesting that nothing could have been more affectionate than the conduct of Millicent and the Captain ; and then going on to declare that Mrs. Duke had fallen prostrate on the snow, bewailing her bitter fortune and her husband's return ; and further relating how she had never addressed a word to him, except once, when she suddenly cried out, and asked him why he had come back to make her the most guilty and miserable of women.

Here the innkeeper came to an abrupt finish, in nowise encouraged by the terrific appearance of his wife Sarah, who sat shaking her head at him fiercely from behind the shelter of her apron.

It took a long time, therefore, altogether before the examination of Samuel Pecker was concluded, and that rather unmanageable witness pumped completely dry. Enough, however, had been elicited from the innkeeper to establish Darrell Markham's innocence of the charge brought against him, inasmuch as he had quitted Compton Hall in the company of Samuel, leaving Captain Duke alive and well at ten o'clock, and had gone straight to his chamber at the Black Bear. Between that hour and the time of George Duke's disappearance, Millicent and the deaf housekeeper had been alone in the great house with the missing man. Montague Bowers congratulated the young man upon his having come so safely out of the business; but Darrell neither heeded nor heard him. He stood close against the chair in which his cousin sat, watching that still and patient figure, that pale resigned face, and thinking with anguish and terror that every word which tended to exonerate him only threw a darker shadow of suspicion upon her.

Darrell Markham, being acquitted of all participation in the crime, was competent to give evidence, and was the next witness examined. All was revealed in the course of that cruel interrogation, to which the witness was compelled to submit. He was on his oath, and must needs tell the truth, even though the truth might be damning for Millicent. Who shall say that he might not have been ready to perjure himself for her dear sake, if perjury could have saved her? But in such a case as this it generally happens that the truth, however fatal, is safer than falsehood; for the man who swears to a lie can never tell how long and complicated may be the series of deceptions in which he involves himself, or how difficult it may be for him to sustain his false position.

The magistrate asked his pitiless questions; and all was told—the marriage at St. Mary's church, Ringwood's letter, the return to Compton, the surprise and horror caused by Captain Duke's reappearance, the hard words that had been spoken between the two men, Millicent's despair and shuddering terror of her husband, and then the long blank interval of many hours, at the end of which Mrs. George Duke came to the Black Bear to tell of a murder that had been done.

" And did she appear agitated ?"

" Yes, very much agitated."

" And was there blood upon her dress ? "

" Yes."

" And were her hands stained.with blood ? "

Again Darrell must needs say yes. Her hands were stained with blood. She had cut her hand ; the magistrate might see the wound if he pleased.

The magistrate shook his head with a sad smile. A surface-wound like that might be so easily inflicted, he thought, to account for the blood upon the wretched woman's dress.

All this the clerk's busy pen recorded, and to this Darrell Markham afterwards signed his name in witness of its truth.

Hugh Martin the constable was next sworn. He described the appearance of the house. The absence of any sign of pillage or violence, the unbroken fastenings of the heavy oaken door, the undisturbed plate on the sideboard, and lastly, the blood-stained razor found by him in the bureau.

From Mrs. Meggis, the deaf housekeeper, very little information of any kind could be extorted. She remembered having admitted Captain Duke on his arrival at the Hall, but was doubtful as to the hour ; it might have been between seven and eight, or between eight and nine ; she was quite sure that it was after dark, but she couldn't take upon herself to say how long after dark. She remembered Captain Duke striding straight into the oak parlour, and bidding her light a fire : he was a noisy and insolent gentleman, and she was afraid of him, being " timersome by nature, and seventy-five years of age, your lordship, come next

Michaelmas," and he swore at her because the kindling was green and wouldn't burn. She remembered preparing the garden room for him, according to Mrs. Duke's orders. She had prepared no other room for Mrs. Duke, and did not know where she meant to sleep. She remembered getting the wine and brandy, which Mrs. Duke carried to the Captain with her own hands. This must have occurred, she thought, at about eleven o'clock, and immediately after this she, Mrs. Meggis, went to bed, and remembered no more till she was awakened next morning by the constable, and nigh frightened out of her poor old wits by seeing him standing at her bedside.

This was all that Mrs. Meggis had to tell; and she, like Samuel Pecker, gave a great deal of trouble to her questioners before she could be induced to part with her information.

Sarah Pecker was also examined, but she could tell nothing more than her husband had told already, and she broke down so often into sobs and pitying ejaculations about her old master's daughter, that Mr. Bowers was glad to make the examination as brief as possible.

All these people duly examined, their depositions read over to them, and signed by them, there was nothing more to be done but to ask the accused, Millicent Duke, what she had to say. She was informed that she was not obliged to speak, and was warned that whatever she might say would perhaps be hereafter used in evidence against her.

She told her awful story with a quiet coherence, which none there assembled had expected from her. She described her horror at the Captain's return, and the distracted state of her mind, which had been nigh

upon madness all that dreadful night. She stated, as
nearly as was in her power, the time at which she bade
him good night, and retired to the chamber farthest
from the garden room—the chamber which had been
her mother's. She grew a little confused here, when
asked what she had done with herself between that
time—a little after eleven o'clock—and the discovery
of the murder. She said that she thought she must
have sat, perhaps for hours, thinking of her troubles,
and half unconscious of the lapse of time. She told
how, by-and-by, in a passionate outburst of despair,
she thought of her father's old razors lying in that
very chamber within reach of her hands, and remembered how one deep gash in her throat might end all
her sorrow upon this earth. But the sight of the
murderous steel, and the remembrance of the sinful-
ness of such a deed, had changed her purpose as suddenly as that purpose had sprung up in her heart, and
she thrust the razor away from her in a wild hurry of
terror and remorse. Then—with but little questioning
and with quiet self-possession—she told how that other
purpose, almost as desperate as the first, had succeeded
it in her mind; and how she had determined to appeal
to George Duke, imploring of him to leave her, and to
suffer her to drag out her days in peace. How, eager
to act upon this last hope, she had gone straight to
his room, and there had found him lying murdered on
his bed. The justice asked her if she had gone close
up to the bedside to convince herself that the Captain
really was dead. No, she had lacked the courage to
do that; but she had seen the fearful gash across his
throat, the blood streaming from the open wound, and
she knew that he was dead.

She spoke slowly, faltering a little sometimes, but never embarrassed, though the clerk's pen followed her every word as unrelentingly as if he had been a recording angel writing the history of her sins, and too severe an angel to blot out the smallest of them with a tear. There had been a death-like silence in the room while she told her story, broken only by the scratching of the clerk's pen and the ticking of the solemn-faced clock.

"I will but ask you one more question, Mrs. Duke," said Montague Bowers; "and I beg you for your own sake to be careful how you answer it. Do you know of any person likely to have entertained a feeling of animosity against your husband?"

She might have replied that she knew nothing of her husband's habits, nor of his companions. He might have had a dozen enemies, whose names she had never heard, since his life had been altogether a mystery to her. But her simple and guileless mind was powerless to deal with the matter thus, and she only answered the question in its plainest meaning:

"No; no one."

"Think again, Mrs. Duke. This is a terrible business for you, and I would not for the world hurry you, or deprive you of the smallest opportunity of exculpating yourself. Do you know of no one who had any motive for wishing your husband's death?"

"No one," answered Millicent.

"Pardon me, Mr. Bowers," interrupted Darrell; "but my cousin forgets to tell you that the Captain of the Vulture was at the best a mysterious individual. He would never have been admitted into our family but for a whim of my poor uncle, who at the time of his daughter's marriage was scarcely accountable for his actions. No one in Compton knew who George Duke was, or where he came from, and no one but the late squire believed him when he declared himself to be a captain in His Majesty's navy. Six years ago I made it my business to ascertain the truth of that matter, and found that no such person as Captain George Duke had ever been heard of at the Admiralty. Whatever he was, nothing of his past life was known to either his wife or her relatives. My cousin Millicent is not, therefore, in a position to answer your question."

"Can you answer it, Mr. Markham?"

"No more than Mrs. Duke."

"I am sorry," said Mr. Bowers gravely, "very sorry; for under these circumstances my duty leaves me but one course. I shall be compelled to commit Millicent Duke to Carlisle gaol for the murder of her husband."

A woman's shriek vibrated through the chamber as these words were said, but it came from the lips of Sarah Pecker, and not from those of the accused. Calm as if she had been but a witness of the proceedings, Millicent comforted her old friend, imploring her not to give way to this passion of grief; for that Providence always set such things right in due time.

But Sarah was not to be comforted so easily. "No, Miss Millicent, no," she said; "Providence has suffered innocent people to be hung before this, and Heaven forgive us all for thinking so little about them! Heaven forgive us for thinking so little of the poor guiltless creatures who have died a shameful death! O, Mr. Darrell," exclaimed Sarah, with sudden energy, "speak, speak, Mr. Darrell dear; Samuel Pecker, speak, if you're not struck dumb and stupid, and tell his worship that of all the innocent creatures in the world, my old master's daughter is the most innocent; that of all the tender and pitiful hearts God ever made, hers is the most pitiful. Tell him that from her birth until this day her hand was never raised to harm the lowliest thing that lives; how much less, then, against a fellow-creature's life. Tell him this, Mr. Darrell, and he cannot have the heart to send my innocent darling to a felon's gaol."

Darrell Markham turned his face to the wall and sobbed aloud, nor did any of those present see anything unmanly in the proceeding. Even that recording angel, the clerk, was at length moved to compassion, and something very much like a tear dropped upon the closely written page of evidence lying before him. But whatever pity Mr. Montague Bowers might feel for the helpless girl, who awaited his will in all quiet patience and resignation, he held to the course which he considered his duty, and made out the warrant which was to commit Millicent Duke to Carlisle prison, there to await the spring assizes.

Millicent started when they told her that she would leave Compton for Carlisle as soon as the only post-chaise in Compton, which of course belonged to the inn and posting-house kept by Samuel Pecker, could be prepared for her; but she evinced no other surprise whatever. The written depositions were folded and locked in the justice's desk; the clerk retired; and the prisoner was left in the safe keeping of Hugh Martin and his fellow-constable, to await the coming of the postchaise which was to carry her the first stage of her dismal journey. Darrell and Sarah remained with

her to the last, only parting from her at the door of the
chaise. The young man took her in his arms before he
lifted her into the vehicle, and pressed his lips to her
cold forehead.

"Listen to me, Millicent, my beloved and my darling," he said, "and keep the memory of my words
with you in your trouble, for trust me they are no idle
promises. I dedicate my life to the solution of this
mystery. Remember this, Millicent, and fear nothing.
I have powerful friends, and can get all needful help
in the unravelling of this dark enigma. Trust me,
darling, trust me, and rest in peace. Think every
day that I am working for you; and sleep tranquilly
at night, knowing that even in the night my mind will
be busy planning the work of the morrow. The mystery shall be solved, darling, and speedily. Believe
this, and have no fear. And now, God bless you, my
own dear love, and farewell!"

He kissed her once more before he lifted her into
the vehicle. In the last glimpse which Darrell and
Sarah had of her, she was sitting quietly, with Hugh
Martin by her side, looking out at them through the
window of the chaise.

The dusky afternoon closed about the horses as they
galloped off; the wheels of the vehicle rolled away
through the snow as noiselessly as if it had been
some ghostly chariot drawn by spectral steeds; and
she was gone.

It was to be observed that neither Millicent Duke
nor the old woman, Mrs. Meggis, had made any allusion
to the stranger who called at the Hall a few hours
before the discovery of the murder. The truth was,
that this circumstance, being apparently unconnected

with the terrible event of the night, had been completely blotted out of the addled brain of the deaf housekeeper, as well as from the mind of Mrs. Duke.

CHAPTER XXI.

THE FOREIGN-LOOKING PEDLAR PAYS A SECOND VISIT TO THE BLACK BEAR.

THREE days after Millicent's removal to Carlisle, an unlooked-for visitor made his appearance at the Black Bear. This visitor was no less a personage than the West-country baronet, whom Sarah Pecker had last seen close against the doors of St. Mary's church, London.

This distinguished guest arrived in the dusk of evening by the Marley Water coach, alone and un-attended, but wrapped in a princely travelling cloak bedizened with fur, and wearing the flaxen wig and velvet coat, the glittering sword - hilt and military boots with clanking spurs, and all those braveries which had made such an impression at the Black Bear a short time before.

Striding straight up to the bar, where Samuel Pecker sat in an attitude of melancholy abstraction staring at the fire, the West-country baronet inquired if his friend Captain Duke had left any message for him.

Samuel, overpowered by the sudden mention of this name, which since the murder seemed to carry a ghastly significance of its own, had only strength to murmur a feeble negative.

" Then," said Captain Fanny, " I consider it d——d unhandsome of him ! "

He looked so fiercely at Samuel Pecker, that the landlord, being, as we know, of a nervous temperament, began to think that he might be in some way held accountable for Captain Duke's shortcomings, and felt himself called upon to apologize.

" Why, the truth of the matter is, sir," he stammered, faltering under the light of the West-country baronet's searching black eyes, " that when people have their throats cut in their sleep—no notice being given as to its going to be done—they're apt to leave these little matters unattended to."

" People have their throats cut in their sleep ! " echoed the highwayman. " What people ? Whose throat has been cut ? Speak, man, can't you ? "

" Don't be violent," said Samuel ; " please don't be violent. We've been a good deal shook by what's been going forward these last few days at Compton ; for there *are* shocks that the strongest constitution can't stand against. My wife Sarah keeps her bed ; and my nerves, never being overmuch, are of very little account just now. Give me time, and I'll explain everything."

" Give you time, man," cried Captain Fanny ; " can't you answer a plain question without beating about the bush for an hour ? Whose throat has been cut ? "

" Captain Duke's."

" Captain Duke has had his throat cut ? "

" From ear to ear ! "

" Where ?—when ? "

" At Compton Hall—on the night of his return."

" And that was——"

" Five nights ago."

" Good heavens! this is most extraordinary," exclaimed Captain Fanny. " George Duke returned five nights since, and murdered upon the very night of his return! But by whom—by whom?"

" Ah, there it is," cried Samuel Pecker piteously; " that's what has upset everybody at Compton, including Sarah, who took to her bed the day before yesterday, never before having been a day out of the business since she first set foot in the Black Bear, whereby there's everything at sixes and sevens, and Joseph, the waiter, always the most sober of men while Sarah kept the keys, drunk two nights running, and shedding tears about poor Mrs. Duke, as is now in Carlisle gaol."

" Mrs. Duke in Carlisle gaol?"

" Yes, for the murder of her husband, which never harmed a fly," said Samuel, with more sympathy than grammar.

" Mrs. Duke accused of her husband's murder?"

" Yes, poor dear! how should *she* do it,—a poor delicate creature with scarce strength in her wrist to carve a chicken, let alone a turkey? How should she do it, I should like to know; and if she did do it, where's the body? How can there be a murder without a body?" exclaimed Mr. Pecker, returning to that part of the question which had always been too much for him; " why, the very essence of a murder is the body. What is the worst inconvenience to the murderer? Why, the body! What leads to the discovery of the murder? Why, the body! What's the good of coroner's juries? Why, to sit upon the

body! Then how can there be a murder without a
body? It's my belief that Captain Duke is alive
and well, hiding somewhere — maybe nigh at hand
to this very place — and laughing in his sleeve to
think of his poor wife being suspected of making
away with him. He's wicked enough for it, and it
would be only like him to do it."

Captain Fanny was silent for a few moments, thinking deeply.

"Strange—strange—strange!" he said, rather to
himself than to the innkeeper; "some men are unlucky from the first, and that man was one of 'em.
Murdered on the night of his return; on the very
night on which he thought to have fallen into a
good thing. Strange!"

"Don't say murdered," remonstrated Samuel; "say
missing."

"Missing or murdered—it's pretty much the same,
if he never comes back, man. Then, supposing Mrs.
Duke to be tried and found guilty, the Compton Hall
property will go to the Crown?"

"I suppose it will," answered Samuel; "these sort
of things generally falls to the Crown. The Crown
must feel an uncommon interest in murders."

"Now, look you here, Samuel Pecker," said the
distinguished guest; "the best thing you can do is to
bring a bottle of decent Madeira with you, and show me
the way to a snug sitting-room, where you can tell me
all about this business."

The innkeeper desired nothing better than this.
He had sprung into popularity in a most sudden and
almost miraculous manner since the murder at Compton Hall, and that examination before Justice Bowers

in which he had played so prominent a part. And now he found himself called upon to relate the story of Captain Duke's disappearance to no less a person than the elegant West-country baronet, whose appearance was in itself enough to set the Black Bear in a flutter of excitement.

Samuel Pecker was perfectly correct in his description of that hostelry. It was indeed at sixes and sevens. Betty the cook abandoned herself to the current of popular feeling, and was flurried and uncertain in all her movements, thinking a great deal more of the murder than of her culinary operations, and making perpetual blunders in consequence, encouraging gossips and slovenly loitering women to hang about the kitchen of the Black Bear, wasting half an hour at a time talking to the carrier at the back door, and altogether falling into an idle slipshod way, utterly out of the ordinary course; while the waiter Joseph added his quota to the general confusion, by getting up in the morning in a maudlin and reflective stage of semi-intoxication, lurking about all day in strange corners, wiping dirty glasses upon a dirtier apron, breaking four or five articles of crockery-ware per diem, and going to bed early in the evening crying drunk. Sarah Pecker had been the keystone of this simple domestic arch; and without her the whole edifice fell to ruin. The honest creature, unable to bear up against that bitter parting with her old master's daughter, had taken to her bed, and lay there, refusing to be comforted.

Poor Sarah had no stronger mind on which to lean for consolation than that of her husband Samuel, for Darrell Markham had quitted the Black Bear upon the night of Millicent's removal from Compton, leaving a brief note addressed to Mrs. Pecker, and worded thus:

"DEAR SARAH,—I leave you on an errand which, I trust in Providence, may save my poor Millicent. Keep a good heart, and pray God to shield and comfort my afflicted darling.

"DARRELL MARKHAM."

Invalid though Mrs. Pecker was, she was not destined to remain long undisturbed; for upon the very night on which Sir Lovel Mortimer arrived at the Black Bear to keep that appointment with his friend, Captain Duke, which death had stepped in to break, there came another and equally unexpected visitor to the head inn of the quiet Cumbrian village.

Joseph the waiter, after weeping plentifully, and relating a new version of the occurrences of the night of the murder to a select party of listeners, content to hear him in the absence of his master, who was closeted all that evening with his distinguished guest in the white parlour—Joseph the waiter had bade good-night to the ordinary customers of the Black Bear, locked the doors, and retired to rest. The infallible clock upon the landing-place had struck eleven; Samuel and Captain Fanny were still drinking and talking in the sitting-room above-stairs; Sarah lay awake listening to the sign before the inn-door flapping to and fro in the night wind; and Betty the cook, waiting lest the distinguished visitor in the white parlour should require supper, sat by the fire in the kitchen, nodding every now and then over the grey worsted stocking she was trying to darn. Presently the hand armed with

the needle dropped by her side, her head fell forward
upon her ample bosom, and Betty the cook fairly gave
up the struggle and fell fast asleep.

She seemed to have enjoyed a slumber of some
hours, during which she had dreamed strange and
complicated dreams—amongst others, one wherein she
had headed a party of searchers, who found the body
of Captain George Duke standing bolt upright in the
little closet under the stairs of her grandmother's
cottage in a neighbouring village—when she was
awakened suddenly by a cautious tapping at the
kitchen door. The clock upon the stairs chimed the
quarter after eleven as she darted bolt upright in her
chair, and with her eyes fixed in a stare that was
almost apoplectic. It was only a quarter past eleven,
and the slumbers which had seemed to occupy hours
had only lasted twenty minutes.

Honest Betty's first impulse was to scream, as the
best thing to be done under all extraordinary circumstances; but remembering that this was no ordinary
time at the Black Bear, and that for the last five days
all sorts of strange visitors had been coming at all kind
of abnormal hours, she thought better of it, and going
to the door quietly, unbolted it and looked out. A
dark figure stood close against the threshold, so muffled
in the garments it wore, and so shrouded by the hat
slouched over its eyes, that, though there was a feeble
new moon shining faintly high above the roofs of
stables and outbuildings, the visitor, whoever he might
be, was not easily to be recognized. The heart of Betty
the cook sank within her; and a death-like chill, com-
mencing at that indispensable organ, crept slowly upwards to the roots of her hair.

It would have been some relief now to have screamed, but the capacity for that useful exercise was gone, and the terrified woman could only stand staring blankly at the figure on the threshold.

How, if this mysterious visitor should be that horrible shadow or double of Captain George Duke, which had appeared three times before the murder.

It had come, no doubt, to show the way to the hiding-place of the body, as is a common practice with the ghosts of murdered men, and it had selected Betty as the proper person to assist in the search.

Even in the agony of her terror, a vision of possible glory shaped itself in the mind of this simple country-woman, and she could but remember how she would doubtless rise in the estimation of all Compton after such an adventure. But as a humble-minded member of the corporation will refuse some civic honour, as a weight too ponderous for him to bear, so Betty, not feeling equal to the occasion, sacrificed the opportunity of future distinction, and sounded the prelude of a long scream.

Before she could get beyond this prelude a heavy hand was clapped upon her open mouth, and a gruff voice asked her what she meant by making such a d——d fool of herself.

Now as this is by no means the manner in which phantoms and apparitions are accustomed to conduct themselves—those shadowy folk generally confining themselves to polite pantomime and courteous beckonings towards the lonely places in which their business ordinarily lies—Betty took courage, and drawing a long breath of relief, asked her visitant what his business was, and if he wasn't ashamed of himself for turning a poor girl's "whole mask of blood." Not deigning to enter into any discussion on this remarkable physical operation, the stranger pushed the cook aside, and strode past her into the great kitchen, which was dimly lighted by the expiring fire and one guttering tallow candle.

Relieved from her first terror, Betty was now able to perceive that this mysterious stranger was a taller and a bigger man than George Duke, and that his figure bore no resemblance whatever to that of the murdered sailor.

He stood with his back to the hearth, slowly unwinding a great woollen shawl from his neck, when she followed him into the kitchen. This done, he threw off his hat, pushed his great hand through his short grizzled hair, and stared defiantly at the girl.

The stranger was the foreign-looking pedlar who had robbed Mrs. Pecker of her watch, purse, and silver spoons, in that very kitchen, six years before. Yes, he was the foreign-looking pedlar, but by no means the same prosperous individual he had appeared at that period. His hair, then hanging in sleek greasy blueblack ringlets, had lost its purple lustre, and was now coarse and grizzled, and cropped close to his head in a manner by no means becoming. His gaunt frame was strangely clad, his coat-sleeves torn from cuff to shoulder, only held together here and there by shreds of packthread, his dingy blue striped sailor's shirt hanging in rags upon his broad chest, which was protected by neither coat nor waistcoat, for the first-named garment was too much tattered to meet across his breast, and the last was altogether missing. One foot was

shod in a great leathern boot which came above the
wayfarer's knee, the other in an old shoe tied about
his naked ankle with rags and packthread. The pedlar
had been fat and comely to look upon six years before,
but now his massive frame was strangely wasted, the
torn coat and wretched shirt hanging loosely about a
bony angular form. No earrings now glistened in his
ears; no massive rings of rich barbaric gold adorned
his big muscular hands. A gaunt terrible half-starved
desperate-looking vagabond stood upon that hearth
where once had stood the smart and prosperous foreign
pedlar.

Betty was preparing to begin scream number two
when the intruder thrust his hand suddenly into his
pocket, and taking thence a great clasp-knife, exclaimed
fiercely,—

"As sure as I do stand here, woman, if you lift your
voice above a whisper, I'll put such a mark upon that
wizen of yours as will stop your noise for ever."

He opened the knife with a sharp snap, like the report of a miniature pistol, and looked admiringly at the
weapon—not as if he were thinking of it in connection
with the particular threat he had just enunciated, but
rather as if he were reflecting what a handy thing it
was in a general way. Then remembering himself, he
shut the knife with a second sharp snap, dropped it into
his capacious pocket, and looked again at the cook.

"Sit you down there," he said, pointing to the chair
upon which Betty had dropped her work when she rose
to open the door. "Sit you down there, my lass, and
answer the questions I've got to ask—or——" He
thrust his hand back into his pocket, by way of a finish
to his sentence.

Betty dropped into the chair indicated as submissively as if she had been before Mr. Montague Bowers, justice of the peace.

"Where's your missus, my lass?" asked the pedlar.

"Ill abed."

"And your master?"

Betty described Samuel's whereabouts.

"So," muttered the man, "your missus is ill abed, and your master is in the white parlour, a-drinking wine with a gentleman. What gentleman?"

Betty was not particularly good at remembering names; but after considerable reflection, she said that the gentleman was called Sir Lovel Summat.

The pedlar burst into a big laugh—a harsh and hungry kind of cachinnation, which seemed to come from a half-starved frame—a hoarse grating noise, as of human machinery which had grown rusty and out of order.

"Sir Lovel Summat," he said, "it isn't Mortimer, is it?"

"Yes, it is," replied Betty.

The pedlar laughed again.

"Sir Lovel Mortimer, is it? Well, that's strange! Very strange, that of all nights out of three hundred and sixty odd as go to a year, Sir Lovel should pick this night for being at Compton-on-the-Moor. Has he often been here before?"

"Never but once; and that were last Christmas. He's a rare riotous gentleman, but pleasant-spoken, and uncommon free with his money," said Betty, emboldened by the pedlar's hoarse laughter. The cookmaid had never heard of that class of assassins who can "murder while they smile," and fancied herself safe, now that the pedlar was disposed to be conversational.

"Uncommon free with his money, is he?" repeated the tramp. "He's a lucky dog to have money to buy folks' good word. And he's here to night? It's a strange world. I know Sir Lovel Mortimer; and Sir Lovel Mortimer knows me—intimately."

Betty looked rather incredulous at this assertion.

"Ay, you may stare, my lass," muttered the pedlar; "but it's gospel truth for all that. I suppose this barrownight of yours wears a fine gold-laced coat now, don't he?"

"It's silver lace," the girl answered; "and the handle of his sword shines like diamonds; and his eyes is blacker than his boots and brighter than the buckles in his lace cravat; and ain't he a daring one too!" added Betty, recalling a skirmish she had had with Captain Fanny in a dark passage on the occasion of that gentleman having attempted to kiss her.

"O, he's a daring one, is he?" growled the stranger. "I'm afraid his daring will carry him a step too far one of these days, if he don't take care what he's about, and not make ill-friends with those that can blow him—ay, and has the will to do it, if he turns contrairy. I suppose he's in high feather, eh, my lass?"

Betty stared at him vaguely. The figure of speech was beyond her comprehension.

"He's in the white parlour," she said, "along with master."

"Look you here, missus cook," said the pedlar; "talking's poor work on an empty stomach, and I haven't had a mouthful to put into mine since the break of this cold winter's day; so I'll trouble you for a bit of victuals and a drop of drink before we go on any further."

Seeing something like hesitation in the girl's face, he brought his hand heavily down on the table with a terrible oath.

"Fetch me what I want!" he roared; "d'ye hear? Do you think there's anything in *this* house that I can't have for the asking?"

In her confusion and terror Betty brought a strange selection of food from the well-stocked pantry. She disappeared for a few minutes, during which she could hear the terrible guest growling threateningly in the kitchen, and then she came back to the hungry stranger laden with a cold sirloin, the carcase of a chicken which had been cooked for Captain Fanny's dinner, a couple of raw onions, a bunch of dried herbs, half a jam tart, and a lump of fat bacon. But the pedlar had no mind to be critical. He pounced like some ravenous beast upon the viands set before him, hacking great slices off the joint with his clasp-knife, and not waiting for so much as a grain of salt to give relish to his food. He ate with such savage rapidity that his meal lasted a very short time, and then, after pushing the dish away from him with a satisfied grunt, he gasped fiercely the one word, "Brandy."

Betty shook her head. She explained to nim that drink of any kind was impossible, as the bar was locked and the key in her master's possession.

"You're a nice hospitable lot of people," said the pedlar, rubbing his hand across his greasy mouth "Now look you here: it's double business that has brought me all the way from the county of Hampshire to Compton-on-the-Moor, tramping through frost and snow, and sleeping under haystacks and in empty barns, until I've been as nigh being froze to death as ever a man was that lived to tell of it. That business is first and foremost to see your missus; and secondly, to meet a friend as I parted company with above a fortnight back, and as promised to meet me here, but I expect I've got here before him. Now that friend is a gentleman bred and born, and his name is Cap'en George Duke, of the Vulture."

Betty the cook clasped her hands imploringly.

"Don't!" she cried, "don't! This makes two this blessed night; for him as is upstairs said he came here by appointment with the murdered gentleman."

"What murdered gentleman?"

Betty told the story which had been so often told within the last five days. She told it in rather a gasping and unintelligible manner, but still with sufficient clearness to make the pedlar acquainted with the one great fact of the Captain's murder.

"His throat cut from ear to ear on the very same night as he came back," said the man; "that's an awkward business. He'd better have stopped where he was, I reckon. So there was no money took nor plate, and his pretty young wife is in Carlisle gaol for the murder. That's a queer story. I always thought that George Duke had the devil's luck and his own too, but it seems that his luck and the devil both failed him at last."

Now the reader may perhaps remember that, on the hearing of the murder, Captain Fanny had made an

S

observation to the effect that the murdered man had been an unlucky fellow from first to last; whereby it may be perceived how very widely the opinions of two people may differ upon a given subject.

" So Cap'en Duke is murdered—a bad look-out for me !" muttered the pedlar ; " for I had a hold upon my gentleman as would have made his house mine and his purse mine to the end of my days. I'd best see your missus, without losing any more time, my lass. Is her room anywhere nigh the parlour where your master and the barrownight's a-sittin' ? "

" No ; missus's room is at the other end of the corridor."

" Then go and tell her that him as come here six winters ago, and took the little present as she was kind enough to give him, has come back, and wants to see her without loss of time."

Sarah Pecker lay awake, with a great family Bible open upon the table by her bed. She lifted her head from the pillow as Betty ran, breathless, into the room, for she saw from the girl's face that something had happened.

" Again !" she cried, when the cook had told her of the man waiting below ; "again! How cruel, how cruel, that *he* should come at such a time as this ; when my mind is full of the thoughts of poor Miss Millicent, and when I've been praying night and day for something to happen to clear her dear name. It does seem hard."

" There's many things in this life that seems hard," said a voice close against the half-open door, as the gaunt pedlar strode unceremoniously into the room. " Starvation's hard, and a long tramp through the snow with scarce a shoe to your foot is hard, and many things more as I could mention. You may go, young woman," he added, addressing himself to Betty, and pointing to the door, "you may go; and remember that what I've got to say is more interesting to your missus than to you, so you've no need to listen outside; but just keep a look-out, and give us warning if either your master or his guest leave the white parlour. You understand; so go."

Lest, after all, she should fail in comprehending him, the pedlar laid his rough hand upon that particular part of Mistress Betty's anatomy commonly called the scruff of the neck, and put her outside the room. This done, he locked the door, walked across the chamber, and seated himself deliberately in an arm-chair by the sick woman's bed.

"Well, Mistress Sally," he said, staring about the room as he addressed Mrs. Pecker, as if looking for any articles of value that might lurk here and there in the shadowy light; "I suppose you scarcely looked to see me in such trim as this?"

He held up his gaunt arm and shook the torn coat-sleeve and the wretched rags of linen, to draw her attention to the state of his garments.

"I scarcely looked to see you at all after these six years," Sarah answered, meekly.

"O, you didn't, didn't you, mistress?—Mistress Pecker, as I believe they call you hereabouts? No thanks to you for the compliment you paid my good sense. You thought that, after happening to come by chance into this part of the country, and finding you living in clover in this place, with money put by in the bank maybe, and silver plate, and good victuals, and prime old wine, and the Lord knows what—you thought I was such a precious fool, after seein' all this, as to take about fifteen poundworth of property, and go away contented, and stay away for six year. You thought all that, did you, my lady ? "

People had called Sarah Pecker a shrew. If they could have seen the white entreating face turned towards the stranger, the hand lifted with such an appealing gesture, they might perhaps have altered their opinion of her.

"I thought," she said, falteringly—"I thought you might be pitiful enough, knowing what I had suffered from you in years gone by, and seeing that it had pleased Providence to give me peace and comfort at last—I thought even your hard heart might have taken compassion upon me, and that you would have been content to take all I had to give and to have gone quietly away for ever."

The pedlar looked at her with a fierce scornful smile. He lifted his arm for the second time, and this time he pushed back the rags and showed his wasted flesh.

"Does this look like as if I should have much compassion on *you* ? " he cried savagely—"on *you*, wallowing here in comfort and luxury, with good feed to eat and good wine to drink, and fires to warm you, and clothes to wear, and money in your pocket? Why, if I was to sit here from now till daylight talking to you, I could never make you understand what I've passed through in the six infernal years since I last came to this place."

"You've been away at sea ?"

"Never you mind where I've been. I haven't been

where men learn pitifulness, and compassion, and such fine sentiments as you've just been talking of. I've been where men are treated worse than dogs, and where they learn to *be* worse than the fiercest bloodhound that ever turned against his master. I've been where human beings are more dangerous to each other than savage beasts; where men use their knives oftener than their tongues; and where, if ever there was a bit of love or pity in a poor wretch's heart, it gets trampled out and changed to hate. That's where I've been."

"And you've come here to me to ask for money," said Sarah, looking shudderingly at the man's gloomy desperate face.

"Yes."

"How much will satisfy you?"

"A hundred pound."

She shook her head despairingly.

"I haven't thirty," she said; "every farthing I own in the world is in that box yonder on the chest of drawers with the brass handles. The key's in the pocket of the gown that's hanging on the bed-post. You can take what there is, and welcome; but I've no more."

"But you can get more," answered the man; "you can ask Mr. Samuel Pecker."

"No, no!"

"You won't ask him?"

"Not for one penny."

"Very good, mistress; then I will. I'll ask him fast enough; and if he sets any value on his faithful wife, he'll give me what I ask, when I tell him——"

"O, Thomas, Thomas!"

She raised her hands imploringly, and clung about the man as if to stop him from uttering some dreaded word; but he flung her back upon the pillow.

"I'll tell him that I'm your lawful husband, Thomas Masterson; and that at one word from me you'll have to pack out of this house, and tramp wherever I please to take you."

For a moment poor Sally lay back upon the pillow, her whole frame convulsed by tempestuous sobs. Then suddenly raising herself, she looked the man full in the face, and said deliberately,—

"Tell him, then, Thomas Masterson! Tell him as how you're my lawful husband as deceived and deluded me when I was a poor ignorant girl—as beat and half-starved me—as took me away from friends and home. Tell him that you're my lawful husband, as stole my dear and only child away from me while I was asleep, and as stayed away for seventeen long years, to come back at the last and claim me when I was a good man's happy wife, not for any love of me, but with the hope to rob my true and faithful husband of his money. Tell him that you're Thomas Masterson, smuggler and thief. But let me tell you first, that if you dare to come between him and me, I'll bring those up against you as will make you pay a dear price for your cruelty."

The pedlar tried to laugh at this speech, but failed signally in the attempt.

"You've your old high spirit, Mrs. Sarah," he said; "and even sickness hasn't taken it out of you. You won't ask Samuel Pecker for the money?"

"Not for one farthing."

"Suppose I had a secret to sell, and wanted a hundred pounds for the price of it, would you raise the money?"

"A secret?"

"Yes. You spoke just now of your son, as you were so uncommon fond of. Suppose I could tell you where he is—within easy reach of you—would you give me a hundred pounds for the information?"

Sarah shook her head mournfully.

"I know you, Thomas Masterson," she said; "it's poor work to try and deceive me."

"Look here," answered the pedlar; "you're uncommon suspicious to-night; but I know if you take your Bible oath you won't break it. Swear to me upon this book, that if I tell you where your son is, and bring him and you together, you'll let me have the hundred pounds within a week."

He closed the Bible and placed it in her hands : she pressed her lips upon the cover of the volume.

"I swear," she said, "by this blessed book."

"Very good. Your son is now sitting with Samuel Pecker in the parlour at the other end of the corridor. He calls himself Sir Lovel Mortimer, and a very dashing gallant fine-spoken gentleman he is ; but his friends, companions, and the Bow Street runners call him Captain Fanny, and he is one of the most notorious highwaymen who ever played fast and loose with Jack Ketch."

CHAPTER XXII.

MOTHER AND SON.

SAMUEL PECKER and his guest, seated over their wine in the white parlour, between the hours of eleven and twelve, were startled by the violent ringing of the bell communicating with Sarah's bedchamber. Samuel was too good a husband not to recognize the vibration of that particular bell; and Samuel was too true to the instincts of the past not to quail a little as he heard it. Without stopping to apologize to his distinguished visitor, he hurried from the room and along the corridor to Sarah's chamber. The pedlar had left this apartment under the convoy of Betty, who had been ordered by Mrs. Pecker to find the gaunt-looking wanderer sleeping room in one of the garrets in the roof, or in some loft over the stable.

Sarah was alone, therefore, when the landlord entered the room in answer to the loud summons of the bell.

" Samuel," she said, clasping her hands upon her forehead, as if to steady the bewilderment of the brain within, " have I been mad or dreaming? Who have you yonder in the white parlour ? "

" The gentleman that came at Christmas, Sarah; the gentleman——"

" The eyes—the restless, restless black eyes, like **my** baby's," cried Sarah, in a voice that was almost a shriek. " I ought to have known him by his eyes. I ought **to** have known——"

Her terrified husband thought that she was raving in some paroxysm of delirium.

"Sarah," he said—"Sarah, what is it?"

"The eyes," she repeated—"the eyes of the child you've heard me tell of; the child I lost long before I knew you, Samuel; the child whose cruel father was my first husband, Thomas Masterson."

"But what of him to-night, Sarah?"

"Ay, what of him to-night?" she repeated wildly, pushing the hair off her forehead with both her feverish hands; "what of him to-night? Who is there in the white parlour?"

"Sir Lovel Mortimer," answered Samuel, more and more convinced that his wife was distraught by the fever.

"Sir Lovel Mortimer, known to his friends, companions, and the Bow Street runners as Captain Fanny," said Sarah slowly, repeating the words of Thomas Masterson; "let me see him."

Samuel stared aghast.

"Let me see him," she repeated.

"See him—Sir Lovel Mortimer—the West-country baronet?"

"The youth with the black eyes; the poor unhappy boy; the——Let me see him, let me see him."

Samuel shrugged his shoulders hopelessly. We know that he was a simple and faithful creature. If his sick wife had asked him to carry the moon to her bedside, he would, no doubt, have made some feeble attempt to gratify her. It was a small thing, then, to shuffle along the corridor and request the baronet to visit the invalid's chamber. Sir Lovel might, perhaps, be skilled in blood-letting and pharmacy, as some country gentlemen were in those days, thought the landlord, and he might be able to reduce this terrible fever and delirium. Samuel accordingly did as his wife bade him, and went and brought the West-country baronet to her chamber.

It did indeed seem as if his presence had some soothing influence upon the sick woman, for Sarah quietly motioned him to a seat by her bedside, and then turning with a white but tranquil face to Samuel Pecker, bade him leave the room.

Being left alone with the young highwayman, she lay perfectly still for some moments, looking—ah, Heaven only knows with what vague maternal love and yearning!—at the sharp profile of that young face, worn thin by many a midnight brawl and revel, until at last the restless gentleman fairly lost patience.

"I don't suppose you sent for me for the pleasure of staring at me, ma'rm," he said. "I'm no ill-looking fellow, perhaps; but I'm not like the waxen images in Westminster Abbey, only good to be looked at. It's getting late, and I've had a weary day of it," he added, with a yawn: "have you nothing to say to me?"

"I have heard ill news to-night," said Sarah, slowly; "sorrowful news of an only child that I thought was dead and gone."

Captain Fanny made no reply. He thought the speaker's wits were bewildered, and that it was best to let her have her say without making any attempt to question or contradict her. But the next words she uttered brought the blood to his face and set his heart (which was not that of a coward) beating at a gallop.

"There has been one here to-night," she said, "who has told me who and what you are."

Who and what he was! This sick woman, in this lonely wayside inn, in a quiet Cumbrian village, where he thought himself safe in playing the baronet and fine gentleman—safe in hiding from the justice that was rarely off his track—this feeble woman knew him and might denounce him. From his very boyhood his life had been a game of fast and loose with the gallows, and after those few brief heart-beats of surprise he recovered himself and was able to make light of the danger.

"You know me?"

"Yes; you are a highwayman, and they call you Captain Fanny."

He clutched her wrist in his thin nervous hand.

"You'll not peach upon me?"

She shook her head, looking at him with a mournful smile.

"Of all the creatures on this wide earth," she said, "I should be the last to do that."

"Not that it would so much matter," he muttered, speaking not to Sarah, but to himself. "A few months —maybe a few weeks—more or less. It wouldn't matter, if it wasn't for Jack Ketch. I'd rather make an end of it quietly, without the help of the hangman."

"Henry Masterson," said the sick woman, "tell me where and how your life has been spent."

She called the young highwayman by a name which he had not heard for seventeen years, and the faint hectic flush faded away from his hollow cheeks, leaving them white as the coverlet upon Sarah's bed.

"You wonder that I know your name," said Mrs. Pecker; "but, O, my boy, my boy, the wonder was that when I saw you this Christmas lately past, I did not guess the reason of my trouble at the sight of you. As if there could be but one reason for that trouble! As if there could be more than one face in all the world to set my heart a-beating as it beat that night! As if I could feel what I felt then at sight of any face but one, and that the one that was a baby's face four-and-twenty years ago, and looked up at me out of my own baby's cradle."

The young man drew his breath in short fierce gasps, and turning suddenly upon Sarah, spoke to her in a thick husky voice.

"What do you mean?" he said; "what do you mean? I have heard my father say that I was born in Cumberland, and that he deserted my mother, carrying me away with him when I was but a child in arms. What is it you mean by this wild talk?"

The Bible, which Sarah had kissed a short time before, lay open on the table by the bedside. She stretched out her hand and laid it upon the page, as she said solemnly,—

"I mean, Henry Masterson, that *I* was the wretched wife and mother whom that bad man deserted, and that you are my only child."

The young man dropped his head upon the coverlet and sobbed aloud, his mother weeping over him and caressing him all the while with unspeakable tenderness.

"My boy! my boy!" she cried; "have they told me the truth? Is it true——"

"That I am a thief and a highwayman? Yes, mother; and that I have never been honest since my babyhood, or lived with honest people since I can remember.
My father cuffed me and beat me, and half-starved me
and neglected me, and left me for days and days together in some wretched den, while he sought his own
fortune, and well-nigh forgot that such a creature as his
son lived upon the earth: but he did not forget to teach
me to steal, and I was quick to learn my lesson. I ran
away from him when I was ten years old, and lived with
gipsies and tramps, and thieves and vagabonds and beggars, till I was cleverer at all their wicked businesses
than those that were three times my age; and they
made much of me and pampered me for my pretty looks
and my cleverness, till I left them for a higher way of
life, and fell in with a man who was my master first
and my servant afterwards; but who, from first to last,
was the one to stifle every whisper of conscience and to
laugh at any hope I ever had of being a better man.
The history of my life would fill twenty volumes, mother, but you might read the moral of it in three lines.
It's been a straight race for the gallows from beginning
to end."

He had lifted his head to say all this. The tears
he had shed were already half dried by the fever of his
flushed cheeks, and his eyes glittered with a burning
light.

"Tell me, my boy," said Sarah, clinging fondly about
this new-found son, "tell me, is there any danger—
any danger *for your life?*"

He shook his head mournfully.

"I've never cared much how or when I risked it,"
he answered. "I've well-nigh thrown it away for a

wager before this; but I feel to-night as if I should like to keep it for your sake, mother."

"And is there any danger?"

"Every danger, if they scent out my whereabouts just yet awhile. But if I can only cheat the gallows for two months longer, Master Jack Ketch will be cozened of his dues."

"As how, my darling?"

"Because a learned physician in London told me a couple of weeks ago, after sounding my chest and knocking me about till I was fairly out of patience, that my lungs are for the most part gone, and that I have not three months to live."

Sarah looked in his face; and in the hollow wasted cheeks, the parched lips, burnt pale with fever, the glassy lustre of the great black eyes, the pinched and sharpened aspect of every feature, she saw the signs and tokens from which it needed no physician's skill to read the dismal verdict—Death.

CHAPTER XXIII.

THE FINDING OF THE BODY.

THE body of George Duke was found.

Nigh upon two months had passed since that January night on which Millicent Duke rushed half distraught into the hall at the Black Bear to tell her horrible story; for nigh upon two months the unhappy lady had languished in Carlisle gaol, waiting the spring assizes, and the assembling of those grave and learned gentlemen, and those wise and honourable jurymen,

who were to decide whether that feeble hand had been
lifted to destroy the life of a fellow-creature.

The Captain's body was found in a dismal pond
behind the stables at Compton Hall. How the hiding-
place had come to be overlooked in that general search
which had been made immediately after the murder,
no one was able to say. Every man who had assisted
in that search declared emphatically that he had looked
everywhere; and yet it seemed clear enough that no
one had looked here; for, as the end of March drew
nigh, and the inhabitants of Compton were busy talking of Mrs. Duke's approaching trial, the draught-
horses on the Compton Hall farm refused to drink the
stagnant water of this pool, and a vile miasma rising
from its shallow bosom set the slow brains of the farm-
labourers at work to discover the cause of the mischief.
A dismal horror was brought to the light of day
by this search. The body of a man, rotted out of
all semblance to humanity, was found lying at the
bottom of that stagnant pool, as it had doubtless lain
ever since that night in January when the falling
snow blotted out the traces of the murderer's feet,
and fell like a sheltering curtain upon the footsteps of
crime.

The stable-yard lay behind the prim flower-beds
and straight walks of the little pleasure-ground below
the garden chamber in which George Duke had been
murdered. Between the stable-yard and this neglected
flower garden there was no barrier but a quickset
hedge and a little wicket-gate. From this gate to
the pond behind the stables the distance was about
thirty yards.

It was a likely enough place, therefore, for the murderer to choose for the concealment of his victim; but whoever had dragged the body of George Duke from the garden chamber to this pool, must have had another task to perform before his hideous work was done. Every piece of water in Compton had been frozen over on that January night; so the murderer must have broken a hole in the ice before throwing the body into the pond; and this hole being frozen over the next morning by daybreak, and the pond, moreover, being thickly covered with a bed of snow, it was scarcely so strange that those who searched for the body should have overlooked this hiding-place.

The remains were carried into one of the empty chambers in Compton Hall, and a coroner's inquest was there held upon them.

The particulars of the murder were already so well know to all present that there was no need to reca- ·
pitulate them.   So there was little evidence to be heard, except such brief statements as were made by the farm-labourers relative to the finding of the body.

No one seemed for an instant to entertain a doubt that this was the body of George Duke, although there was little enough about these decomposed remains by which to prove identity.   The few rotting rags of clothing still hanging about the corpse consisted only of the shreds of a shirt, breeches, and stockings. There was no trace of the shabby coat with the naval buttons, the three-cornered hat, waistcoat, and boots which the Captain had worn on the night of his return to Compton.   Yet these things had disappeared at the time of the murder.

The coroner's jury took no pains to unravel this branch of the dismal mystery.   Neither did they puzzle themselves by attempting to understand how feeble Millicent Duke could have contrived to drag the body of a strong man from the garden chamber to the pond behind the stables. Justice in those days did her work briefly enough. The coroner's jury pronounced a verdict to the effect that a body—supposed to be the missing body of George Duke—had been found in a pond on the premises belonging to Compton Hall.

Two months had passed since Millicent's examination before Mr. Justice Bowers, and nothing had been seen of Darrell Markham. Brief letters came now and then for Sarah Pecker, telling her how the young man was hard at work for the good of his cousin; but each of these letters was less hopeful that the last, and Sarah began to despair of any help from that quarter for the hapless prisoner languishing in Carlisle gaol.

Sarah had travelled to that city several times to see her old master's daughter, and on every occasion had found Mrs. Duke equally calm and resigned. She was pale and thin and faded, it is true, but less altered than Sally had thought to find her by this long imprisonment.

Once, and once only, Millicent uttered some words that struck a shivering horror to the very heart of the stener.

It was towards the close of her dreary incarceration that Mrs. Duke thus terrified her honest-hearted friend. Sarah had been reading Darrell's last letter—in which, though evidently wrestling hard with despair, he promised that he would labour to the very death to clear his cousin's name—when Millicent began wringing her hands and crying mournfully :

"Why does Darrell take this trouble for me? Let

the worst that can befall me; I am prepared to suffer
my fate with patience.   And after all, Sarah—after all,
who can tell that I am really guiltless of George Duke's
blood?"

"Miss Millicent!—Miss Millicent!"

"Who can tell?   I know that I was nigh upon
being distraught that cruel night on which my husband
came home.   The magistrate asked me what I was
doing in all those hours that I was alone in my room,
and I could not tell him.   My mind was distraught,
and I had no memory of that time.   Who knows if it
may not be, as Mr. Bowers thinks, that I killed George
Duke in a paroxysm of madness?   Heaven knows I was
close enough to madness that night."

Sarah Pecker fell upon her knees at the feet of Mrs.
Duke.

"O, Miss Milly!" she cried, "for pity's sake—for
the sake of the merciful God who looks down upon you
and sees your helplessness, do not utter these horrible
words.   Do you know that to say in the court of justice
one week hence what you have said to me this day,
would be to doom yourself to certain death?   *I* know,
Miss Millicent, that you are innocent, and *you* know it
too.   Never, never, never let that thought leave your
brain ; for when it does, you will be mad!   Remember,
whatever others may think of you—however the wisest
in the land may judge you—remember through all,
and until death—if death must come—that you are
innocent!"

Sarah Pecker did not content herself with this adjuration, she waited upon the governor of the gaol, and
being admitted to his presence, implored of him that he
would place some kind and discreet woman in the cell

with Mrs. Duke as nurse or watcher, for that the poor lady was in danger of losing her wits from the effects of long and solitary confinement. " I would ask leave to stay with her myself, poor darling," Sarah said, " but that I have one lying ill at home whose days are well nigh numbered."

Mrs. Pecker spoke with a heartfelt energy that carried conviction with it; and although those were no great days for mercy, and though the glorious fiction of the law which pretends to hold a man innocent until the hour of his condemnation, was then little attended to, the governor acceded to Sarah's prayer, and a woman (herself doing penance for some petty offence) was placed with Millicent to lighten the horrors of her cell.

That modern saint and martyr, John Howard, had not yet shed the light of his noble intellect upon the darkness of the felon's gaol, and in those days a prison was indeed a den of wretchedness and despair, an earthly Inferno, in which guilty creatures suffered tortures that may, perhaps, have been sometimes accepted by a merciful Heaven as an expiation of their crimes.

Sarah had her hands full of trouble this melancholy spring. She had told so much of her son's story as she could safely venture to reveal to Samuel Pecker. She had informed that honest creature that the pedlar was the brother of her dead husband, Thomas Masterson, and had given him very little information about her son's delinquencies. She also told Mr. Pecker that which is apt to soften the sternest of us towards the sinning—she told him that whatever Henry Masterson's failings might have been, he would soon be beyond the chance of making any earthly atonement for them, and before a Judge who is wiser, and yet more pitiful, than any justice of the peace in the county of Cumberland, or on the face of the wide earth.

So, simple and soft-hearted Samuel Pecker opened his arms to the dying son of the vagabond Thomas Masterson ; and the worthy Thomas, having enjoyed a good night's rest and a hearty breakfast, strode away in the dusky dawn of the February day ; after leaving behind him a message for Mrs. Pecker, to the effect that he should return before the week was out to fetch that little matter they had talked about.

Betty delivered this message with laudable accuracy, and Mrs. Pecker fully understood that the little matter in question was the hundred pounds she had promised as the price of the pedlar's secret. She obtained the sum with little difficulty from her confiding husband, who went by coach to the market town one afternoon within the week, to draw the money from the bank. But it happened that on that very afternoon Thomas Masterson, dressed in a new suit, bought by him out of a handful of ready cash obtained from Sarah on the night of their interview, swaggered through the High Street of the same market town, and was betrayed into the natural weakness of putting his big hand into somebody else's pocket. Whether from long residence in a foreign land and want of practice in the art, I know not, but Thomas on that particular afternoon was so very far from up to the mark in his performance, that he was caught in the act by his intended victim, and delivered over to the constables, who handed him on to Carlisle gaol to await his trial at the ensuing assizes, with many other culprits of the same calibre.

This unfortunate circumstance of course hindered Mr. Masterson from appearing to claim the reward promised by Sarah ; and the worthy woman, after living for several days and nights in perpetual dread of his arrival, began to hope that some happy chance had befallen to send him out of her way.

She had enough to do in watching by the sick-bed of her son, who lay in a comfortable garret chamber under the gabled roof of the Black Bear, and whose whereabouts were known to none but his mother, Samuel Pecker, and the doctor who attended upon him.

The brilliant Sir Lovel Mortimer—the notorious Captain Fanny—could scarcely have had a safer hiding-place than the garret chamber in this old inn. Bow Street had grown weary of counting on the reward which was offered for his capture. His old comrades— fine fellows, of course, every one of them, but any one of whom might, in some unlucky moment, have taken it into his head to turn king's evidence—had entirely lost sight of him ; and it seemed almost as if the highwayman had dropped out of the troubled sea of human life and crime, without leaving so much as a bubble to mark the spot where he had gone down.

CHAPTER XXIV.

THE TRIAL OF MILLICENT DUKE.

DARRELL MARKHAM had not 'been idle. The noble
Scottish gentleman whom he served was ready to give
him all help in his hour of need, and three days after
the examination before Mr. Montague Bowers, the case
of Millicent Duke was in the hands of the most distinguished criminal lawyers of the day. Busy Bow Street
runners—better known as Robin-redbreasts—had been
placed upon the scent; but look which way they would
at the case it had an equally sinister aspect.

Endeavours to throw light upon the antecedents of
George Duke resulted in the discovery that the Captain
of the Vulture had well deserved the worst fate that
could befall him. Inquiries, which occupied much time
and caused a great deal of trouble in the making,
revealed the fact that the good ship Vulture had been
seized and burnt by a vessel belonging to the French
Government off the coast of Barbary; and that her
captain, George Duke, together with his first mate, one
Thomas Masterson, had been sent to the galleys by the
same French Government as slavers, pirates, and suspected assassins; from which dismal captivity they had
escaped in conjunction upon the first of January last
past.

The attorney employed by Darrell Markham for the
preparation of his cousin's defence deemed it expedient
to discover the whereabouts of this very Thomas Masterson, in the hope that some clue to the mystery might
be extracted from this, the familiar companion of the
murdered man.

An advertisement, inserted several times in the *London Gazette,* resulted in a letter from the governor of Carlisle gaol, containing the information that this man, Thomas Masterson, was confined in that prison for some petty theft, awaiting his trial at the same assizes which were to decide the fate of Mrs. George Duke.

One of the best men at the Old Bailey was retained for Millicent's defence by the solicitors intrusted with the case. Darrell Markham implored the worthy gentlemen to spare neither trouble nor money in compassing the acquittal of his unhappy cousin ; but the advocate, shook his head over the contents of his brief, and freely told Mr. Markham that he saw but little hope in the dreary business.

So, on the eve of Millicent's trial, the northern mail carried Darrell Markham to the city of Carlisle, where he met Mr. Pauncet, the solicitor, and Mr. Horace Weldon, barrister-at-law, who went circuit on horseback, according to the fashion of those days, and who was quartered with his fraternity at the chief inn. Darrell looked sadly at the great grim court-house, past which the coach carried him, remembering how upon the terrible morrow a delicate woman of seven-and-twenty years of age was to be within those walls charged with the crime of wilful murder.

The eve of the trial brought Sarah Pecker from the bedside of her dying son. The poor woman came to Carlisle attended by Samuel, who was one of the witnesses for the Crown, and whose brain was well-nigh turned by the responsibilities of his position.

The cold March sunshine lighted up every corner of

the crowded court when Millicent Duke was led to her place in the criminal dock to answer to the charge of murder. She had been brought so low in health by her long imprisonment, that her custodians, out of pity for her weak state, allowed her to sit throughout the proceedings.

Fifty years after that day there were people living in Carlisle who could tell of the pale golden head, lighted by the faint spring sunshine, and the delicate face, worn and wasted by trial and suffering, but very beautiful in its white tranquillity.

"Not guilty!"

The clear and silver tones in which those two words were spoken penetrated to the farthest corner of the court. There was a general conviction amongst those present that this feeble woman had actually committed the horrible crime of which she had been accused. The belief in witchcraft had not yet died out in that far northern county. Who could say that this fair woman, sitting there in such almost superhuman tranquillity, was not supported through her trial by the evil one himself? Her very youth and beauty were used to her prejudice by the simple north-country folk. Had not such as she been burned at the stake for offences very similar to the murder of George Duke? and who but the devil or his imps could have given her power to do the deed, and to carry the body of her husband down a flight of stone steps and over nigh upon forty yards of ground? For it was a notable feature of this wise and popular belief that the more incredible—nay, impossible —was the crime supposed to have been committed, the more determined people were in their conviction of the guilt of the accused.

The evidence given by the witnesses for the prosecution was much the same as that already recited before Mr. Montague Bowers. Again Samuel Pecker became vague and obscure as to the identity of George Duke of the Vulture with that ghost, or shadow, which had appeared at three divers times to three separate individuals in the course of seven years.

The story of the ghost was listened to with breathless interest by the country folk ; but there was nothing to be made of it that could throw any light upon the foul murder which had been done at Compton Hall.

Samuel Pecker, under a rigorous examination, faithfully narrated the first appearance of the shadow in the cold twilight of the October evening, and went on to tell how the same ghostly shade had been met three months afterwards on the pier at Marley Water by the prisoner at the bar, and how the shadow had again appeared upon the very night of the murder, bringing with it a horse of lean condition, but of actual flesh and blood; which horse had been afterwards fetched away from the Black Bear by a morose stable-lad, who refused to tell whence or from whom he came, but who paid the money due for the animal's keep, mounted him, and rode away.

All this savoured so very strongly of the scarcely exploded belief, that it perhaps influenced the minds of the spectators rather against Millicent than in her favour. There was witchcraft evidently at the root of the business, and very likely this wicked enchantress with the yellow hair had power to cause her victim to appear in two or three places at once for the furtherance of her unholy ends.

Now, while the facts recorded by Samuel Pecker produced this effect upon the more ignorant portion of the
assembly, the more enlightened hearers were inclined
to consider the whole story some confused creation
emanating from the maze and fog of Samuel Pecker's
intellect, just as vaporous shadows and will-o'-the-
wisps arise from a low and marshy soil. Mr. Weldon,
the barrister retained for Millicent's defence, was entirely of this opinion, and had little hope in following
up a thread which only led away from the business in
hand. Had a dozen ghosts of Captain George Duke
appeared simultaneously in a dozen different places,
the fact of their appearance could not have lessened
that other fact of the sailor's disappearance, the pool
of blood upon the floor of the garden chamber, and
the terrible chain of circumstantial evidence which connected Millicent Duke with the foul deed that had too
surely been done.

It was hard for Darrell Markham to take his place in
the witness-box and answer the questions put to him by
the counsel for the Crown, knowing full well that every
word he spoke went to condemn his unhappy cousin.
When asked if he had ever seen the captain's double,
he told of the encounter upon Compton Moor, in which
he had been robbed and wounded, and further related
the story told by Ringwood Markham of the young
squire's meeting with a man whom he mistook for
George Duke in the house at Chelsea.

Mrs. Meggis, the deaf housekeeper, Hugh Martin,
the constable, and Sarah Pecker, were then examined,
with the same result as on the former occasion; and the
case for the prosecution closed. A terribly strong case
against the pale woman at the bar.

A clock outside the court struck three as the counsel for the Crown sat down. More than half the day had been spent in the examination of these witnesses.

After reading the deposition made by Millicent before Montague Bowers, the counsel for the defence summoned the first of his witnesses.

The law, which even in those hard days—popularly known as the good old times, by the way—was supposed to regard an accused person as innocent until his or her guilt was duly established, did not afford the suspected individual much opportunity of proving that innocence. The prisoner's counsel was not allowed to plead for his client. The counsel for the Crown might thunder forth what denunciations he pleased against the supposed criminal; a hanging judge might bully the jury into the finding of a fatal verdict; but the counsel of the accused had no chance of serving his client save by the cross-examination of witnesses, and by hazarding an objection now and then to some unfair question upon the part of his opponent.

Thus it was that the one strong point in favour of Millicent was insufficiently demonstrated to the jury who were to decide the awful question of her guilt or innocence. That one point was the physical weakness of the accused, and the improbability, if not impossibility, that such a woman could have carried the body of a stalwart strongly built man down a flight of stone steps, and across a space of forty yards, to a frozen pond, the ice upon the surface of which she must have broken before throwing the corpse of her victim into the water. That even the unnatural strength of madness could have enabled the accused to do this unassisted was surely impossible; but this impossibility the prisoner's counsel could only attempt to demonstrate in an indirect manner, by cross-examination of the witnesses who had found the body, and by the exhibition to the jury of a plan of the Compton Hall premises.

Nor was he able to raise a doubt which might have saved his client— a doubt as to whether a murder had actually been committed in the absence of all direct proof as to the identity of that disfigured corpse which had been found in the pond. What proof was there that a murder had been committed? And if a murder had been done, was it not more likely to have been the work of practised robbers and assassins, who had entered Compton Hall in search of the late squire's massive old plate ; who had made their entrance by the garden chamber—so fatally easy of access—unaware of the presence of Captain Duke ; and who, finding him there, and alarmed by some sign of awakening on his part, had assassinated him thereupon? The fact that no property had disappeared was proof that a robbery had not been perpetrated. What more likely than that the burglars were startled by the footsteps of Millicent in the corridor outside the garden chamber?

But Mr. Weldon was not allowed to set forth all these possibilities. The laws of a hundred years ago were hard and bitter laws ; and if to-day society is apt to pamper the criminal, it has good need to atone for past cruelty. Who shall say that poor innocent Eliza Fenning might not have been saved from the gallows, if an eloquent counsel had been permitted to plead her cause?

Thomas Masterson **was** the first witness called for the defence.

It was no very easy matter to get the truth out of this gentleman: he fenced with the questions put to him in a manner which would have commanded considerable admiration at the Old Bailey; but he had an Old Bailey practitioner to deal with, and he was made to declare how he and George Duke had contrived to escape together from the watchful guardians of the galleys.

Every ear was listening to this man's words, every eye was fixed upon his face, as he told his story, and every creature in that court recoiled with a thrill of horror at sight of a change which suddenly came over the aspect of the speaker's countenance towards the end of his examination.

In the very midst of a sentence Thomas Masterson stopped, and with ashen cheeks and dilated eyes stared across the heads of the lawyers and the multitude at the doorway of the court, which was in an elevated situation, communicating by a flight of steps with the main body of the building.

A man who had just entered the court was standing at the top of these steps apart from all other spectators. He was speaking in a whisper to an official close to him —speaking as if he was charging the official with a message, and it seemed by the man's air that the intruder's business was no common one.

"Why do you pause, Thomas Masterson?" asked the barrister.

The witness slowly raised his hand, and pointed to the stranger at the top of the steps.

"Because Cap'en George Duke has just come into the court," he answered.

There was a simultaneous movement amongst the

vast body of spectators, and a simultaneous cry of astonishment broke from every lip. Millicent Duke had been sitting quietly in the dock, with her head drooping forward, and her hands loosely folded in her lap, throughout the whole length of the proceedings, very much as if she were an uninterested spectator, to whom the issue of that day's business mattered little; but as Thomas Masterson spoke these words she lifted her head, and looked in the direction to which the hand of the witness pointed. She looked full at the figure standing on the threshold of the door, and then uttered a feeble cry of horror.

She did not fall into a swoon, but she sat as one transfixed, and, with her blue eyes opened to their widest extent, stared aghast at the intruder.

"Again," she murmured, "again, again!"

The official to whom the new comer had been speaking made his way through the crowd, and whispered some message into the ear of Millicent's counsel.

The barrister turned to the judge with a sudden gesture of surprise.

"My lud," he exclaimed; "convinced as I have myself felt of the innocence of my client, I must freely confess that my list of witnesses for the defence was not a strong one; but I am now in a position to call a new witness—I am now in a position to declare that no murder has been committed, and that George Duke now stands in this court."

"No, no, no!"

It was from the lips of the prisoner that this feeble murmur came; but at that moment every eye was fixed upon the brown-eyed stranger in the shabby naval uniform, who was now placed in the witness-box, Thomas Masterson giving way to the new comer.

"Stop where you are, Mr. Masterson," said Millicent's counsel; "we may want you presently."

The mariner stepped a few paces from the witness-box, staring with a peculiarly puzzled expression at the face of the new comer, and scratching his closely shorn head with a slow and reflective gesture.

The new witness was duly sworn, after some little discussion as to whether his evidence could be admitted in the course of that trial. The judge could urge no precedent against such a proceeding; for in no criminal case that either experience or reading had made him familiar with had the supposed victim of a foul murder appeared to give his evidence during the trial of his supposed assassin. It was altogether a business out of the ordinary line, and judge and king's counsel allowed Mr. Weldon to have his own way.

"May I ask, Captain George Duke," said the barrister, "for what reason you have been pleased to keep out of the way until your wife was placed in a criminal dock under the charge of wilful murder?"

The dusk was gathering in the furthermost corners of the court, and creeping slowly up towards the benches, the dock, and the witness-box. Two or three officials began to light the candles in the brass sconces; but the red sunlight had not yet faded out of the building, and the great windows glowed with the last glory of the day.

In this half-light the man in the witness-box looked slowly round the court, scanning the eager fac's turned towards him. But while making this deliberate survey, it was to be observed that he carefully avoided meeting the eyes of the accused—those widely opened blue eyes, which were fixed as the eyes that gaze upon a ghost.

" I stayed away," said the man, " because I got no pleasant welcome from my wife yonder. We quarrelled before I went to rest ; and having drunk more than was good for me, and being disheartened by my uncivil reception, I thought life was so little worth having, that I made a gash in my own throat, thinking to finish with it. But though I let blood enough to cure twenty fever patients, I did no more harm to myself than was enough to bring me to a more reasonable way of thinking. So I stanched the wound by tying a thick woollen handker-chief about my throat, and walked straight out of the house, never meaning to set eyes on yonder lady again. I made a cut of nine miles across country, and con-trived to meet the York mail. From York I went to London, where I've been staying ever since. Three days ago a chance paragraph in a newspaper informed me of the mischief caused by my absence. I lost no time in booking my place in the North coach, and here I am to clear my wife yonder of the charge brought against her."

The man looked round defiantly as he finished his statement. Millicent's counsel crushed the papers in his hand. There was no little sense of disappointment amongst the unconcerned spectators. The business had come to a very shabby and commonplace termination, people thought, and Captain Duke ought to have been ashamed of himself for playing such tricks upon a British public.

The counsel for the prosecution rose at this juncture. " My learned friend forgets," he said, " that the person stating himself to be Captain Duke has been only recognized by one man, and that man a witness for the defence. The gentlemen of the jury will require stronger proof of this person's identity before they admit that there has been no murder committed."

"The gentlemen of the jury shall be satisfied," replied Millicent's counsel. " Call Samuel and Sarah Pecker, Darrell Markham, Martha Meggis, and Hugh Martin."

The witnesses were called.

" Be good enough, Captain Duke, to step forward into the strongest light the court will afford," said the barrister.

The man advanced into the full glare of the candles. He wore the very clothes he had worn upon the night of his arrival at Compton; the shabby blue coat, adorned with naval buttons and shreds of tarnished gold lace, the jack-boots, the threadbare waistcoat, and the weatherbeaten three-cornered hat. He wore the chestnut wig, which had replaced the captain's flowing curls, and his brown eyes had the same cruel light in them which every one could remember in the eyes of George Duke.

One by one the witnesses swore to his identity. Hugh Martin the constable was the last to swear.

"I knew Captain Duke well," he said; "and I can take my oath the man at whom I am now looking is no other than he. If a better proof of his identity is needed, I think I can give it."

" Let us have it, then, by all means," answered Millicent's counsel.

The constable took something from his waistcoat-pocket and handed it to the barrister. It was a naval

U

button, with a fragment of shabby blue cloth still fastened to the hank.

"I picked that up in the oak parlour at Compton Hall on the night of the supposed murder," said Hugh; "and it strikes me that you'll find it to correspond with the other buttons on that gentleman's coat."

On examination, the buttons were found to correspond. They were of a foreign make, and bore the arms of the King of Spain. No such buttons had ever been bought in England.

"Gentlemen of the jury," exclaimed Horace Weldon—"what need can there be to delay you any longer upon this business? We have no occasion to press Captain Duke as to the motives of his strange conduct. He has been identified in open court by six witnesses. My client's innocence is so self-evident that I call upon you to acquit her without leaving your seats."

The judge spoke very briefly.

"Gentlemen of the jury," he said—"I fully concur in the words addressed to you by the counsel for the defence. The case appears to me to be a very simple one, and your course in the matter sufficiently clear.

There was a little whispering amongst the jurymen, a suppressed murmur of applause from the crowd, and an hysterical shriek of delight from Sarah Pecker. The foreman of the jury rose to address the judge.

But, before he could speak, Millicent Duke rose from her seat for the first time since the trial had begun. She stood up, calmly facing the eager crowd, which had been so ready to condemn her for a witch and a murderess, and which was now as ready to applaud and pity her as an innocent victim.

She turned to the judge, and said, with quiet deliberation,—

"I thank you, my lord, for your goodness to me;
but that man is not my husband!"

Millicent's counsel had seated himself, and was
busy collecting his papers. He rose to his feet as
she spoke.

"My lud, and gentlemen of the jury!" he said,
"this day's proceedings have unsettled the mind of
my client. I beg of you to pay no attention to this.
Captain Duke, remove your wife."

"I repeat," said Millicent, "that man is not my
husband!"

"O, I saw it, I saw it! I know how it would be
the day she spoke to me in her cell, poor innocent
lamb!" exclaimed Sarah Pecker, wringing her hands,
as she and Darrell advanced to take Millicent from the
dock; "I knew that her sufferings were driving her
mad."

"Let Mrs. Duke's friends remove her from the
court," said the judge.

"I will not stir until I have spoken, my lord," cried
Mrs. Duke. "Do I look or speak as if I were mad?
That man is not my husband. George Duke was
murdered upon the night of the 30th of January last.
It was his dead body which I saw stretched on the
bed in the garden chamber, with the blood streaming
from a great gash in his throat. As for that man
standing there, it is no new thing for to see the
shadow of my husband. I saw it seven years ago,
upon the pier at Marley Water, as the church clocks
were striking twelve."

The story of Captain Duke's ghost, narrated by

Samuel Pecker, flashed upon the spectators, and many
a cheek grew pale at the thought that the man standing
under the light of the flaring candles might be something more or less than mortal.

The man himself looked at Mrs. Duke with a savage
scowl.

" My wife is mad," he said.   " Are we to stop here
all night to listen to her ravings ? "

" Will anyone ask that man two or three questions ? "
said Mrs. Duke.

The barrister who had defended her replied.

" If you really desire it, madam," he said ; " but I
warn you that—— "

" I do most earnestly desire it."

" Then I am at your service."

" Ask him if he has in his possession a single earring—a diamond set in Indian filigree work ? "

The man took a little canvas bag from his waistcoat,
opened it, and picked out the jewel, which he handed
to the counsel.

" Perhaps that'll satisfy my wife," he said.

" The gem corresponds with your description, Mrs.
Duke," said the barrister.   " Are you satisfied ? "

" Not yet.   Be so good as to ask that man what
my husband said when he took that earring from
me."

The man laughed.

" What should a husband say when he takes a
keepsake from his wife," he answered, after a moment's hesitation ; " what could he say but promise
to keep the treasure faithfully, and not to give it
away to any sweetheart he may pick up in foreign
parts ? "

" You hear, you hear!" cried Millicent; "he cannot tell me what George Duke said when he took that trinket from me seven years ago. He told me that whoever came to me, calling himself my husband, and yet was unable to produce that earring, would be an impostor."

" Then," said the barrister, shrugging his shoulders in evident impatience of his client's folly, "the very fact of this person being able to produce the jewel is in itself a proof of his identity."

Millicent put her hand to her forehead, and was silent for some moments. After a pause she said slowly,—

" Whoever murdered my husband carried away his clothes. That earring was in the pocket of his waistcoat."

There is an earnestness in the sincerity of the speaker which carries conviction to the listener. Fully as Mr. Horace Weldon believed the man standing before him to be George Duke of the Vulture, he was, in spite of himself, shaken by the words and by the aspect of this quiet woman, who seemed bent on knotting afresh the rope which had just been loosed from about her neck.

Accustomed to the study of the human countenance, Millicent's advocate bent his grave eyes upon the face of the man in the witness-box. From him he looked a little way to the right, where stood the worthy Thomas Masterson under watch and ward of one of the officials, being, as we know, only temporarily released from prison to attend this trial. The two men were looking earnestly at each other, and Thomas Masterson's mouth was moving in a peculiar contortion, which might be either a convulsive motion of that feature or a signal.

It was a signal, for it was accompanied by a rapid gesture of the hand—a kind of gesture common amongst French thieves and vagabonds.

"How dare you make signs to that gentleman, sir?" exclaimed the barrister, fixing his eyes sternly upon Thomas Masterson.

"Let the *gentleman* give me the countersign," answered Thomas, "*if he can!* If he can't, he has never been in the galleys, and he is not George Duke."

"He is not George Duke?"

"No. I've had my suspicions ever since I first swore to him. If he is George Duke, let him strip off his clothes, and show his bare shoulders in open court If he is George Duke, let him show the mark of the branding-iron on his back. Let him show such a mark as I can show, for George Duke and I were taken the same day and branded the same day."

"I suppose you will have no objection to do this, Captain Duke?" said the barrister, after a pause.

The stranger's face flushed with an angry red.

"Egad!" he cried, "I have an objection, and a strong objection too. Curse me, gentlemen! must a man strip off his clothes in open court, and show a shameful mark burnt into his flesh by the enemies of his country, in order to prove his identity, after having been sworn to by half-a-dozen competent witnesses? Is a man to do this because his mad wife chooses to deny her husband? Gad's life! it's enough to rouse the spirit of the veriest milksop that ever trod British ground."

He looked round defiantly as he spoke, and there was a murmur of applause in the court.

"Come, come, sir," said the judge; "I do not wish you to do anything unpleasant to your own feelings; but this case is becoming involved in such a mystery as we may never be able to clear up. Here are five people who swear that you are George Duke, and here are two other people who swear that you are not George Duke. The question must be settled before you leave the court; for it is a question upon which hinges the guilt or innocence of the prisoner at the bar. You have no need to bare your shoulders in open court; you can withdraw with two gentlemen appointed by me, and show them the mark of the branding-iron."

The man was silent. Then, after a long pause, he looked about him with a scowl, and said,—

"Suppose I deny that I ever was in the galleys?"

"Then you throw fresh difficulties into the business," replied the judge. "This man, Thomas Masterson, has sworn that he and George Duke were taken together on board the Vulture the day she was burnt and sunk by the French; that they were sentenced together, and escaped together early in last January."

"Every word of which is gospel truth, my lord," said Thomas, sturdily.

At this juncture a weak voice interposed—a pale face made itself conspicuous amongst the crowd round about Millicent, and Mr. Samuel Pecker, of the Black Bear inn, claimed the attention of the court.

"I know who it is," he said. "It's the ghost! The ghost that asked the way to Marley Water—the ghost that met Master Darrell upon Compton Moor, and robbed him of his purse and his horse, and was near taking his life—the ghost Miss Millicent saw on the pier—the ghost Squire Ringwood met in London—the ghost that called for a glass of brandy, and paid for it, on the night of the murder!"

The little innkeeper was wonderful to look upon in his excitement. Thomas Masterson slapped his clenched fist violently down upon the wooden ledge before him.

"Ghost!" he cried. "Lord save us! the man's no ghost. I know who he is. It's come upon me all in a moment, and I was a fool not to think of it before. That man is the bitterest enemy George Duke ever had in his life."

A ghastly change came over the man's face as Thomas Masterson said these words, and he looked furtively round as if seeking some easy egress from the court. But he was hemmed in by the crowd, which had closed round him like a sea; and he could no more have escaped than if he had been bound hand and foot by bands of iron.

"What! what! Thomas Masterson?" exclaimed the judge, while the breathless spectators stared all agape at the mariner.

"I say that this man is the man George Duke hated worse than he hated the French captain who burnt his ship, or the French judge who sent him to the galleys. I'd a'most forgotten the story, for I've led too hard a life to think much of other men's family histories, but it comes back upon me to-night. That man is George Duke's twin-brother!"

"His brother?"

" Yes, his twin-brother; born in the same hour, and so like him that the mother that nursed them could never tell the two apart. Cap'en Duke told me the whole story one night when we lay off the coast of Africa in a dead calm. He told me how he and his twin-brother had fought together as babies in the cradle, and hated each other as helpless orphan boys. They were the sons of a mate on board a merchantman, and their father died of yellow fever off the coast of Jamaica before they were six years of age. The mother was a drunken jade, who turned her sons out to play in the gutters of Portsmouth, while she drank with any one who would pay for her liquor. George took to the sea, and ran away when he was fifteen years of age. The other boy, James, was a thief and a rascal as soon as he could run alone ; and George had many a time to pay for his brother's delinquencies, for there wasn't a magistrate or constable in London that could tell one of the boys from the other. James was a liar and a coward, always ready to sneak out of harm's way, and leave brother George in the lurch ; and a few such tricks as these didn't go far to mend the hatred there was between 'em. So when George Duke took to a seafaring life, his last word on leaving England was the word that cursed his only surviving kinsman and twin-brother. Mind," added Thomas Masterson, "I give the story to you as the Cap'en give it to me. James Duke and me never clapped eyes on each other before to-day, but I know of them that know him."

" A singular story," said the judge, " and a story that goes to prove this man guilty of perjury, unless he can contradict it."

" Which I dare swear he cannot, my lud," interposed

Millicent's counsel. " If this man, who has upon his person the clothes worn by George Duke upon the night of his disappearance, is not George Duke, how does he account for the possession of those clothes, my lud? I venture to say that this man is the murderer of his brother. He is identified by the witness Sarah Pecker as the man who called at the Black Bear within a few hours of the murder. He left a horse at the inn for three days, and sent a messenger to fetch the animal instead of returning himself to do so. He comes into this court to-day with an improbable story, in order that, by passing himself off as the husband of Mrs. Millicent Duke, he may obtain possession of her fortune. Where has he been, and what has he been doing since the night of George. Duke's disappearance? Let him bring forward witnesses to answer these questions, and in the mean time let him be placed in custody on suspicion of having committed perjury and murder. I call upon you, my lud, to order the arrest of this man."

The judge expressed his concurrence in the opinion of his learned friend ; and George Duke's shadow, or double, or twin-brother was removed from the court to lie in Carlisle prison until further inquiries should set him free, or justify his detention until the following assizes.

The jury then retired, and deliberated on the strange and conflicting evidence that had been put before them. The tide of popular feeling had completely turned as regards Millicent Duke ; and the twelve honest citizens of Carlisle were not slow to agree to a verdict in her favour. This verdict was received with unanimous applause.

Millicent Duke was carried out of the court in the strong arms of her cousin Darrell. The feeble frame had given way at last, and she had fallen into a swoon while Thomas Masterson was telling his story.

Early the next day they took her back to Compton-on-the-Moor; not to the roomy old mansion in which the murder had been committed, but to a pleasant chamber at the Black Bear, where she was faithfully served by Phœbe the pretty chambermaid. Faithful Sarah would have gladly tended her dear Miss Millicent, but she had her hands full of sad work at this time, and could spare no time from her attendance on the sick bed of her son.

The race of Henry Masterson, *alias* Captain Fanny, *alias* Sir Lovel Mortimer, was well-nigh run. Before the spring flowers should bloom in the woods and hedgerows about Compton-on-the-Moor Sarah's newly-found son had passed away from this pleasant earth. He lingered for upwards of a fortnight after Millicent's trial, and died in his mother's arms, conscious to the last, resigned to his early death, and honestly peniten⁴ for the wickedness and folly of his brief career.

He was thunderstruck upon hearing an account of the proceedings at Carlisle.

" I fully thought that it was James Duke who was murdered," he said, " and that the unhappy lady had done the deed in some paroxysm of madness or despair. I can do much to throw a light upon the business, and to clear the lady's name, and thus do one act of justice before I die; but I had best tell my story on oath before competent witnesses, as it may help to hang this man James, who, for that matter, is better out of the world than in it, having never been of any service to a living creature."

That evening, in the presence of his mother, Samuel Pecker, and Attorney Selgood, Captain Fanny made a deposition, which was carefully written down by the lawyer, and afterwards signed by the sick man.

In this statement the highwayman told how James Duke had been first his comrade and afterwards his servant. How he had been from first to last an ill-conditioned fellow, nicknamed by those who knew him Sulky Jeremiah, and sometimes, by reason of his constant bad fortune, Unlucky Jeremiah. How the hatred between the twin-brothers was well known to all who were acquainted with either of them; and how, on hearing of George Duke's disappearance, he, Henry Masterson, had thought that James might profit by the circumstance to pass himself off for his brother, and thus get possession of the wife's fortune. This plan had been discussed and matured in London, when the highwayman chanced to meet the wedding party upon the steps of St. Mary's church. This chance meeting decided James Duke upon immediate action. He started that night for Compton-on-the-Moor, having been furnished with money for his journey by Captain Fanny; and having appointed to meet the highwayman, a week afterwards, at the Black Bear, and share with his old comrade and master the fortune acquired by the imposition.

This was all that Henry Masterson could tell; but it formed a powerful link in the evidence against the man lying in Carlisle gaol.

Captain Fanny was sleeping under a turf-covered mound in Compton churchyard when James Duke was placed in the dock, where Millicent had so lately stood, to take his trial at the Midsummer assizes for the wilful murder of his brother George.

Link by link the chain of circumstantial evidence was forged. Every step of the accused from London to Compton-on-the-Moor was tracked by one witness and another ; but the most damning of all the evidence against him was that given by the ostler of a small inn on a cross-road thirty miles from Compton, where James Duke had hired a horse, and whither he had returned on foot at dusk on the evening after the murder, carrying with him a bundle, and sneaking into the inn-yard like a thief, with his clothes all bespattered by blood and clay ; the foul marks being caused, he said, by a fall from his horse, which he had left for that reason at Compton-on-the-Moor.

The boy who had been sent to fetch the horse also gave evidence, and told how the prisoner had promised him a guinea on condition that he refused to answer any questions that might be asked him at Compton.

So James Duke was hung at Carlisle ; and a fair headstone was set up by Millicent's command over the disfigured remains that had been found in the pond, bearing a brief inscription to the memory of George Duke, who was cruelly murdered by his **twin-brother** on the night of the 30th of January 17—.

EPILOGUE.

NEARLY a twelvemonth elapsed before Millicent had any mind to return to Compton Hall. She lived during that time in the little cottage which she had inhabited during the seven years of her husband's absence. The garden chamber was razed to the ground, and a new wing in red brick built in its stead, called at first King George's, and subsequently the Nursery wing. The pool behind the stables was filled and planted over with laurels and holly-bushes. It is to be recorded that the simple villagers declared that no shrub ever flourished upon that accursed spot; but it is also a fact that the place was an exposed corner lying open to the east wind.

There were grooms and stable-boys of nervous temperament who declared that strange noises were to be heard after dark in the neighbourhood of this mound of earth, and that Captain Duke still "walked" amidst the scene of his assassination. But Millicent was never troubled further by the shadow of her husband, and blushed for her own superstitious folly when she remembered how she had mistaken a form of flesh and blood for a spectral apparition.

Before George Duke's widow returned to the house in which her ancestors had lived and died, she took her part for the third time in the marriage ceremony, and was united by the curate of Compton to her cousin Darrell Markham.

Thomas Masterson, convicted of a petty theft, died
of gaol-fever in Carlisle prison a few months after the
death of his son.   So it fell out that Samuel Pecker
never to his dying day learned the true history of the
foreign-looking pedlar who stole the spoons and Sarah's
oumpion watch.

Is there any need for me to tell of the peaceful happiness that reigned at Compton Hall?   There is a picture still to be seen in the dining-room of the old mansion—a family group, common enough in such houses,
but surely never displeasing to look upon, whether the
painter is the mighty Sir Joshua himself, or only some
poor imitator of the great artist.   It is the picture of a
young mother, dressed in an open gown of light blue
satin and a petticoat of embroidered muslin, with her
pale golden hair turned back from her innocent forehead under a matronly cap of lace and cambric.   A
sweet and gentle creature, who bends over the cradle of
a sleeping child, while a stalwart gentleman in a hunting costume stands in the background, with a sturdy
urchin of some three years old seated upon his shoulder, and a leash of hounds at his feet.

THE END.